FINDING
SAFEHAVEN

A novel

BEVERLY MARQUART

Raintree Publishing
Fort Collins, Colorado

Finding Safehaven
Copyright © 2017 Beverly Marquart – All Rights Reserved
Raintree Publishing, Fort Collins, Colorado

ISBN: 978-0-9986066-0-6

Cover images © 2017 istock.com | rglinsky
Author Photo © 2017 Agnieszka Wormus
Cover design © 2017 DeAnna Knippling
Interior design © 2017 DeAnna Knippling

Printed in the United States of America

First Printing, 2017

For information about special discounts available for bulk purchases, sales promotions, fund-
raising and educational needs, contact Beverly Marquart at marquartbeverly@gmail.com.

Visit the author's website at www.beverlymarquart.com.

FINDING
SAFEHAVEN

Acknowledgments

I am deeply indebted to the following individuals for their invaluable contributions:

To the people who actually lived the events depicted in this book. Sadly, most are no longer with us, but without them and their grit and determination, the way we live today would look much different.

❧❦

Ernest Hemingway once said there is nothing to writing—all you do is sit down at a typewriter and bleed. The following people stanched the bleeding and kept me on writing life-support: Brian Kaufman who launched the critique group Raintree Writers. Without its members (past and present), this book would not have been written. I owe a great deal of gratitude to: Kenneth Harmon, April Joitel Moore, Melissa Pattison, Laura Powers, Sidna Rachid, Patricia Stoltey, and Carolyn Yalin who all provided steadfast assistance with a much-needed kick in the butt from time to time. Their honesty and encouragement is without equal.

Early readers whose reassurance and insight was vital: Donna Axelson, Julie Chen, Melissa Farrand, Susan Harness, Ted Olsen, and especially my sister-in-law Judy Marquart who believed in me before this project ever began.

Dawn Marano, developmental editor, for her unbiased appraisal and guidance.

DeAnna Knippling who designed an amazing cover to disprove the old adage, "You can't judge a book by its cover." And also to DeAnna, copy editor extraordinaire, for helping to bring this project to its tangible conclusion.

Finally, I am forever grateful to my daughter, Brittany, and my son, Reid, and to each of their families for the love and devotion that makes this project and others worthwhile. Thanks to my brother-in-law, John Shull, for his historical perspective; and to my sister, Bonnie for her endless support. And last, but certainly not least, thank you to my husband, Rick, who has always believed in me. You are my foundation. I love you all.

Dedication

In memory of Ervin and Betty, my parents,
who gave me love and strength.

December 7, 1941

Ervin slid his arm around Betty's waist as they walked toward the Strand Theater that stood like a *grande dame* at the corner of Second Street and Burlington Avenue in the small Nebraska town of Hastings. The building's enameled-white exterior matched the snow falling lightly that Sunday afternoon. A train whistled in the distance, the shrill sound hanging in the frosty air.

For Ervin, Hastings held a promise of more prosperity than the poor farming community where he grew up, less than thirty miles away. The country was still struggling to recover from a nasty spell called the Great Depression, and Erv had vowed to make something of himself. He'd spent the latter part of summer and early fall trailing harvesters from Kansas all the way to North Dakota. He didn't have a car. Not many people did. So he hitchhiked or rode the rails to get to the next threshing job. Now in the clutches of winter with no farm work available, he worked nights at Lincoln Telephone & Telegraph to make ends meet.

The twenty-five cents for admission to see Gary Cooper play *Sergeant York* was a splurge but worth every penny. Betty had just announced she was pregnant with their first child. This called for a celebration. He might even spring for a chocolate malt after the show from Brooke's Drugstore with its fancy tin ceiling and marble counter.

They had married six months earlier at the Lutheran Church parsonage with his sister and brother-in-law standing up for them. Erv picked a rose from the pastor's garden that June day and pinned it on her flower-print dress. Betty was much prettier than the dress or the flower.

The popcorn machine at the Strand erupted with creamy white puffs trickling down the steel kettle and piling in a heap inside its steamy glass sides. The aroma of melting butter drifted through the lobby. No time to stop for something from the concession stand. Hand-in-hand they hurried past the dark-paneled walls and gave their tickets to the young, red-haired usher. Smiling at each other, Ervin and Betty parted the heavy blue velvet curtains and found a place to sit. They leaned back in the wooden seats and waited in the darkness. With her fingers woven between his, he brought their hands to his lips and gently kissed the back of her hand.

Upside down numbers scrolled on the screen. The familiar black-and-white newsreel began with a recap of the war in Europe. Images flashed of Italy taking sides with the Germans, France knuckling under to the Nazis with the signing of the armistice at Compiègne, and London suffering heavy bombing attacks.

"I feel sorry for the people over there," Betty whispered. "It doesn't look like there's hardly anything left standing."

"Yeah, it's a mess. I'm glad we're right smack-dab in the middle of this country."

Betty placed Erv's hand on her belly. "I hope you'll never have to go. I don't know what I'd do without you here."

By the middle of the newsreel, it seemed as if the rest of the world was falling apart. But the United States had vowed to stay out of it. That was, until the red-haired usher opened those blue velvet drapes and the flap, flap, flap of the film hitting the projector reel signaled the end of the sound and picture. The theater, dark and chilly, was filled with the shouts of the red-haired boy, "Pearl Harbor's just been attacked! The Japanese bombed Pearl Harbor!"

❧❦❧

Fifteen-year-old Catherine and her mother sat in their small salon with heavy blackout blinds tightly drawn and the radio tuned to Radio-Londres, the broadcast of the Free French Forces. Of course it was illegal to listen, but they removed the wooden box from its hiding place and hunched in front of it every evening since Catherine's father's death, waiting for news of France's resistance or the war's end. Catherine's father had been taken months ago by the Germans from their home town of Colmar to fight the Nazis' war. His death had generated only a telegram from the Vichy government, without so much as a body to grieve over or bury.

"I'm going to bed. Goodnight, *mon ange*," Maman said. She seldom referred to Catherine by name after her husband's passing. Catherine had become *mon ange*—my angel.

Maman went upstairs to bed, but Catherine stayed and listened, occasionally dozing off as the commentator droned on. Eventually the embers in the coal stove lost their crimson color, a sign she should get ready for bed. Catherine yawned. Tomorrow would be a long day in preparation for the upcoming holiday break from school.

Often, at the end of a news piece, music played. It soothed Catherine and eased her into slumber that blocked out the war. Tonight, without warning, Anna Marley's clear, sweet voice stopped. Then, as quickly as the broadcast ended, it started again. This time a man's slow, measured words filled the room, "We interrupt this program with an important announcement. The Japanese have bombed the United States at Pearl Harbor, Hawaii."

Catherine bolted up the stairs two at a time and rushed into Maman's bedroom. She gulped at the air, trying to catch her breath. "They bombed the United States!"

Maman sat up in bed. "What? What are you talking about, child?"

"The Japanese. They bombed the United States! It just came over the radio!"

Maman's mouth turned up in a slight smile. "The Americans have been drawn in, and now the Germans will have to fight them. There is a chance for us, for France. Let us ask God to help the Americans."

Catherine and Maman sank to their knees beside the bed and prayed.

BOOK I: CATHERINE REVAUX

THE LINEN FACTORY 1944

Chapter 1

The linen factory in Colmar where I work had been closed for months because of bombing, which kept supplies from reaching us. Maman and I exhausted our limited savings by the time it reopened in July of 1944. Boys who'd not yet been forced to join the army, and elderly men who escaped conscription and continued to avoid the notice of observant military officers, signed up for any available post. As long as you worked, people didn't seem to notice as much, especially if you kept your nose out of others' affairs. Sometimes men fled the confines of the military and hid in out-of-the-way places like the factory, emerging from the shadows and seeking work. Those types of men were increasingly rare because the sharp eyes of Nazi sympathizers constantly scanned the streets and sent those who were caught to the front lines or worse.

On a crisp day in September, one such stranger appeared at the linen factory looking for a job—any job. No one asked questions. It was obvious by his tall, sturdy build he could handle the heavier work. The supervisors didn't need to know any more about him. Muscle was in short supply in our French town filled with women. He satisfied a need as he loaded crates of gray-green uniforms and blankets onto pallets that would eventually be taken by train to a German headquarters. In the dark corners of the warehouse he could elude the occasional surprise inspection of a Nazi officer. To me, he was utterly mysterious, with hair the color of dark caramel and his haunting, deep-set eyes.

He had only worked at the factory for a brief time before the whispering began. The far-away look in his smoky-colored eyes intrigued me, and I wanted to know more about him, so I listened to every rumor that came my way. A small circle of women, who almost always gathered on the front steps before work, gossiped between puffs of cigarettes they had most likely traded for favors with German soldiers. I'd slow down and strain to hear their latest reports as I walked past them each morning. It didn't take long in a factory of mostly females to find out about the handsome new worker—especially one with an exotic air about him.

It takes Nina, my best friend, two days to discover his name. She breathlessly divulges it as we trudge to work this chilly morning.

"Renier."

"Oh," I say.

Nina giggles, no doubt delighted at my reaction. Judging by her response I must sound quite interested.

"That's all you can say? 'Oh.'" She giggles again.

"I have no idea what you're talking about." A crooked smile from Nina forces me to stop defending myself. "All right. I am interested in him. Who isn't? Every girl stops what she's doing whenever he comes upstairs to the workroom."

Knowing each other from the time we were little girls, few secrets lingered between Nina and me. We eat lunch together every day at the factory. I welcome my time with her as a respite from the repetitive work. She always laughs—always enjoys life even though lately our joy has disappeared like thread sliding off the factory's spools. Despite Nina's playful attitude, we live in constant fear the German soldiers or the Army's police will take whatever they want, including us, the women.

This morning our walk takes a sinister turn. I gasp and point to the red stain on the cobblestones in front of us. "There."

Nina's too busy daydreaming to take notice. "What? What is it?"

"That's the place. The place where they beat the old man to death."

It doesn't seem to faze Nina. She's the cheery one. I'm the one with a bank of dark clouds hanging over my head. Maman says I was born somber and serious.

The old man had spoken out about the German occupation and said France had become a puppet government for the Nazis. Using clubs, they attacked him on these stones in front of his house and left him choking in a pool of his own blood. A brutal reminder there was no room for freedom—not then and maybe not ever again. But when bad things happened, the people of Colmar seemed more interested in what next year's crops might bring than in the chaos exploding in our world in Alsace-Lorraine. Life was simpler if you didn't think about what was going on right before your eyes.

We cross the canal toward the center of town when three soldiers round the corner of the market. They see us and walk with a sudden urgency in their steps. German soldiers frequently stand outside the shops and taverns to watch people come and go, always ready to stop and question. We move quickly and keep our heads down. I pull my scarf closer to my chin. With my other hand, I draw my baggy work clothes around my waist and hunch over. Apparently, I didn't look as inconspicuous as I had hoped. The tallest of the three soldiers approaches with a definite stagger and blocks our way. Keeping our heads bowed, we scoot left to go around him.

"Halt, meine frauleins."

I lift my head without looking directly into the soldier's eyes. His breath smells of alcohol. Trying not to show fear in my voice, I speak in my best accent-free German, *"Guten tag. Entschuldigen Sie uns, bitte."* We try again to maneuver out of their way.

"You girls should not be out walking these streets," one of the other soldiers warns, grabbing Nina's shoulder.

The short one steps in front of me with tiny beads of drink still clinging to the top of his lip. "What are you doing in this part of town?"

"We're on our way to work. We'll get in trouble if we're late," I say.

"*Mach schnell*," he orders with a tone of exasperation. He breaks the other soldier's grasp on Nina and tilts his chin upwards, gesturing us to move on.

"*Danke schön.*" I momentarily close my eyes as I imagine what could have happened. My body shivers from the coolness of the morning and the unsettling experience.

"I'm surprised they let us go," Nina says when we are a safe distance away.

Although the incident frightened me as much or more than it did her, I stick to a false bravado. "They probably wanted to get back to their drinking."

We step up our pace as if evil will latch on to us if we tarry too long. Needing to get away from this section of Old Town where soldiers congregate, we move from the towering buildings with their sweeping archways and spacious openings. Turning at the next street, we wind up at the Musée Bartholdi. The irony of this location does not escape me. The museum is the birthplace of Frédéric Auguste Bartholdi, the man who sculpted the Statue of Liberty—the keeper of the flames of freedom.

Now more aware of watchful eyes, we dart along the hidden recesses of the canal. Colmar is sometimes referred to as *le petit Venice* because of the similarity of the canals—only without the gondolas. The water is the lifeblood of our community. Everything circulates along the water system and runs through the Centre, the heart of Colmar. The flow eventually joins the Rhine River and then crosses into Germany. The water is a valuable asset we share with Germany—the only good thing we have in common, to my way of thinking.

The stones under our feet are slick and dirty. The street cleaner had long ago been called up and taken away. Hundreds of panes of glass in the mullioned windows of the once-beautiful buildings stare blankly at us. Many of the windows are sealed with wooden shutters, as if they have closed their eyes, not wanting to look out. Maman often remarks that the city has avoided the ravages of war. I argue neglect is destructive enough.

When we arrive at the factory, Nina and I climb the steps leading to the main workroom and hang our cloaks on the black metal hooks, which have smooth, shiny tips from years of wear. I stick my lunch in one of the pockets. It will be easier to retrieve on the way out of the building.

Usually, my job is to keep bobbins from falling off the spindles and replace empty spools with full ones. Sometimes, however, I am relegated to the looms, a task I dislike even more. But unlike the threads quickly whirling around the spools, for me, time feels as if it stands still.

My mind wanders as my throbbing fingers pull heavy thread from spindle to spindle on the bobbin line. Every day at the linen factory reminds me of the exquisite fabrics we once produced for tables of grateful customers. Now we are mostly a group of young girls forced to make dreary military uniforms for German soldiers who eat from their laps while listening to the crackle of gunfire. There was a time when I shared pride in the intricate patterns of the beautiful cloth; now my heart aches at the memory.

Reliving conversations with Maman keeps me from going mad from the mundane work. My mind drifts to this morning's routine, which had started out like any other workday.

"Get out of bed, *mon ange*," Maman had called.

I'd gotten up and eaten a piece of bread and a slice of cheese left over from dinner. She'd baked three loaves—one for us and two for the workers in the grape fields. Their labor had no value for the Nazi war effort, but it remained part of the fabric of our region. We honored the field hands' determination and grit with what little we could offer. Our bread would hold us for several days. I hoped theirs would last until someone else could share.

From the kitchen window, I saw the grapevines on the hillside showing signs of drying in the late summer sun. This piece of France had been in

Maman's family for generations, and constantly stirred up feelings of life with Papa. I thought about the war and how different everything was. Like us, the grapes were hanging on for dear life.

It seemed such a long time ago when happiness filled us, filled Colmar, and filled our country. The only thing we had left seemed to be fear. I tried to remember life before the war, but like Nazis guarding French boundaries, pleasant memories were held tightly within imaginary barricades even I could not open anymore. The summer's heat and the German occupation had scorched our lives, but we held onto the promise and hope that life would be bountiful again.

Just then, the harsh clang of the factory bell signals our break and rips my worries out of reach. I hurriedly finish what I'm working on and grab the lunch I'd made this morning. Holding the plain cloth bag, I think of times when Nina and I were in primary school and on nice days would pull our lunch sacks from the wooden shelf next to the classroom door and run outside to eat. We talked and shared our schoolgirl hopes and dreams. Now I rush to our usual place under a large tree near the storage cellar and wait for her.

Within a few minutes, she joins me and we sit in the shade not far from the building, freeing our hair from the scarves we are forced to wear inside the factory. Nina looks like one of the delicate porcelain dolls from her collection. Sunshine catches the highlights in her hair, drawing attention to her beauty. I feel homely by comparison. Her honey-colored curls fall to her shoulders and cinnamon freckles are sprinkled across her fine-boned nose. At the factory, she wears her golden hair tightly pulled from her face, which showcases her striking features.

During lunch, our conversation centers around the recent news of the liberation of Paris almost a month before. The Allied forces had helped reclaim the city, and in turn gave us hope they might be moving in our direction. However, at this point, we see no signs of freedom coming, only tightening of the already stifling restrictions.

As Nina describes the ruffled dress she dreams of buying when the war is over, Renier walks up the steps from the storage cellar. My heart races.

He looks surprised to find us sitting here. He walks toward us, his confidence overshadowed by the scruffy and dingy clothes he wears. He approaches and then kneels, looking directly at me.

"*Bonjour.* How are you this afternoon? Would you mind if I sit here to eat?"

He tilts his head as if waiting for an answer, but I am like a nervous young girl on a first date, not knowing what to do or say around a man. It has been a long time since I spoke with a male even close to my own age. Men are scarce and younger men something of a novelty.

Instead of waiting for a response, he attempts to cover for my shyness and lapse of good manners and says, "I noticed you girls and wondered if I might share this cool spot."

Nina giggles as she does after anyone says anything. Her infectious laugh makes him smile, which lights his dark gray eyes and shows off his inviting mouth. I can't stop looking at him.

"Of course," I say to draw attention away from my fixed stare.

He sits with his legs folded, crossing them at the ankles. "And you ladies are?"

Nina is more courageous and makes the introductions. "I'm Nina. And this is Catherine."

My face feels like it's on fire. I'm too flustered to eat, let alone engage in small talk about the weather, so I nod along here and there and try to keep my wits about me. I am already suffering from this morning's meager breakfast churning inside me.

Nina quickly moves the conversation to what we both want to know. "So, what brings you to Colmar, Renier?"

"You know my name?" he says with surprise.

"Oh, I overheard the older busybodies talking," Nina quickly explains. "Go ahead. Tell us what brought you to our little village."

"I needed to find work. That's all."

The tone of his voice is soft and low. He looks at the bread in his hand, peels away a small piece and chews it slowly. When he glances up, a faraway look in his eyes tells me he has been asked this question before. He seems hesitant to say more.

I don't want to pry into his life, afraid he has a terrible past. If he does, I don't want to know about it—and don't care, for that matter. However, it doesn't stop all the questions from tumbling around in my head. Where is he from? Why did he come to Colmar? Is there someone else in his life? And why am I having these thoughts?

Nina also seems to sense his unwillingness to provide details and politely offers him her dried apple, as it appears his lunch consists only of bread. "It's from my *tante*'s tree. She stores them in the cellar, and they keep until winter. They're quite good."

"*Merci.*"

Nina hands him another piece. I feel foolish and selfish for not giving him some of my food. Every shred of decent manners has left me.

"Have you two known each other a long time?"

"We practically shared a crib," Nina says. "Our mothers grew up together and are still good friends."

"Sounds like you have a lot of history." There is a certain melancholy in his voice.

"Our fathers were also friends," I tentatively offer. At his smile of encouragement and interest, I continue, "My father was a supervisor at the linen factory until a few years ago, when the Germans mobilized him and others they wanted for their fight. I had just celebrated my fourteenth birthday. He was one of the older *Malgré-nous* to be taken. Men whose jobs could be done by the women were forced to go. We were told he died but never received any other word, let alone his body for a proper burial. Maman says he died of a broken heart. Everything is different because of the war—men fighting against their own flesh and blood."

I can't believe my babbling. And why did I have to mention anything about my age? The words flooded from my mouth as if someone had opened one of the canal gates in town. I mentally scold myself for talking so much.

"Many things are different now. It has changed all of us. *C'est la vie*," Renier says in a deep, smooth voice.

He's holding something back. I hear it in his tone. Even though it seems foolhardy to be so open with someone I've just met, his comment conveys empathy and understanding for what we've all been through. I feel a bond of friendship between us.

We finish our lunches with little conversation. Much has been shared in this short time away from the noisy factory. As I sit here, I wonder if I will ever have a chance to find out more about him.

"It's almost time to go back," Nina says, collecting her belongings.

The bell rings and pulls us into the factory's bleak grasp. I'm suddenly aware of how plain I look and tie the simple scarf around my head, gather the remains of my uneaten food, and stash it in the cloth bag that looks nearly as worn as my clothes. As I try to stand, I place one hand on the dry sod to steady myself. Renier reaches down and gently takes my elbow to help me up. I am sure I will float off the ground from his touch.

A wave of magic envelops me as I return to work. I go through the motions, pull the spools on the machines I stand at, and think of nothing other than his company. For the rest of the afternoon, my mind rolls back to the break from the factory, the war, and my life.

Chapter 2

On our way to work the next day, Nina and I agree our lunch with Renier provided an escape and that we were intoxicated by his presence. We debate rumors that had been swirling around the factory—he's a German spy, part of the French Resistance, or a *saboteur* who's been living in the warehouse for weeks. I'm certain if he had been in Colmar for any length of time, the ladies at the linen factory would surely have known about it.

Nina and I also agree we should be more careful because it isn't only the Germans who watch our every move. There are always those who study the way people talk to each other, the places they meet, or things they say and do. People hesitate to gather in groups of more than two or three for fear of arousing suspicion. The Army police are known to arrest people even if they suspect they might have information about a deserter or a spy.

By the time we arrive at the red brick building, workers are streaming into the factory. We hurry inside to the warmth, but it won't be long before I will wish for the cool outside air as I stand and work.

Thinking about Renier being in the same building makes my cheeks flush. I have never experienced such feelings before—it frightens me in one way, and strangely excites me at the same time. My mind jumps between thoughts of him and the drudgery of the spindles.

I've never had a boyfriend. I think of myself as sort of unattractive—an honest face, dark hair, and a straight, almost formless body. I'm the girl with the long braid. Every morning Maman fixes my hair while I sit at the kitchen table. It is our custom. She brushes and patiently listens to my complaints about the trials of having long hair. Sometimes I imagine cutting my hair short, but my braid is as much a part of me as anything I am.

I was thirteen when the war began, and none of the boys from school interested me. Most of them quit by eighth grade and never graduated. Many were needed for field labor. A few left Colmar to find jobs in the bigger cities. Even those who stayed to work in the factories or shops are gone now. Maybe they'll return when the war is over. Maybe some of them can't. I wonder if I will ever fall in love. I want a love like that of Maman and Papa.

Noon eventually arrives and the factory bell clangs its usual midday signal. Nina and I hurry outside, our anticipation as thick as heavy cream. We wait until we are far enough away from all the other workers to start talking.

"Do you think he'll join us again?" Nina asks in her innocent way.

"I don't know. Maybe he has work to finish."

"He wanted to get to know you. I'm sure of it. He's probably just waiting for the chance to talk to you again."

Her suggestion makes my heart drum faster, and heat rises to the surface of my face. Regaining my composure, I try to act nonchalant. "It would be nice to be friends."

Nina sees through me as if I were made of glass. "You're in love with him, aren't you?" she teases.

"Maybe I do feel something when I'm around him, but love? Oh, I don't know. Everything's so confusing. Why do we have to live with this worry about who we talk to? Why can't this war be over? Then maybe Renier and I could get to know each other."

"Maybe there will be a way. Maybe."

Nina's voice, so soft and gentle, makes me believe it might happen. Me and Renier.

For the rest of our break under the tree, Nina and I speak very little. With each bite of bread, I look toward the steps of the storage cellar, imagining Renier walking up them as he did the day before. My longing only makes the time go by more slowly. I realize that it probably wouldn't be wise to sit with him again, but it doesn't make me wish for it any less. I feel certain he would join us if he could.

An idea suddenly strikes me, and I blurt it out to Nina. "I'm going to see if I can find Renier. He may still be in the warehouse. You don't have to come with me, but you can if you want to." My lack of real courage makes me hope she'll take up the offer.

"I'll come. We can put our things away and then go to the stockroom and pretend we're there to gather supplies for Madame Wilbert. The warehouse will be open, and we can see if he's there as we walk by. You should have a chance to talk to him before anyone notices. I'll stand watch and let you know if someone comes along."

"What will I say?"

Nina gives me a quick smile. "You'll think of something. Maybe you won't need to say anything at all."

I smile at her remark. "Let's go before I decide this isn't a good idea."

Approaching the hallway leading to the workroom, we change our minds and agree we should go directly to the stockroom. It might look odd to the floor supervisor if our things were there but we were not at the machines. Instead, we tuck our belongings inside our baggy work clothes and scurry along the corridor and down the stairs. Even from the hallway, the small room gives off a pungent smell of greasy equipment parts and a musty odor of old boxes that have been sitting on shelves for years.

We move along to the warehouse and I peer inside. I see no movement, not even M'sieur Dubois, the tall, gray-haired man who has monitored parcels sent from the linen factory for nearly thirty years. I step around the doorway and look at the shipments labeled for places I have never heard of before. For a brief moment, I imagine being sent to one of those far away destinations. Sadly, the crates will most likely end up at German military posts.

Dubois steps out from behind a stack of boxes. The burden of heavy work without assistance of younger, able-bodied men shows on his weathered face and sinewy limbs.

"M'sieur Dubois. I—Nina and I—we were just down the hall fetching supplies for Madame Wilbert."

"Are you sure supplies are what you came for?" he says with a tinge of suspicion, yet with a layer of kindness in his tone.

He speaks again before I have a chance to stammer out a response. "Renier isn't here. He didn't come to work this morning. Such a shame he's gone. He could do five times the work of young girls or old men."

I am embarrassed my intentions were so obvious. "*Merci*, M'sieur Dubois."

As I back out of the doorway, he murmurs, "Be careful, girl. There are many eyes and ears here. Not everyone is to be trusted."

I start to feel lightheaded. I can't believe Renier has gone. Why didn't he come to work? Could someone have questioned him? Did he decide to go away? Despair overtakes me, and I feel as if the air is too thin to breathe.

Nina pulls at my arm. "Catherine, the bell, the bell. We'd better go before Madame has our hides. Neither one of us needs to draw her wrath nor the fine she might inflict."

We head to the workroom. "Why don't you tell her you're not feeling well? Your work is caught up, and she can do without you for an afternoon. Go home and get away from this place. The soldiers will be in the taverns while everyone's at work; and you'll be safe walking alone this time of day."

Nina's plan is too tempting to resist. "Yes, maybe that's what I should do."

I remove my scarf and walk slowly to Madame's office. I tap on the door frame. She waves me in. I hold on to the edge of her old wooden desk with one hand as if to keep from collapsing.

"Madame Wilbert, I don't feel well. I'd like to ask your permission to leave."

"You do not look good, *ma chèrie.*"

"If I could just go home for this afternoon."

"*Oui.* I will have Sylvie cover your station, if need be."

"*Merci.*" I lower my head and make my way to the door.

To make my exit more believable, I touch the wall as I leave her small office. Because I have never left work for any reason, and unsure if my acting fools her, I continue out of the building slowly, with an unsteady gait. I'm relieved she had not suggested someone see me to my house. For now, I prefer to be alone.

As I travel along my familiar route, I think about Renier. Have the German soldiers found him and taken him away? Or, worse yet, have they suspected him of being a deserter and shot him? The last possibility is more than I can bear. All this worrying has actually made me feel ill. I'm glad to be almost home and hope Maman will be in the house when I get there. I will tell her about everything—the soldiers stopping me and Nina, Renier not being at work. Everything. She will understand. She always does.

When I arrive, I open the front door and go inside. There are no savory smells— no sounds of her clattering dishes or humming as she usually does while she cooks. Something is different. As I reach the kitchen, she looks up with surprise.

"You startled me, Catherine. Why aren't you at the factory?"

I see relief in her face when I lie and tell her I am simply a little tired, but there is something else happening. I can sense it. What is it? What's going on?

"The man you told me you had lunch with yesterday is here."

"Renier? In the house?" I am unable to conceive how this could possibly be true.

"In the root cellar. Apparently, you made quite an impression on him. He trusted you and took a chance in coming here."

I find myself concentrating on the word impression. What could have impressed him? Did he feel the way I did? Or was he simply looking for a safe haven?

"He told me that when he returned to his hideout at the factory last night, he could tell someone had been there. Someone looking around. Maybe a neighbor who lives in the area. Maybe even German soldiers. He couldn't be sure. We must all be careful. They say the trains run day and night with loot and war prisoners," she cautions.

I'm still reeling from the thought of Renier being in the root cellar.

"Catherine. Are you listening to me?"

"I'm sorry. I was thinking about what you said."

"We must be careful," she repeats. "We'll wait until dark to bring him into the house. You can find some of your father's old clothes for him to wear."

"Why is he hiding?" I make note of all the other questions I want to ask.

"He's running from the Nazis. If they find him they will kill him. We have to give him a safe place to stay. They took him just like they did Papa."

Though I'm frightened for myself and for Maman, knowing he's so close sparks something inside me. We'll provide a sanctuary for him as long as we can, even at our own peril. Someone would have done the same for Papa if he had run. I'm sure of it.

"You cannot say anything to anyone, not even Nina. What people don't know, they can't tell."

"Yes, Maman."

Waiting for night to come proves agonizing with time ticking by even more slowly than it does at the factory. I help Maman with the usual household chores, plus a few rarely done except in spring. I rearrange dishes on the shelves behind the fabric that serves as colorful fronts for the cabinets in the kitchen.

It is, of course, too dangerous to bring Renier from the cellar until nightfall, so we find more to busy ourselves. I wipe the shelf above the stove, cleaning behind and under everything in sight. When I lift the sugar and flour bins, my stomach lurches. They are nearly empty. Our rations are scarcely enough to feed two people. With a sinking feeling, I realize we will only be able to help Renier for a short while.

With nothing else to do, I sit and watch Maman from the divan as she guides fabric under the sewing machine's shiny metal foot, working on uniform jackets even though she has already completed her weekly quota. She looks up and smiles, her dark hair framing the lines that fan out like spokes from the corner of her eyes, a marker from years of close work at the machine. Despite the tension I feel from waiting, the smooth, rhythmic sound of the treadle soothes my nerves.

"Go ahead and stoke the stove so we'll have a warm drink ready," she suggests.

Even with her attempt to distract me with a routine task, I find it impossible to take my mind off Renier. As a result, I pay little attention to the flames in the firebox and reach to open the door without protecting my hand. I quickly pull away as the heat penetrates. The burn on my finger, slight but painful, brings me to my senses. I find a towel and place it around the handle and swing the door open. A wrought iron poker rests on a hook beside the stove, and I use it to adjust the coals before adding larger pieces. The orange embers give off a pleasant glow, making the small room more inviting. Although we have electricity in the house, it remains unreliable. We are thankful for the scant amount of coal we are able to buy to keep the stove going. Others, we know, are not as fortunate and huddle together during the cold evenings.

I pump water to fill the cast iron pot and place it on the stovetop. Coffee, a rare commodity and far too expensive for us, won't be served. Because imports have been greatly reduced in order to make use of supply ships for the armies, our tea rations consist of two ounces every two weeks. We'll have watered-down tea tonight. I decide that when the war ends, if it ever does, I will make tea as dark as the heavy blackout blinds we've been issued to cloak the light when Allied air forces rumble overhead, and I will savor every sip.

Maman pulls the inside layer of weathered curtains along the thin metal rod, arranging them carefully now that the sun has almost set. Drawing a shade before dusk would seem strange, so we don't vary our nightly routine. We can't afford to have anyone take notice of something different, so we sit quietly and wait for the long day to steal into the evening's darkness.

When the night is an inky black, she calmly says, "Why don't you go to the cellar and get him?" It's as if she's asking me to bring clothes in from the lines strung between two poles off the back porch. Regardless of how composed she sounds, the suggestion makes my heart flutter like a butterfly in summer.

"Go without light," she cautions.

Grabbing my shawl from behind the door, I swing it over my head and wrap it around my shoulders. I go outside and walk around the corner of the house to the cellar, thankful a piece of moon illuminates the yard. The chill of fall air makes me shiver—or is it the anticipation of finding Renier? After looking around to make sure no one is watching, I carefully push the large hook from the latch and slowly pull up the weathered wooden door.

"Renier?" I quietly call, hoping he will still be there.

He stoops over as he inches forward to keep his head from scraping the dirt ceiling. I hold the door while he climbs the steps. Emerging from the dark cavern, he looks much less confident than he'd seemed the day before. Once up the last step, he moves into the shadows. I check around again and then quietly lay the door down, making sure it remains latched.

I move toward the house. He follows close behind like a lost child, so close I feel his soft breath on my neck.

Despite our efforts to remain silent, the porch steps creak under our feet. As we enter the warm kitchen, Maman pours tea into the blue-rimmed cups decorated with tiny sunflowers. She hasn't used the good dishes since we last ate with Papa. A solitary candle burns in the middle of the table. This feels like a special occasion. It has been a long time since we had company.

We sit at the table as Renier tells me and Maman about the camps where Nazis take Jews and undesirables, as they are called. He gazes at his tea and keeps both hands around the cup for warmth. An awkward silence settles in the room like a dense fog. I try not to stare at him while Maman rummages through the cupboards fixing something to eat. When I look up, my eyes meet his. His intense gaze flows though me as if I'd been shocked by electric current. Trying to regain my composure, I push my chair to get up and help, but tip it over.

"Are you all right, Catherine?" Maman asks.

"*Oui*, I'm fine. This old chair has always been tottery." The blush heats my neck and creeps up my chin. I keep my face lowered as I right the chair. Not daring to see what Renier thinks of my clumsiness, I retreat to the sideboard and gather the silver.

She brings out cheese, dried meat, and bread. I place it on the table and then take a seat at my usual place, which happens to be next to Renier.

We sit quietly as he consumes the meat and cheese. Despite being at a loss for words, several questions bounce around in my head. The candle between us flickers as a passing draft catches the flame. The dimple on his chin deepens with the shadows. While he eats, a thoughtful frown appears on his face, perhaps considering how much to tell us.

He sets the piece of bread on his plate. "I'm originally from Holland," he begins, as if reading my mind.

His voice fills the kitchen. The last male voice in this room belonged to my father. I yearn for him and the life we knew. Consumed in the mind-dulling routine of home and the factory, I finally grasp how much I have been isolated from the magnitude of this loss.

The candle flame flutters again, and it seems even the walls strain inward toward the caress of his deep, baritone voice. I notice Maman soften at the sound.

"Maybe I should tell you about myself, but I'm not quite sure where to start."

Maman smiles. "Perhaps the beginning."

"Yes, the beginning," he says with a sheepish grin. "I am from Rotterdam. My given name is Dedrick."

"Your French is very good. I would never have guessed you weren't French," she says with astonishment, her tone quietly feminine in comparison.

"Being able to speak French has been very useful. After I escaped from the *Arbeidsdienst*, I decided to call myself something less German-sounding. The name Renier seemed safer."

"What's an *Arbeidsdienst*?" I ask, intensely curious at the recognition of a German word, but from Renier's lips it takes on a menacing tone.

"It's a German labor camp. I mostly did farm work there, like harvesting potatoes."

"When were you taken?" I ask.

"Early in 1941. I was almost twenty at the time. They invaded Holland and began to apprehend young men to work so they could feed the giant appetite of their army. Before that, I worked alongside my father on our farm."

I quickly do the math. Four or five years doesn't make him so much older. Lost in my private thoughts, I almost miss Maman's question.

"Didn't your father try to stop them from taking you?" she says, lines of concern furrowing her forehead.

"My father and mother were afraid for themselves and for me and my two younger brothers. Nothing they could say or do would have changed anything. They saw what happened to those who resisted."

"How many men did they take?" I want to know as much as I can about his life, to experience what he had gone through in my imagination, and to heal the wounds I supposed had been inflicted. It also offered the chance to confirm many of the stories we'd heard over the past several years.

"I'm not sure exactly how many there were, probably a couple hundred or so. We were separated into different crews according to the jobs we were given. With all the people and confusion, I managed to escape within a few days."

I lean closer to him as he tells his story, my knee brushing his thigh.

"Eventually, I headed back to Rotterdam by the underground, staying with people I knew or friends of friends. There must have been an informer because they captured me and took me to their base camp, this time as a deserter. I waited there until the commander decided what to do with me. He locked me up for a couple of weeks—enough time to teach me a lesson, but not too long to keep me away from the work. I spent every minute planning my next escape."

Maman fills his cup with tea. "You weren't afraid?"

"Yes, but too young to know how afraid I should have been."

"What happened then?" I ask.

Maman cuts another slice of cheese and places it in front of him.

He stares at the plate. "*Merci.*" After he takes a bite, he looks up and begins again. "I left with two other fellows from Holland. We agreed it would be better if we stayed together, but Ernst, the youngest, changed his mind and headed for home. I doubt he made it on his own. Jakob, the friend who escaped with me, figured it wasn't safe in Holland, so we decided to make our way through northern France. We planned to end up in Britain. Our weeks of travel ended when we were discovered by the *Maquis*, the French Resistance fighters. One of the officers advised us to abandon our plans to go to England because he said it was much too dangerous."

"Or did he say it to keep you as a soldier for the Resistance?" Maman says with a suspicious tone. The past years have given her an understanding of the ways of war. "Even those on the side of good can be corrupt for a cause. There are few who can be trusted, and many who have hidden motives."

Renier leans forward in the chair. "Looking back on it, I'm sure you're right. They couldn't afford to lose any able bodies. Patrolling forests in the unoccupied zones made it difficult to keep track of everyone, so I'm fairly certain they wanted us to believe staying with them would be the only way we would have a chance to survive."

We sit in silence for a moment, each alone with our thoughts. Yet, like a moth drawn to a flame, Maman shifts in her chair and finally asks, "But what brought you to Colmar?"

"We often acquired provisions from farmers by convincing them they were fighting against the Germans if they gave us supplies. On one such trip near La Mure, we were overtaken by German soldiers. I eventually escaped from them and have been hiding since. The choice was to escape or die there. Colmar seemed big enough to get lost in, at least for a while, and I was sure I could find work."

I turn uneasily in my chair. "Did Jakob get out with you?"

He closes his eyes for a moment as if reliving the difficult events. "No, he and I were separated. I found a way out by hiding in one of the transport trucks. I fled when the truck stopped. I had no way to get word to him."

"You have been through much, Renier. My husband's experience might have been similar."

I imagine men like Papa working long hours and being almost starved to death—fed only bread and cabbage soup as he described. I ask how the Nazis could expect a day's work if they didn't give them enough to eat. He gives me a half-smile. But before he can respond, Maman interrupts. I suppose she hopes I can keep my innocence.

At the end of the evening, Renier watches as Maman gets up from the table. "Good night and thank you for supper. Your kindness will be repaid someday."

"No need to thank me. Knowing one man has escaped the tyranny of the Germans is payment enough for me."

She putters in the kitchen putting things away as I collect the dishes from the table. "It's late, and we can clean in the morning when we won't need to use the light. For now, we need to make a place for Renier to sleep. We'll use the extra blankets from the dresser. It will be warmer there by the stove."

"*Oui*, Maman."

She retrieves the tattered, worn blankets from the bureau drawer. "You should go upstairs to bed, Catherine. You need your rest. You don't want to miss any more work." She had heard my stammer and seen me blush. Perhaps, too, she had sensed something in Renier and was uneasy about leaving us alone.

Before retiring to her bedroom, she helps me arrange the blankets on the black-and-white tiled floor. I imagine what it might be like to lay there with him. Would he be kind and gentle, or commanding like his deep voice?

She straightens the top cover and then turns to go upstairs. "Goodnight, Renier."

"Goodnight," he responds.

"Goodnight," I say as I leave the room, following her.

I head down the hall to my bedroom. "Night, Maman."

"*Je t'aime, mon ange.*"

I lay on my bed, staring at the ceiling, which arches to a peak. After waiting for a reasonable amount of time to pass, I get up and stand outside her room, listening for her rhythmic breathing. When I'm satisfied she's asleep, I sneak downstairs.

I watch Renier from the doorway as he sits at the table with his hands clasped in front of him. It's as if he's praying. I can't resist reaching out to comfort him and go sit at the table, placing my hand on his. He looks up as if he was expecting me and turns his hand over, lightly grasping my fingers. He stares at our intertwined fingers as though puzzled about how they got there. With his skin against mine, heat rushes through my body. When he shifts his gaze and looks into my eyes, my heart thuds painfully. My lips part to allow trapped air to escape. His hand tightens around mine. From his reaction, I feel courage I have never known before. I lean forward, gently push the candle away, and press my lips against his.

He releases his hand from mine and glides it along my arm. Goose bumps follow its path. There's a struggle between what my mind tells me I shouldn't do and what my body tells me to give in to. I can't believe what I'm doing, but when our lips part, I reach over and cup his face in my hands. He pushes his chair from the table, inviting me to come closer. I settle myself on his strong legs. He hesitates for a moment. I lean into him and run my hand through his hair. I softly utter the only word that comes to my mind. "Please."

Accepting what I offer as a gift, his hand slips around my back, and he presses me close. His mouth consumes mine. I never knew lips could be so soft and yet so strong at the same time.

Probably realizing where we are headed, he pulls away. "Catherine, we need to think about what's happening. I want you more than anything, but I don't want it to be like this."

Disappointed, I draw back. As much as I want him, I'm embarrassed and find it difficult to look at him. "I don't want you to think badly of me, Renier," I say with my head lowered.

"No, please, Catherine," he says, lifting my chin. "It's not that I don't want you. I want you more than I've ever wanted anything. But I must be respectful. I have to think about your maman and what she's done for me. I don't want to betray her kindness."

I'm nearly in tears. "What if you have to leave again like you've had to do all the other times? What if they find out you're here? This is the war, and no one knows what will happen to us. All I want is to be with you."

He kisses me on the forehead and tucks a wisp of hair behind my ear. "You're so young, Catherine."

"I'm almost eighteen." With his face between my palms I feel older. I seem powerful, as though I'm the more experienced one. I lean toward him again and slide my tongue under his earlobe until he groans and gathers me close for a second time.

He swings his arm under my legs and stands up from the chair, carries me to his make-shift bed, and lays me down. The coldness from the tiles penetrates the blanket, and I feel the hard floor against my shoulders. Lost in passion, I only vaguely realize my sweater is pushed up under my arms. Impulsively, I pull it over my head, casting it aside.

He looks at my breasts. His hot stare sends a chill through me. My fingers find the buttons on his shirt. With his shirt gaping open, I smother my hands over his broad chest. He leans into my touch, arching over me. Heat against heat, we are lost in each other. I gladly say goodbye to my innocence.

Nestled in his arms, I awake with a warm stickiness between my legs. I shift out of his clutch and carefully remove the blanket from under his arm and wrap it around myself. Fortunately, he hasn't roused from my movement. A glimmer of light from the candle droops into a puddle of wax and reveals a red stain marking the inside of my thighs. Blood is smeared on me and the blanket.

To control my panic, I decide to deal with the situation by figuring out a way to clean up before Maman finds out. I pour water into a pan and pull a rag from the box that sits by the back door. I wash the inside of my legs, being certain to rinse the scrap of cloth and hang it on a nail to dry. Finding a way to remove the stain in the tightly woven wool blanket will be another matter. Should I stash the blanket under the other ones in the bureau? Or should I try to wash it now? I opt to hide it from sight. I carefully fold it with the stain well-hidden and place it at the bottom of the pile. Hopefully, she will not see it before I think through this predicament.

Even though I hate to leave Renier and the comfort and warmth of his touch, I gather my clothes and tiptoe to my own bed with the cold from the floor shooting through the soles of my feet. I wince at each step. I snatch my nightgown from the peg and slip it over my head, letting it cascade over me. Pulling on a pair of heavy socks hurries the thawing process.

As I lay there, I worry about facing Renier in a few hours. In the silent darkness before I fall asleep, I think about what he said—how special he felt with me and that I was beautiful. The second part hadn't seemed real. Me, a beautiful girl? No man, except Papa, ever told me that before. I lowered my head when he whispered the words, but he tilted my chin upward and repeated the phrase and looked into my eyes as if he wanted to be sure I knew he meant everything he said.

He told me about his family—how he missed them and didn't know if he'd ever see them again. It hurt him to be so far away. He explained that no matter what happened after the war, he would return to Colmar and find me and Maman. I am sure he meant that too.

Chapter 3

Waking to the muffled sounds of Maman and Renier talking in the kitchen, I hurry to get dressed and stare into the silver mirror Papa gave me for my twelfth birthday. Do I look different? I think I look older, more mature. I run the brush through my hair. One last glance in the mirror and I nervously go downstairs. I hope Maman won't notice the change that seems so obvious to me.

I rush through breakfast, doing my best to keep Maman from noticing the looks he and I share. As I get ready to leave for the factory, I pluck the kerchief from the sleeve of my coat and loosely tie the plaid square under my chin. I ask Renier if he'll be here when I return. The question is already out in the room before I can capture it and safely store it with my other thoughts. Out of the corner of my eye, I see Maman turn to look at me. I quickly say goodbye and sneak another look at him. Looking over my shoulder, I catch his attention. He seems sad when I had expected a smile.

As soon as I open the front door, I see Nina walking along the path that runs between our houses. I pull in a deep breath and try to clear my head. Having shared every secret, I know keeping my new feelings from her will require avoiding the subject of Renier as much as possible. When Nina sees me, she gives me a tiny wave, barely taking her hand out of her pocket. Standing at the point where the path and the lane meet, I wait until she approaches.

"Salut."

Ignoring my greeting, Nina scowls. "I can't believe how cold it is this morning. It feels like winter. This coat gets thinner by the day."

"I hadn't really noticed, I guess."

"You must be numb. Your coat is more threadbare than mine."

Thinking about Nina's words, I realize I probably am numb. The world looks different today, as if nothing could scare me or even make me angry. I feel something I wasn't sure I would ever feel or might even have the chance to feel again. But oh, how I wish I could spill all my thoughts to Nina and describe every detail about Renier! Instead, I work deliberately to chatter about insignificant and everyday things to keep my mind on anything but him.

Nina's question comes out of nowhere and startles me with just the sound of his name. "Have you heard anything about Renier?"

I pause, trying not to sound anxious. "No, I haven't. Have you? Maybe he'll be at the factory today."

Nina pokes my arm with her elbow. "I hope so. I think he really likes you. Anyway, I trust he's not in some kind of trouble."

"He probably had business to take care of yesterday."

"Wouldn't he have had to ask M'sieur Dubois for permission to leave?"

"I suppose, but it isn't our affair. We'd better get going," I say, trying to discourage any more talk of Renier. I might fool everyone else, but Nina will see right through me.

Arriving at the factory, we hurry inside to the warmth of the red brick building. The looms are already in operation and heat begins to make its way to the large, curved-top ceiling.

I enter the cavern of activity and find my way to my station at the loom. I search the expressions of the women to determine if any of them notices something different about me. I'm certain my new emotions are written across my face like lessons on a chalkboard. If they detect a change, their concentration on the monotonous work never betrays their thoughts.

The morning slowly melts into the lunch break. Normally, I would find a good place to stop, but Madame Wilbert asks me to stay and finish the piece I am working on. Relieved that I can insulate myself from creating more white lies, I gesture to Nina to go ahead and eat lunch without me. I'm not hungry anyway. Maybe this is some form of punishment. You can never tell about Madame's motives. For now, I concentrate on my task and choose to get lost in the repetition of the shuttle as it goes up and down over the strands of thread.

Looking from my vantage point, I watch the door and see the horde of workers trickle to their stations after the break. Nina shuffles through the wide doorway and gives me a quick look. Trying not to call attention to the fact I've worked while everyone else ate lunch, I momentarily slow my pace and work as quietly as I can while the worker bees return to the hive. This day at the factory will not end soon enough for me.

Having spent hours after lunch at the loom, my legs wobble under me and the soreness between my thighs is more noticeable now. The bell signals the end of our shift and I head to the rack of coats, rummaging to find mine. I don't see Nina's. Maybe she was afraid to be seen with me and has already left. When I reach the end of the stone walkway, I spot her up ahead.

"Nina." I call. "Nina," I call again, striding toward her.

She stops and waits for me to catch up.

"I'm glad I saw you." I say as I gasp for air.

"When I grabbed my things, I saw Madame watching from her doorway, so I decided not to wait around. What's going on? Why didn't you leave for lunch?"

"She wanted me to finish what I was working on, and by then, everyone was coming back, so I continued to work. Maybe she was having one of her bad days."

"She seems to be acting strange lately."

We walk in silence along our usual route. I think about getting home and seeing Renier. As we arrive at the fork in the path separating our houses, we each head for home. It's almost dark, and the dim light coming from the front window radiates a glow that immediately warms me. But why aren't the curtains drawn? When I'm at home, I know I'll feel safe from any kind of scrutiny, but now I'm nervous Renier will not be as anxious to see me as I am to see him.

I enter the house and look around expecting to see Maman sitting at the table. She is not even in the kitchen.

"Maman?" I call out. "Maman?" I shout from the bottom of the stairs.

"Up here."

Her soft voice drifts from her bedroom. I hurry up the stairs and stop at the door. She's sitting on the bed holding a stack of papers. "What are you doing?"

She looks up and places the papers in her lap. "Did you know your father wrote letters to me before we were married? He never sent them. I imagine he wrote things he felt too embarrassed to say. After we were married and you came along, he gave them to me bundled with a piece of twine. I hadn't read them for such a long time."

"Why are you reading them tonight? Why is it important right now?" I am helpless to understand what's going on.

"Renier's gone," she says, her words penetrating me like a sharp knife. "I knew you would be hurt. I know you care about him. I can see it in your face, Catherine."

It takes a moment to digest her words. My throat is as dry as ash and I can barely speak. "When?" I drop next to her on the bed. "When, Maman?"

"I don't know. He didn't say anything about leaving. I sewed most of the afternoon while he tinkered around the house. He went outside once, but he came back in and we talked for a while. After I finished sewing, I got up to start supper, and he was gone. I checked everywhere. It felt like I had lost Papa all over again. I came here and found these letters. They remind me of how much we loved each other, and I thought of you and Renier. I'm so sorry, *mon ange*."

I stare into her eyes. "There must have been something that alarmed him. Did anything unusual happen?"

"No, nothing."

"Did he take anything with him? Any food?" I don't wait for her to answer and dash to the kitchen with her following behind. Could it be she hadn't heard him say he would return?

I go through every drawer and cupboard, hoping that if he hadn't taken something to eat maybe he would be coming back. A chunk of bread and a block of cheese are missing. I feel as though someone threw a punch I didn't see coming. My legs crumble underneath me, and I slide down the side of the cabinet until I'm on the floor with my knees almost touching my face. Pressing my forehead to my crossed arms, I sit and weep.

Maman leans over me. "He wouldn't leave unless he had good reason. But he'll be back. I'm sure of it."

"He told me if he had to leave, he'd return to find me when the war was over," I say through my tears.

She touches my shoulder. "He will. I know he will."

When I have no tears left to shed, I get up from the floor and coil my arms around Maman's tiny frame and hug her for a long time.

After releasing my embrace, she straightens her clothes and hobbles to the basin, pulling a pot from the shelf and then setting it on the stove. "I'm going to fix soup. Why don't you peel some potatoes?" she directs, probably hoping to usher me to a normal routine.

A strange feeling surrounds the kitchen as we work. The night before, we listened to Renier and welcomed his stories and presence. Now I look at the woodstove in the corner and recall the time he and I spent together. The house feels as if we are closing it up and leaving.

The soup's aroma stirs my hunger and forces me to think about something other than Renier. Maman and I eat in silence, each of us knowing exactly what the other is thinking. There is no need for words, not for now at least.

After we finish, I help clear the dishes and clean up. It's difficult to work with my thoughts constantly returning to Renier. I can't help but think something scared him away. I play out scenes in my mind about what I'll say when I see him again.

Eventually, the chill of the night begins to penetrate the house after the warmth from the cooking stove fades. Finding the coal bin empty, I decide to go out to the shed next to the cellar and bring in a load for tonight and the next several evenings.

"I'm going for some coal, Maman."

"I thought Renier made sure it was full."

"No, it's empty. I'll fetch some and be right back. Go on to bed, Maman."

I grab my faded coat and the key to the shed and hurry outside. Clenching one hand tightly around the collar to keep out the crisp September air, I hold on to the skinny black handle of the scuttle with the other. Maman and I have always kept the coal shed locked to deter unwanted scavengers from helping themselves to our cache of black gold. Approaching the tiny building, I find the rusted lock hanging open and threaded through the latch. My heart stops. Slowly, I open the door, not sure what I'll find. For a split second the hair on the back of my neck bristles. An uncanny feeling tells me there is something I need here, and my feet are frozen in the doorway. Moonlight enters through the cracks of the boards. Inside the rickety building, someone shares the darkness with me. A shadowy figure stands in the far corner.

A small breath catches in my throat. The open door beckons behind me. *Run, Catherine, run!* But I cannot.

The outline of a man in a uniform steps forward. "Catherine?"

I drop the scuttle. "Renier! Thank God it's you!" Relief overwhelms me as he takes me into his strong arms. "I'm so thankful to see you, but what are you doing in here?"

"I needed a place to hide until dark and counted on you coming for coal. I killed a man, Catherine—a German soldier—the one who drove the transport truck. They won't stop until they find me. I'm not safe in Colmar anymore. I have to leave, but I couldn't stand the thought of not seeing you again."

Hearing him say the same things I feel fills me with a sense of joy. I always dreamed of having this kind of chance at love, but never truly believed it would happen. When I'm with him the world appears so different. He is the piece of me I didn't know was missing.

Tears pool in the corner of his eyes which seem to release a raw sadness and sorrow that surprises me. We hold each other as if it might be the last time we'll be together. Maybe it will be. We have no way of knowing.

Chapter 4

Early in the morning as Nina and I stash our cloaks in the factory workroom, Madame Wilbert comes out of her office and heads straight toward us.

"*Bonjour*, Madame Wilbert," I say, unable to read her expression.

"*Bonjour*, Catherine." She tips her head to Nina, acknowledging her before turning her piercing eyes on me. "I need you to work late today."

"*Oui*, Madame."

"Good. There is much work to be done. I can't afford to get behind now. We're already short in the warehouse. Seems the man who worked for M'sieur Dubois has disappeared. You haven't heard anything about him, have you, Catherine?"

My throat tightens and I try to keep my voice from cracking. "No, I haven't. I know who you're talking about—all the women here do—but this is the first I've heard he's gone." I attempt to sound aloof and uninterested, but Madame's relentless stare makes me believe she's not fooled. Even so, she dismisses us both with a wave of her hand as if to shoo flies away. She turns and makes her way to her office and closes the door.

"What could have happened? It's as though she thinks you know something about him."

Nina's statement momentarily stops me. "If she thinks I know anything, she'll make me wish I didn't."

"What are you going to do?" Nina says under her breath.

"I'm going to continue to tell Madame and anyone else who asks that I know nothing," I lie. I see relief in Nina, but feel ugly for having to be dishonest. This is the first time I can remember ever saying something to her that wasn't true. With this double life I'm leading, I am positive there will be more deceptions in the future. "I'm not sure what's going on, but we'd better get busy." I hurry to my place at the station.

Our encounter with Madame Wilbert leaves my stomach twisted into knots. Why did she ask me if I knew anything about his disappearance? Why had I been singled out? Nina and I were both seen with him. I chastise myself for being a foolish girl who flirted openly with a man. How could I have been so stupid? Why wasn't I more careful? I have to be mindful of my actions and conversations with Nina from now, and everyone else for that matter.

My mind drifts in and out from thoughts of Renier to the questions I might have to answer from Madame. After making an error in a weave, I command myself to focus on the task at hand.

Then suddenly, the sound of boots clacking in unison on the wooden floor fills the factory. Madame slinks out of her office and stands next to the doorway as German soldiers congregate around her.

"You are in charge of these workers?" the German officer growls, presenting it as more of an accusation than a question.

Madame takes a few steps from the door. "Yes, but only the women who work in this part of the factory," she answers evenly. "What can I do for you, *Kommandant?*"

"We're looking for a deserter. We have information he's here."

"I know nothing of such a person. We would never disobey orders of the German Army and hide a fugitive." Madame Wilbert uses a firm voice but with enough deference to show the officer he has complete control.

I never know what to think about Madame. Her expression is as changeless and stern as the French winter. I often wonder if she intentionally pulls her straight hair tautly back to keep the corners of her mouth from lifting in a smile. However, at this moment, she looks colder and more ominous than I have ever seen her.

The officer waves his arm toward the upstairs and then in the direction of the warehouse. "Search the building!" The half dozen soldiers milling around him look like hound dogs waiting to fetch a piece of meat. "Find him!" He returns his harsh gaze to Madame. "No one leaves this building until I say."

Madame Wilbert straightens her back and purses her lips. "Of course. Anything you need. Anything at all."

The slender commander with a pistol strapped to his hip crosses his arms across his chest and stands with his feet apart, a human barricade to the workroom entrance. In any other circumstance, his small build would make his stance laughable. The residents of Colmar, however, have learned to fear even puny German commanders in exceptionally crisp uniforms that suggest self-importance and ambitions of cruelty.

Overhearing pieces of their conversation, I grip the shuttle of the loom firmly to keep my hands from shaking. I hope the soldiers will question the supervisors and leave the rest of us alone.

For once, I am glad Renier is gone. I pray he has gotten far away from the scum who hunt him. I think about Nina and how tempted I had been to confide in her about my time with Renier. My restraint proves invaluable. Thankfully, she knows nothing about what became of him after his brief time at the linen factory. Still, I wonder what Madame suspects and wrestle with the worry she might direct the Germans to question me.

Not one of us speaks a word. Only the rattle of the automatic machines still in operation make any noise. We freeze at the sound of the Nazis as they tromp up and down the halls and stairways. Terror permeates the room. No one dares look up for fear of being singled out. Maybe our silence and bowed heads will make us invisible.

Within minutes, each uniformed soldier comes from a different area of the building and announces the deserter can't be found. The six men converge around their commander and take turns giving their specific accounts in German, bits and pieces of a language I've learned in order to survive in my own country. From their expressions and words, I can tell they are exasperated by their lack of success. The commander escorts Madame Wilbert into her office and closes the door while the other soldiers stand as sentries outside. Each man glares at us, apparently searching for signs of weakness, or hoping one of us will divulge a clue.

When she and the officer emerge, Madame nods as if in some sort of agreement. The smirk she gives him makes me think she has struck a deal with the devil.

The commander signals two of his men, sending them down the stairs to the warehouse. "Bring me the warehouse supervisor. Now!"

Alice, closest to Madame, starts to cry, but is immediately hushed by those around her. A collective panic spreads across the shop floor like flames devouring stubble in a field.

A soldier at each arm forces M'sieur Dubois up the stairs. We have all heard the horrible stories of Nazi interrogations before, but none of us believed it would play out right before us. How much will the old man be able to endure? Or will he lie to protect his own life?

The commander holds the handle of his whip with one hand and the thin leather tip with the other. "I understand you had a new man working in the warehouse. Is this true?"

"*Oui,*" M'sieur Dubois answers with a shaky voice.

"Where is he?"

"I don't know. He only worked for a few days, and then he was gone."

Extending his leather riding whip, the commander snaps it across M'sieur Dubois' face. A deep red mark appears on his cheek with blood surfacing at the corner of his mouth. "I don't have time for this. I want to know where he is!"

Another crack of the whip hits the old man around the neck. The *Kommandant* tips his chin and one of his young Nazi soldiers strikes him across the shoulder blades with the butt of his gun. M'sieur Dubois crumples to his knees on the floor.

"I know nothing. I don't know where he is."

Another lashing tears across the old man's back. Gritting his teeth, the commander spits out the words, "I want to know where he is. The punishment for harboring a fugitive is death by execution. If you don't know where he is, which one of the other workers does?"

"No one," Dubois says, his voice quavering.

Another blow from the young soldier's rifle explodes to the back of his head, driving Dubois flat on the floor where he moans in agony.

I struggle with the knowledge I was the last one to see Renier before he left Colmar. I hate myself because M'sieur Dubois knows nothing and is being beaten for what I could confess. I want to demand an end to this inquisition, but instead I'm paralyzed with guilt and fear.

Drawing a gun from his holster and pointing it at the old man, the commander delivers each word slowly and deliberately. He releases the safety from his pistol. "One last time. Who else knows the deserter's whereabouts?" He lifts M'sieur Dubois' head with the tip of his jackboot and looks down on him.

"I know of no one."

Frustrated, the commander kicks him in the head. "I will not tolerate your lies."

M'sieur Dubois slowly rises on his elbows and clasps his hands to his chin as if begging forgiveness from a schoolyard bully.

The *Kommandant* pulls the trigger and a shot pierces the stillness of the factory. With a resounding thud, Dubois falls to the floor, lying in an oozing patch of glossy red.

"The old man knows nothing now." The commander calmly turns, gathers his troops and leaves the factory.

We are witnesses to a lesson in Nazi brutality we will never forget.

Chapter 5

The winter gradually pulls patches of daylight from the sky, and my mood darkens with the lengthening nights. I yearn to know if Renier is safe, or if he will ever return. It is all I can think about as each day dissolves into the next. In spite of the fact he's been gone only a few months, I fret about whether he still cares for me. I ache to be with him again and hear him repeat the beautiful things he said that night. With this time apart, will he regret what we shared together? I am so unsure of myself and afraid the closeness, the deep sense of caring I thought he felt, is only in my imagination.

The realities of my dreary existence erase any dreams I might entertain. Rations continue to decrease as the war consumes the basic necessities for survival at a gluttonous rate. Our canned food and other winter supplies dwindle. The cellar reveals extra shelf space each day, but it doesn't matter to me. I don't feel like eating. Even thinking about food makes me sick to my stomach. I survive on bread and little else. At least there will be more for Maman.

"I want you to eat," Maman says, encouraging me to put meat on my bones.

I try to placate her. "Maybe a little bit." These days, we often battle over the subject of food. My arms are scrawny, but my waistband fits tightly. I don't like arguing with her, but I can't bring myself to eat. There seems to be no point.

She fills a small bowl with broth and sets it in front of me. I take the spoon and draw eights on the bottom as if practicing number writing on a chalkboard.

"What's wrong, *mon ange*? You've not been yourself."

"Nothing, Maman. I just want the war to be over. That's all."

"We all do. There is nothing we can do except pray each day will bring us closer to the end."

I am consoled more by the fact she has preserved her faith through death and destruction than by her words that are meant to comfort me. I don't think I will ever know the sense of peace she manages to maintain.

Time at home limps along with an endless repetition of chores, and the days at the factory inch ahead mechanically. The house feels empty even with the two of us here. There is a depth of loss I've never known before, and I wonder if things will ever be good again. But the monotony of each day builds a false sense of security. The reality of the war means only too little to eat, too little to enjoy. We wait every day for news of Allied troop advancements that might release us from this living hell. I have become complacent, but nothing could prepare me for the shattering of my current existence.

This sense of refuge abruptly ends on a bleak, dreary day shortly before Christmas when the German soldiers once again force their way into the linen factory. We are startled into immobility by the sound of screeching brakes and the fast clomping of heavy boots making their way up the stone steps. Staring between the threads that create a simple screen between me and the door, I watch as the elite SS soldiers rush in, their rifles drawn.

The leader orders us to line up as the other soldiers spread around the perimeter of the room. We hurriedly comply. Madame Wilbert watches as we line up against the far wall. We form a tight line, standing shoulder to shoulder, our backs against the brick with the tall row of windows above us. Staying close to one another seems to be our only defense. I feel the trembling of the woman next to me through my skirt.

I wonder how many others like us have faced these same men and failed to walk away. Waiting to learn our fate, afraid to breathe, we stand as still as the marble statues in the town square. The terrifying silence, made more ominous by the clack of a single set of boots methodically making their way to the middle of the room, sends a chill through me like a Northern wind.

Resembling a vulture deciding which piece of meat to pick at, the SS commander moves to the front of us and surveys his prey. He stands with his feet spread wide and stable, his hands clasped behind his back. The SS insignia is stuck prominently to his lapel. The SS are feared more than any of the regular Nazi soldiers. They are Hitler's chosen troops, specializing in getting results with their precision and cruelty. The officer's demeanor indicates he clearly gets his way. He seems confident that not one of the women before him will challenge his authority. Obviously, none of us poorly-nourished factory workers pose any threat to his Nazi war machine.

"Get me a list of all the workers and their documents," he barks at Madame Wilbert.

Eager to endear herself, she hurries into her office, quickly emerging with a folder and hands over the identity and nationality records for the forty-two of us. In that one act, she literally presents our lives to the German SS. And in this moment, I feel as much hatred for her as I felt during the killing of M'sieur Dubois only months ago.

Sifting through the papers, he calls out last names followed by a first.

My name is fifth on the list. Nina's name is called after mine.

"You will be reassigned," he states coldly. "Move forward and stand over there."

Pleading cautiously, Madame Wilbert asks, "Respectfully, *mein Kommandant*, how can I run these machines without many of my workers? How will I be able to keep producing uniforms for the German Army?"

The officer carelessly flips a gloved hand toward the other workers cowering against the wall. "They can make up the extra hours."

With a shove from the end of rifles, the eight of us are herded outside to an idling truck, its gray exhaust plume rising in the late afternoon air. My mind fills with terror. Where are they taking us? What will happen?

Will Maman ever have a chance to know the baby I am carrying?

BOOK II:
ERVIN ACKERMAN

HEADED TO EUROPE

Chapter 6

After twenty-two months of training, the 90th Division finally departs the wide-open, mesquite-filled range country of west Texas and makes a brief stop at Camp Pilot Knob near Yuma, Arizona. Whoever called Arizona blistering hot never spent the night in a fart sack in the desert. I shivered rather than snoozed. I'm pretty sure the desert at dark could freeze the balls off a brass monkey.

My next home away from home will be Camp Granite situated in the Harquahala Mountains—part of the California/Arizona Maneuver Area. In the final weeks of September, we stage large-scale, mock-battles that rage from Needles to Yuma. Airplanes swoop down and strafe the hell out of everything below. Artillery shells cover the ground 'til Hell wouldn't have it, while tanks rumble and blast away. I can't imagine any desert critters ever surviving these live-fire exercises.

Now, with fall temperatures setting in, we finally find relief from the daytime's scorching summer heat and prepare for overseas movement. We'll be headed across the pond. Nobody knows what to expect. We just do our jobs and take each day as it comes.

By late December, obsolete railcars take several thousand of us from three regiments on a coast-to-coast trip to Fort Dix, New Jersey, on what seems like the slowest moving train ever headed east. It feels as though we get sidetracked for every milk-run that comes along. Rumor has it we change our route instead of making a straight shot in case a Nazi spy gets wind of the transfer of troops and supplies. If a zigzag course throws the Krauts off course, it's okay by me, no matter how tiring it gets.

Salt Lake City, our first real stop, has the crew unloading a few cars while we're allowed to get off and stretch our legs for a spell. The train rumbling down the tracks vibrates through the seat of my pants and I gladly take the chance to move around.

"You've got ten minutes. Be back at 0700," the sergeant bellows so no one misses his brief instructions.

"I'm bailing out," I tell my buddy Hank. We'd become fast friends in boot camp with our shared Nebraska roots. "Want to see if we can find something to drink besides this cup of joe? A spoon could stand up by itself in this stuff."

"Nah, go ahead, Erv. The prettiest sight I ever saw was Salt Lake in my rearview mirror."

"Okay, suit yourself. But I've got to get up. I'm not used to this much sitting." I squeeze between Hank and the seat in front, edging toward the side door. I'll find out about his past in Salt Lake City later.

I'd been cooped up for over twenty-four hours, and this provided the chance to feel solid earth under my feet. I plan to take advantage of the break one way or another.

Hank and I are like brothers, depending on each other, sharing the good times and the hard ones. We are farm boys who wound up together for basic training in the 359th Regiment at Camp Barkeley, Texas. Our outfit reactivated into the 90th, originally made up of recruits from Texas and Oklahoma, was dubbed "TO" for the two states. By the time draftees from all over the country rolled into Barkeley in '42 the Texas–Oklahoma tag no longer fit. TO now stood for "Tough Ombres."

Camp Barkeley, a huge base of buildings, hutments, barracks, and even cells for German prisoners of war, had more people than any town I'd ever seen. There were so many of us that when we marched in daily formations the locals reported that clouds of dust we kicked up could be seen ten miles away in Abilene.

At twenty-seven years old, I was drafted into the Army along with two of my six brothers. My oldest brother, married with a family and a farm to run, didn't have to serve, and the three Mama liked to call her babies were too young to get called up. Farming, considered critical in fighting the Nazi menace, spurred every store front in our neck of the woods to post a sign that read, "*Food Will Win the War.*" And if you didn't farm, you did your patriotic duty by tending a Victory Garden in your backyard.

Having three sons from the same family sent off to war wasn't uncommon, especially when the Bohemians sit on the local draft board and make decisions about boys from German families. A history of bad blood between the Czech Bohemians and Germans still lingers in Fillmore County—an uneasy truce that harbors old prejudices. Why the Bohemians control the Board I'll never know, but they seemed to pick a lot of us German-Americans. Guess they think German blood should fight German blood.

The hissing sound from the train's exhaust reminds me of the short time I have, and I quickly work my way through the crush of men searching for freedom from the overcrowded railcars. I set out to find something to drink and spy a familiar red Coca-Cola machine inside the station. I could stand a pop right now—anything besides the rotgut brew they try to pass off as coffee. I grab the shiny chrome handle and lift the lid. "Son of a gun." There's nothing but empty racks where bottles should be hanging.

"You got any more Cokes?" I ask the old man behind the counter.

"Nope. We've been out for a few days. Might try next door." He points to his left. "Go through the hall, down those stairs and into the next building. They've got an icebox. Could have some in there."

"Thanks." Like I have time for that.

I lean against the wall, check my watch, and light one of the free cigarettes doled out daily by the Army. The only tobacco I'd seen before the war came out of a Red Velvet can—the kind my dad used to roll his own. But with the constant offer to "take ten, smoke up," I had started the coffin nail habit.

There must have been a signal to get back on board because all of a sudden everyone scrambles out of the station like kids let out for recess. I drop my cigarette and crush it under the sole of my boot.

Having forgotten to count the number of railcars from the engine, I struggle to remember which opening to climb into and hope I'll find my place in the dozens of dull green boxes that sit waiting. Recognizing a guy I sat behind, I track him as he winds his way through the sea of drab olive uniforms. I won't make the same goof at the next stop, wherever that might be.

"Damn, I couldn't remember which car we were on. I almost had to sit next to another lucky stiff," I say to Hank, stepping over piles of gear to get to my seat.

Hank grins. "Did you find something to drink?"

"Nah, just had a smoke, that's all. Holy crap, it's cold out there."

"Yeah, well, your blood got a lot thinner in the desert, then. You'd better get used to it. I hear our next stop's Cheyenne, Wyoming," he says with resignation.

"How far is that?"

"A long haul." He slumps down and rests his feet on the duffle bag with his name and serial number stenciled in white paint across the side. From what I can tell, Hank could sleep standing up or hanging from a hook if he had to. Guys like Hank can doze for hours on end through the rhythm of the rails. But for those who stay awake, talk always finds its way to a girl back home or the dream of a sweetie as beautiful as Betty Grable. Of course, no remark about Betty Grable is complete without someone bringing up her glorious gams—always followed by an eardrum-breaking whistle. As for me, my wife is the only Betty I need.

During daylight, fellows read magazines or letters from their sugars, or play cards on tables made from anything flat, or simply crouch in the aisle and shoot craps. Having a wife with a baby daughter at home who needs most of my twelve-dollar paycheck, I keep the flying dice at a safe distance. Instead, I look out the window as time and the landscape roll by. Never having been any farther than North Dakota on a threshing crew, I want to take a good, hard look at the U. S. of A. As much as I ache to live an everyday life with my new family, I know this country is worth fighting for.

Wyoming moves past my window with an occasional herd of antelope sprinting through the sagebrush. The stops, starts, and coded whistles that are routine railroad shorthand for the crew never phase the pronghorns. They seem to ignore the green snake winding its way through their territory. I look forward to seeing anything besides flat prairie out this dingy square of glass. It feels like it will take forever to get across this state.

Occasionally, a guy slides a window up from its tight frame and clears the smell of sour armpits and smelly feet from the crowded railcar only to replace the odor with sulfur fumes of burnt coal from the engine. The rush of cold air and the sharp stench always wakes everyone up and a howl echoes through the traveling coach.

A poor sap sitting directly behind the opening hollers, "What? You born in a barn?"

Hearing the mention of a barn makes me think about home as the train sits on a siding, waiting for another west-bound freighter to pass. I imagine the milk separator humming on the back porch and the sweet aroma of fresh cream drifting throughout the house.

Mostly, it seems as though we sit and wait more than we move. Eventually we'll be on our way through Nebraska, and I watch for a familiar landmark.

Snow-swept stubble fields mark the beginning of farm country, and a bunch of leafless cottonwoods suggest we are getting close to a river. Sure enough, there she sits—big, wide and frozen rock solid.

"Looks like the Platte, if you ask me," I offer to Hank and anyone else who might want a geography lesson. As a kid, I remember going down to the river in the summer to look for sunken logs and then slowly feeling the hiding places of a slick-skinned channel cat. I'd grab them behind the head and toss them onto the bank. I always knew what we'd be having for supper those nights.

Hank snaps me out of my daydream. "Yeah, we probably aren't far from the town of North Platte. Maybe we'll be stopping there. I sure hope so anyway. I heard about some ladies who started a thing called a canteen for troops who roll in."

"A canteen? Where'd you hear that?" I imagine another one of Hank's stories that starts out seriously but ends in a punch line. He can say anything with a straight face and reigns as the king of practical jokes.

"I ain't *always* sleeping," he says. "I keep my ears open. Never know when there might be something worth knowing about."

"Yeah, well, a lot of stuff is latrine rumor. I don't believe much of what I hear."

"I didn't hear it from a G.I. My mom has a cousin in Broken Bow, and she said ladies from miles around are baking stuff and taking it to the depot for the soldiers. They meet every troop train coming through with snacks and magazines and such."

Saliva pools in my mouth from the thought of good homemade cooking. "Geez, Hank, why didn't you say something before? What kind of snacks?"

"I guess they make sandwiches, fried chicken, doughnuts. Things like that. If the trains don't stop to let the guys get off, the women hand it to them through the windows." Hank has my full attention as well as the ears of all the men sitting around us. "I heard tell there are young gals who make popcorn balls and hide their name and address on a slip of paper in the middle for a fella to find."

I'm not interested in one of those popcorn pen pals, but those other goodies sure sounded swell. I close my eyes and snag forty winks, picturing food that doesn't come in green cans with black lettering on it.

I wake to the sound of two long and one short whistle, and translate the code. We're approaching a station. I sit up straight.

"You getting off this time, Hank?"

"Wouldn't miss this one for anything. That's for sure," he says like a kid waiting for the signal to file downstairs on Christmas morning.

"I sure hope they'll let us get out of here."

Hank twists in his seat and looks out the window. "If they don't, I'm going to claw my way out of this tin can."

Staggering between the cars as the train slows, Sergeant Lewis grips anything he can find to steady himself before coming to a stop at the front of our car to make an announcement. "Ten minutes, gents. Make the most of it," he says, as if delivering a last request before execution.

"Ah, come on, Sarge. Give us a little extra time," a man in the rear pleads.

"I'm not running this train. The engineers have their schedule, and the crew will grease the wheels and fill the water tender. When that's done, we're on our way."

Not wanting to waste any precious time, we scramble off and head to the big white sign with black letters. *Canteen.* The cold hits my nostrils and stings my lungs.

Hank is dead-on about this place. There are sandwiches, plates of fried chicken, hard-boiled eggs, pies, doughnuts, canned pickles, and fresh milk to drink. Ladies in aprons and flower print dresses who look a lot like my mama and five sisters stand behind jury-rigged tables—wood planks on top of saw-horses—piled high with so much food you can hardly see the tablecloths on top. This must be what Heaven is like.

Because things have to move at a brisk pace to get everyone fed, the ladies fill plates with food and serve them as fast as we can snatch them. Their assembly-line precision would challenge any conveyor belt you'd see in a factory. My mouth waters with the taste of fried chicken and homemade bread with butter so thick it must have been spread with a trowel. They treat us like rich relatives staying for Sunday dinner.

Besides a banquet rivaling a feast at a church social, there are tables of free cigarettes and stacks of magazines with a few Bibles sprinkled in, comic books, song sheets, and playing cards scattered around—even a supply of writing paper and envelopes for those who want to scribble a note.

An older woman with eye glasses perched low on her nose calls out to the crowd, "Any of you boys need to get a letter home?" With the invitation, several guys rush the table where she stands by the door, all talking at the same time.

"Eloise," she summons. "Come help me jot down addresses for these nice young men." A good-looking young lady hustles over, picks up an envelope and writes an address as fast as she hears it.

A piano in the corner comes alive with a jazzy tune I don't recognize. The G.I. playing has a look in his eyes like he's forgotten all about home. It's a good thing someone has musical talent because all anyone ever wanted me to play was far, far away. My dad and uncles took up the mouth harp but music was never my strong suit. With the good times and a belly as full as a tick, my worries melt away, even if it's only for a little bit.

A soldier plucks Eloise from behind the table and steers her out to a clear area to shake a leg. She has a big smile on her face until the woman in glasses gives her a disapproving look. I'd seen Mama give my sisters that same stink-eye when she didn't think they were acting like proper ladies. Eventually, he whisks her back to her mail duty, but she gets a quick lecture from the older woman just the same.

The train's whistle blows, piercing the cold air. Our ten-minute break has come to an end. The North Platte Canteen will be nothing more than a sweet memory. I leave the building and move with the mass of men. We are so tightly packed that we shuffle instead of walk. Once near the train, men cross in a hundred different directions to get to their cars. The lively spirit we had when we got off the train is nowhere to be found now.

We've already spent almost two days traveling from the West Coast, and it will be three or four more before we make it to Fort Dix. I'm not sure if leaving my home state or the prospect of going to New Jersey and eventually overseas has got me a little down, but before I hop back on, I kneel and run my hand over the familiar cold, black dirt of Nebraska.

Chapter 7

On New Year's Day 1944, I arrive at Fort Dix, twenty miles southeast of Trenton, and am immediately processed into military quarters—my first time bunking in a real building since being drafted. I'm assigned a barrack and given a physical (or turn your head and cough) and issued a few pieces of new clothing and necessary supplies. I have to try on each piece of winter clothes as soon as possible and exchange the items that don't fit. I hope to hell these G.I. duds are bulletproof. A canteen, first aid pouch, some Hershey's chocolate bars, matches, a couple of cartons of Lucky Strikes, some long johns, and a pair of skivvies round out the basics. I have an M1 rifle that I take apart and clean every day whether it needs it or not. Ammo and a few tools like a bayonet and a banjo—or entrenching tool as the Army calls it—fill in the other necessities. My last name, Ackerman, is printed in bold letters on everything I own. Along with settling in, I have a mountain of paperwork that needs to be filled out.

Inside my barrack, a model of Army precision, single beds are evenly spaced with a wide aisle running down the middle. Only a number separates one barrack from another, which means I'd better commit this joint's address to memory. Otherwise, I might risk the nightmare of stumbling around this toothpick village in the cold looking at identical buildings, trying to find the one I belong in.

Months in the desert didn't prepare us for the subzero temperatures we now face in New Jersey. Only one coal-burning stove in each wooden-framed barrack stands between us and frostbite. I have been away from Nebraska almost long enough to forget the winter's bitterness, but it's probably much easier for me than for guys from the South who grew up with fifty degrees and balmy. Wherever we land overseas, I hope it'll be warmer than Deep Freeze Dix.

Because we're all split out by company, Hank and I don't bunk together. I board with Company D and Hank in C. It won't take long to find him, and I plan to do just that.

Within a company, we're broken down into platoons. The forty-four of us in my platoon share a barrack and do everything by the alphabet. No matter where we are, we line up for inspections, chow hall, every coming and going the same way—by last name. There are times when I feel like one of my dad's cows headed to the auction barn on sale day. At least our cows had names. In the Army the only time you hear something other than a last name is if two guys share the same one. One of them is going to get called Slick, or Shorty, or Squirrel, or something else just as goofy. The one exception to the lining-up rule is visiting the latrine. Too bad. I would have been one of the first in line. I'm sure life at Fort Dix won't be any different.

Because we rolled in on a Saturday, I have free time to snoop around and find Hank. As soon as I unpack my things and make my bed, I plan to set out.

"Hey, Erv!" Hank shouts from outside the window, startling me with his tap on the frosted glass.

What the hell? I hadn't even had a chance to pull the stuff out of my barracks bag yet. Just like Hank, always ahead of the game. I motion for him to come in.

"How'd you find me so fast? I planned to track you down as soon as I got settled. Guess you beat me to it."

Shedding his coat, he plops on my bed with his hands locked behind his head. "Yeah, I wanted to check out the area—get the lay of the land, if you know what I mean. Besides, I kinda missed you, seeing as how we were pressed up against each other on the train like two cheeks on a sow's ass."

"Well, you found me." My first thought is that I'll have to smooth out his imprint on the blanket when he gets up, in case the sergeant decides to make a surprise inspection. "Which building is your home away from home?"

He wipes a circle in the glass and flips his thumb out as if hitching a ride. "Right over there. The one that says 'King Henry' above the door."

"Yeah, well, your castle looks exactly like this palace." His barracks, a carbon copy of mine and all the others, has a sickly green coat of paint and rectangular windows spaced exactly the same distance apart.

Hank pops up from my bunk like bread from one of those newfangled toasters. "I'm glad we got here on the weekend. Tomorrow we can make a beeline for the city and take in the sights. I heard some guys talking about catching the train and going to New York City. I think we should go. What do you think?"

"I don't have money to go anywhere. Hell's bells, Hank, aren't you sick and tired of traveling?"

"Come on, by tomorrow you'll feel like coming along. Besides, it won't be that much. Use some of that coin you charge all these schmucks for sewing patches and buttons on their uniforms," he says, in not much more than a whisper. "By the way, where'd you learn how to sew?"

"In my family, we had to do a lot for ourselves. My ma worked from sunup to sundown and barely had time to feed the family, let alone mend all our clothes."

Hank heads toward the door and then turns around. "Think about it, okay?"

He'd go whether I went or not, that's for sure, but I hate to even spend two bits when I know Betty had to move to York to live with her sister because she couldn't afford a place of her own. I try to send as much extra money from each paycheck as I can. Hank doesn't have kids, so things are different for him.

Flopping down on my rumpled bed, I pull out the latest letter I'd received from Betty and rub my fingers over the words she'd carefully written. I take in the scent on the paper—*Evening in Paris*—the perfume she wore when I first met her at the roller rink. I read it for an untold time.

Dearest Ervin,

I hope you're doing well and that you're safe. I miss you and hope by some miracle you might be able to come home on leave. Bonnie loves the teddy bear you sent for Christmas and drags it everywhere she goes. It's almost bigger than she is! Ha ha!

Maxine and I drove the coupe down to the farm last week and your dad filled it with gas. He gets extra stamps because of his machinery. I hope he doesn't run short because of me. Don't know what I'd do without his help from time to time.

I saw Ada, and she said your mother wants to know if you've had any of your favorite kuchen lately. I suggested your mother bake a batch and I'd send it to you in New Jersey. I'd ask her myself, but my German is worse than her English! I know she worries about you and your brothers. We all do. I'm praying for all our soldiers, but mostly I pray for you.

I'll close for now and write again soon.

All my love,

Betty

I refold the paper and tuck it in the envelope, cherishing each word. I'll have to destroy all her letters before going overseas. None of us will be allowed to carry any personal items the enemy could use to their advantage if we were to get captured. Getting rid of these letters will be like saying goodbye all over again.

I decided against going into New York City, but Hank went with a bunch of men from his platoon. They rode a subway train, saw *Something for the Boys* on 52nd Street, and roamed around Times Square. Probably got liquored-up too. They must have had a pretty good time. They talked about it constantly for the next few days, always bringing up the set of pipes on Ethel Merman. Still, I don't really know what a farm boy wants in a place like that.

With all the traipsing to and from the big city, the Army gets a wild hair that it's time for a short-arm inspection, or a pecker-check, in crude terms. The Staff Sergeant shouts "Fall out in raincoats and jock straps!" We line up and stand at attention, if you catch my drift. I wonder if they go to school for that kind of thing.

Over the next weeks, I serve green beans during mess hall duty, stand guard, march, do push-ups until my nose is callused, practice with a rifle and hand gun, and at night take my turn as fireguard by stoking the coal furnace. There are plenty of housekeeping duties, especially if you want to look top-notch in your uniform. For inspections, it's a good idea to spit-shine your boots and learn how to press your pants and shirt. I've become an expert with a wet towel and iron.

The chow hall is one of the biggest buildings at the Fort. You could probably fit three or four barracks inside. And it never ceases to amaze me how the Army can feed so many men in such short order. Maybe that's where the name Kitchen Police comes from. No shenanigans when it comes to eating in the Army. There are certain rules about eating military-style that take some fellas a while to catch on to. You never reach for food; you ask politely, but only for one serving at a time. One thing's for sure: you'd better eat what's put on your plate.

"How about a big scoop of spuds?" Private McClure, a good old acorn cracker from Kansas, begs.

The cook, overseeing the line, snaps back, "Listen, private, you're not sitting at your mama's kitchen table. The Army's here to feed ya, not fatten ya."

Private McClure dips his head and mumbles, "Sorry, sir."

"You're damn right you're sorry." He points to his sleeve. "You don't see any bars here, do ya? You address me as sergeant. You got it?"

A good ass-chewing practically has McClure slinking behind his stainless-steel tray. "Yes, sergeant."

There are other regs too. You never wear your hat indoors; you fold it and stick it in your back pocket. As the saying goes, "There's the right way, the wrong way, and the Army way."

Growing up with eleven brothers and sisters in the family, I have a definite advantage over a lot of the other mugs. The mess hall and its code of conduct seem pretty normal to me.

For some, there's nothing normal about the Army. Sometimes at night when all the hustle and bustle dies down, I hear guys griping about this or that. A few of them are just plain nervous in the service, but one kid from Hot Springs, Arkansas, is so miserable, he carries on and cries himself to sleep almost every night. Guess he just can't hack it. Wouldn't surprise me if he gets out on a Section Eight. Some of the guys make fun of him, but others avoid him like he has a disease or something. Although thoughts of home are never far from my mind either, I've always believed I have a job to do, so I take whatever gets dished out. No sense "worrying over spilt milk," my dad always said.

I'm headed to get some lunch when I see a notice on the central board that is bound to travel like greased lightning. Companies C, D, and F are given a two-week furlough. It's the last week of February, and it will be our only leave before heading overseas. I have a plan, and I want to run it past Hank as soon as I can.

I find a seat in the chow hall and spot him as he winds his way through the line. "Hank!" I flag him over with his tray piled high with fried potatoes, butter beans, and something that might once have been part of a pig.

He swings his legs in between the bench and the long table, sets his tray next to mine, and plunks down. "What's the skinny?"

"I hear we're getting two weeks' leave," I say before he has a chance to put a fork to his mouth. I find it hard to contain my excitement.

Hank leans toward me and grins as if we're about to swap juicy stories. "Really?"

"Yeah, the sergeant posted it on the board about a half hour ago. What do you think about going home and seeing the girls?"

"Sounds good. Really good."

"We'll have to find a way to get to the station in Trenton. Could hitchhike there if we have to." I make plans as I talk.

"Two weeks. Holy cow! Even counting the travel, we'll have almost a whole week at home," he says.

"I know. I can't wait."

We spend the rest of our meal without saying a word. No need to talk. We know exactly what's zipping around in each other's heads.

When I return to my barracks, I write a quick note to Betty to let her know I'll be coming home. I'll get word to her later about our exact arrival time and date. Probably have to call one of the neighbors and leave a message. I quickly craft a calendar from another scrap of paper. I'll place a big "X" on each square as the days of freedom inch closer.

When our leave finally comes, Hank and I bum a ride from Ernie Beck, a soldier from Allentown. The lucky devil gets a pass to drive home every weekend to see his wife.

"Thanks. Appreciate the ride," I say as we pile out of Ernie's '41 Plymouth. Sure is a doozy of a car.

"Geez, I wish I could take you guys into Trenton. Are you sure you can make it to the station on time?"

"Oh, yeah. No problem. There's always some drifter who feels sorry for a couple of G.I.s," Hank says with a hearty laugh.

"You're welcome to come in for some coffee," Ernie offers.

"Nah, we'd better get going." Hank and I didn't need to horn in on his homecoming with his better half.

Before Ernie steps inside his house, Hank and I have our thumbs out as we walk along the quiet, tree-lined street. We cover almost three blocks before a Good Samaritan stops, reaches across the front seat, and rolls down the passenger window.

"Need a ride?"

"Yes, sir," Hank says, bending over to peer into the shiny black car.

"Where are you going?"

Hank leans on the chrome window frame and smiles at the gentleman behind the wheel.

"To the train station in Trenton. You going that far?"

"No, not really, but we'll figure it out." He gestures for us to pile in.

He offers a gloved handshake first to Hank in the front and then to me in the back seat. "Edgar Jensen." We in turn introduce ourselves. "I'm on my way to work. There'll be someone there who can drive you to the station."

"That'd be great." I thank my lucky stars we're able to get out of the freezing cold.

Mr. Jensen looks like the kind of man who has a lot of responsibility at his job. Underneath his dark overcoat, he wears a tweed suit and a starched white shirt that might not show a wrinkle even if he had it on all day. His wife must spend a lot of time ironing. A whiff of his Old Spice aftershave drifts over the smell of the car's leather upholstery.

After a lot of small talk about where we are from, where we are going, and our estimation of the war's progress, we arrive at the Yardville National Bank, where Mr. Jensen will arrange for our ride. All the ladies at the bank say, "Good Morning, Mr. Jensen," as he strolls through the lobby with its shiny marble floor. Hank and I hang back as he checks to find someone who might be going to the station.

Hank nudges me in the ribs and whispers, "Sure would be nice if one of these good-looking gals would be going our way."

Instead, a gray-haired man clutching a black briefcase offers us a ride. I don't think I ever saw a man with such lily-white hands. We go outside to where the winter sun reflects off his Buick's jet-black, polished shine. It doesn't take long before we arrive at the railroad station.

He hugs the curb and puts the car in park. "Here we are."

"Thanks for the ride," we chime together as we climb out.

"Give 'em hell over there, boys." The old man glances in the rearview mirror and waves as he pulls away.

With our good fortune for catching rides, we arrive about an hour and a half before the train departs for Chicago. We'll catch another rail bound for Omaha, with a final stop at the depot in York. People stream in from all directions, and Hank and I quickly find the ticket counter and dig deep in our pockets to shell out the fare for the trip. I've ridden a lot of trains in the last two years, but this one will rank up there as the best. It might be a boxcar with no seats, but I don't care. I'm on my way home.

After a heck of a long ride, the sound of screeching brakes creates music for my ears. Betty and Florence, Hank's wife, stand at the platform waiting for us as we step off the train. In a little bit, I'll be planting a kiss on Betty that will peel her right out of those stockings with the black lines running up her shapely legs. I can already feel the anticipation throughout my body as if I've been plugged into an electric socket.

"Ervin! Ervin!" Betty waves her hand wildly in the air as I step on to solid ground.

Dropping my duffle bag, I catch her as she leaps into my arms. Time ticks in slow motion like single frames on a View-Master as I hold my wife in my arms. If only I could make this feeling last and take it with me wherever I go.

"I'm so glad you're home. I missed you so much."

"I missed you too. You can't imagine how glad I am to be here. Where's our baby girl?" I say, realizing as soon as I ask that bringing a baby out into the cold wouldn't be such a good idea.

"Maxine's taking care of her at the house."

"I wonder if she'll even recognize me."

"I'm sure she will," Betty assures me.

Hank and Florence, arm in arm, make their way toward us.

"You two have a ride?" I ask.

"Yeah, Flo's dad's waiting in the car over there. Guess we'll see you in about a week. Maybe we can talk the girls into going to Jersey with us," Hank adds with a wink.

"We'll see," I say over my shoulder as Betty and I mosey to our '37 Chevy Coupe. Just like Hank, always letting the cat out of the bag.

Betty raises her dark, perfectly shaped eyebrows until they nearly reach the swirling waves hugging her forehead. "You and Hank want me and Florence to go to New Jersey with you?"

"You don't have to decide right now, but yeah, I'd like it a lot if you could see me off. If you come, we'd have more time to be together before I go overseas. We could take this car. I know it can make it there and back." I let a little time pass to give the idea a chance to sink in before adding, "Let's talk about it later. Right now there are other things I'd rather do than talk." From the look and smile Betty gives me, she knows exactly what I mean. Seeing her sitting next to me gives me the sensation of lightning running through my veins. It's going to be one hell of a great week.

Driving to the pale yellow clapboard house on Delaware Avenue brings a rush of feelings. My chest tightens as if it's being wrung out like a rag. I'd been given leave when Bonnie was born a year and a half ago, but now, seeing the small, well-kept houses is like taking a punch to the gut. My world in the Army feels far removed from this part of the country. The reality of the war smacks me squarely in the face as we round the corner and I see a gold star in a front window. A house displaying a gold star means a family has lost a son. Eerily, each gold point seems to follow us as we drive along the quiet street. I think about my brothers and pray Mama never earns one.

"That's the Duncans' house," Betty says with sadness in her voice. "Their son Albert died in the Pacific last summer," she continues. "Oh, Ervin, sometimes I'm so scared. I don't know what I'd do if you didn't come home." She leans into me and holds on to my arm.

"Don't worry, hon. I'll be back. You just wait and see." I reach for her face and place my thumb at the corner of her eye, trying to keep a tear from falling. She gives me her best "chin up" smile as we drive the last few blocks in silence.

I try to forget about that gold star during the week at home. Putting it out of my mind should have been a lot easier, what with being treated like royalty. I guess everyone realizes I'm headed to an unknown destination and fate, and they want to make my stay a good one. Each meal is one of my favorites. And when we go down to the farm, Mama dotes on me like a sick child. Neighbors and friends from church stop by with all kinds of sweets just for an excuse to say "hello," which accounts for the pounds I've put on from eating and sitting around. I might lose my girlish figure if I'm not careful. I offer to help my dad with chores, but he won't hear of it. Says I need to take it easy. I didn't think my dad knew what taking it easy meant.

About when Bonnie starts getting used to me being around, the time comes to pack up and return to Fort Dix. Maxine, Betty's sister, agrees to watch our little girl so Betty can go along. Maxine claims it won't add extra work for her because she has a toddler of her own. Besides, Betty will return the favor when our brother-in-law has furlough in the next month or so.

Betty pulls on her jacket. "I'm going next door to Mrs. Klineschmidt's to ask if she'll let me use her phone. I want to find out if Florence has decided to go. I don't think I could make a trip that far by myself."

"I know, hon. I don't blame you."

I draw the sheer lace curtain back and watch as she walks along the brick path. It's definitely a long way to New Jersey, and I don't fancy the idea of her traveling halfway across the country by herself, even if I do want it more than anything right now.

While Bonnie takes her nap, I sit on the sofa and think about how I could convince Florence to go along. I quickly realize Hank is probably giving his best sales pitch and doesn't need my help. The thought makes me chuckle.

"Did you talk to Florence?" I ask as soon as Betty returns.

"No, I talked to her mother," she says as she gets out of her coat. "I'm not sure she approves of the idea, though. She's going to have Florence call and let us know. Anyway, she said Hank will meet you at the station at noon on Friday if she doesn't go."

"Florence is a grown woman and should decide for herself," I say with a little more bite to my tone than I intended.

At this point, I know I can't convince anyone, including Florence, about what a great adventure this trip will be, and decide I'll make the best of my last days at home. Even though I feel like a stranger in the house, Betty and I do everyday things, which helps make it seem as though we've always lived like this—doing the dishes together, listening to the radio at night, playing with Bonnie, and watching her haul that big brown teddy bear all over the place.

Betty and I had been over at her folks' house when Florence called, and Maxine had taken the message from Mrs. Klineschmidt.

Understanding the importance of the news, Maxine makes the announcement as soon as we walk in the door. "Florence decided to go. She and Hank will be here on Thursday morning at 7:30."

"Great! That's great!" I whisk Bonnie from the floor and swing her around, my happiness taking form in her delighted giggles. "I only wish you could come, little punkin'."

I strip off my jacket and Bonnie's bunting and carry her on my hip over to the buffet in the corner, opening the drawer and pulling out free maps from the gas station. I sit down and start to plan the route we'll take. Her tiny fingers rub over the paper. We'll go through Cincinnati, Ohio, make our way to Pennsylvania, and then on into Trenton. With a speed limit of no more than forty miles an hour, I reckon the trip will take at least three days.

Florence's dad drops them off at the house right on time. We hurriedly pack the trunk of the car with the small bags we've allowed ourselves. A '37 Chevy Coupe is anything but luxurious. A front seat and a small ledge in the back, curving with the line of the roof, form the tight interior. Four people crammed together on the bench seat in the front will be cozy. We are either going to be best of friends, or we'll never speak to each other again. A nearly fourteen-hundred-mile journey will tell the tale.

I do most of the driving and Betty sits in the middle, with Florence on Hank's lap. When his legs fall asleep, we get out, stretch, and change places. Because Betty is short and Florence is tall and lanky, sometimes Betty crawls up and lies on the ledge to give Hank a break, which in turn gives Florence a spot in the middle. Whenever we come to a city, Betty hops back in the front seat so she can watch the highway signs and recall them for the return trip. Hank starts calling her "Gretel" like in the fairy tale and kids her about looking for a trail of crumbs in case she misses one of the road markers. Betty gets the giggles, and we all laugh and carry on so; the four of us almost forget why we're going to New Jersey in the first place.

Our luck holds without car trouble until we blow a tire in Pennsylvania and have to change it along the highway. We don't want the girls to take a chance on the way home to Nebraska without a spare, so we stop at a local Rationing Board and wait it out until we can get approval to buy a used tire. The sign above the door at the Rationing Board office says it all: "Use it up, wear it out, make it do, or do without." We aren't sure how much sympathy we're going to get from the man sitting behind a gray metal desk with a slogan like that hanging over his chrome dome. He alone will decide if we should receive anything exceeding the government allowance. Fortunately we don't get the runaround, with our military IDs speaking more for us than we could for ourselves. Thankfully we aren't delayed long. The Army would never accept any excuses for reporting late for duty.

Once we reach Trenton, we hook up with another Army buddy whose wife stays in a rooming house close to the post. The gals plan to stay there until it's time to head back. The good times will roll for a few more days.

Chapter 8

For the next month, we train, stand in line, and stand in line some more. By mid-March, the division receives orders to ship out. We say our so-longs to the buddies we've made, load bag and baggage, and quietly clear out of Fort Dix. An hour-long train ride, and the last thread between ourselves and home will officially be cut. It's the end of the line—Camp Kilmer on the Jersey shore—staging area for overseas processing. We are cargo marked for a secret destination.

Immediately upon arriving at Camp Kilmer, we plunge into a flurry of activity. Every man receives a thorough, last-minute inspection which involves counting and examining arms, legs, eyes, and assholes. Equipment is checked and rechecked, hair is clipped high and tight, and instructions are given to discard all personal belongings. We fill out paperwork for life insurance and a last will. I write Betty's name in the first blank and her sister's on the second as beneficiaries; someone will have to look after Bonnie if anything happens to Betty, so I pick her sister. Lord knows my folks don't need another mouth to feed.

I look up from my papers and notice a young kid across the table with a pen trembling in his hand. The reality of being mortal hits close to home.

"I'm sure not planning on having my wife pick up a check and a wooden box," I say, as if thinking out loud. I try to ease the tension and add, "Keep your head down, be smart, and you'll be okay." Being probably ten years older than most of these kids, I feel a need to give them some sage advice in hopes it might serve them later on. It seems to work; the kid stops staring at the paper and starts filling in the blanks.

After turning in paperwork, we train on how to abandon ship in case of a German U-boat attack and endure shots in both arms and both butt cheeks. The Army has a way of making you forget all about your other worries.

Struggling under the weight of our rifles and hundred-pound duffel bags loaded with bedrolls, clothes, and supplies, we are herded like sheep to a ferry at the New York Port of Embarkation in the dark of night. After a short jaunt, the dirty little boat nudges close to the dock, the gangway drops, and we move single-file across a wooden walkway to a pier where Red Cross Gray Ladies hand out black coffee stronger than battery acid, doughnuts tough enough for dunking, and "what nice young men" looks. There are no cheering crowds or brass bands—only towering ocean liners with gaping holes above the water line waiting to be filled with war freight and a human payload.

As we make our way across the sloping ramp, a sergeant calls out last names. We answer with first name and then middle initial.

"Ackerman!" the sergeant roars.

"Ervin H," I answer. With twelve kids in the family, my mother ran out of second names by the time she came to me. The Army requires you to at least have a middle initial, so I'd made up my own. The *H* didn't stand for anything, just had a solid sound, I thought.

A billet is shoved into my free hand, indicating my berthing space on the ship. I inch up the gangplank.

"Matches and electric pocket lamps are prohibited on ship," a G.I. with a clipboard shouts above the crowd. "If you have these items, turn them over to someone in authority as soon as you board. Only patent cigarette lighters are allowed." He reels off a laundry list of instructions and warnings like a drill sergeant during inspection.

I wish I had a cigarette lighter like that. I always light my cigarettes by striking a wooden match across the seat of my pants. Whoever has a patent one on board this ship will be a very popular guy.

Reaching the top of the incline, I have a chance for a clear view of the ship. I look up and there it stands in the cover of darkness, the cold, gray steel side with big white letters: M.S. *John Ericsson.* I've never seen anything that tall in my whole life. I wonder how many pieces of farm machinery she might hold.

"Pretty big boat," I say to no one in particular.

"She's a twenty-thousand tonner. Flagship of the convoy," answers a sailor standing to the side of our shifting line.

I'm not sure why it's called a flagship, but I nod as if I understand his Navy lingo. "As long as she doesn't have a bulls-eye painted on her. All I care about is whether she can turn tail from a torpedo."

Without cracking a smile, he continues, "She's a first-class ocean vessel, built in Germany."

Interesting. A German ship sailing from America to take Americans to fight Germans. The world is a strange place these days.

"How many men can she hold?" I ask, trying to get more information, seeing as how I've never been on a boat before today, let alone an ocean liner.

"In her heyday, she'd have carried fifteen hundred passengers and three hundred fifty crew. Now, she's stripped and fitted to carry fifty-five hundred soldiers plus tons of ordnance for the field. Any remaining space not occupied by troops will carry lifeboats, rubber floating devices, and motor boats."

I scan the Jeeps and mountains of crated supplies waiting to be loaded. I sure hope it can float with all that weight.

The line moves again and I step on board. In a short while, I'll leave America for a long time. I'd be lying if I didn't worry about how this might be a one-way trip for some of us.

As gangplanks are drawn and cables loosened, she slowly drifts away from the blacked-out New York harbor. Most of us miss the chance to see the Lady with the Torch because decks have to be cleared for operational security. But I make a promise to myself that I'll kiss the ground she stands on when the war is over. For now, I close my eyes and imagine what she looks like.

Now on board, I follow the man in front and squirm through a maze of hatches and stairways from one deck to the next.

"Watch your step," a guy ahead warns as he trips over a raised doorway.

I pick up my feet so I won't fall flat on my face. No sense making a fool of myself right off the bat.

Even though the liner had been sold to the Army, stripped and fitted as the sailor had explained, German words still peek through the watered-down paint job. I translate the words underneath. *"Kabine für zwei"*—cabins for two. Given the throng of soldiers I see boarding; I shake any idea I might have of sharing a luxurious space with only one other guy.

Pulling the billet out of my shirt pocket, I check the number to make sure it matches the number on the bunk and the life preserver that will double as my pillow.

Our assigned berths are canvas strips stretched tight by a forest of steel pipes. Pieces of cloth are hemmed along both sides with pipe running through to make a kind of hammock, two feet wide and six feet long, stacked not quite two feet above the one below it. The structures are supported by four iron uprights and stacked three high. The man on the uppermost bunk will stare into a tangle of pipes inches from his mug. The bottom two places don't look much better, because those guys will have to contend with the bulge from a man's butt hanging in their face.

"Home sweet home," I say as I stow my gear on the simple canvas bed and hurl myself on top so the man behind me can get through.

Twenty of us and all our bags are shoehorned into what had been a cabin for two passengers—about twelve feet by fifteen feet.

"Quarters are so close, I bet I'll smell a fella's feet before he even takes his boots off," the soldier in the bunk below declares.

"Yeah, and the first man who farts in here gets buried at sea," I say, giving him a smile. "Unfortunately, I don't think we can open any windows. Ervin," I say, reaching down to shake his hand. "But just call me Erv."

"Nice to know you, Erv," he says, extending his huge hand. "I'm Jack. Jack Fisher."

"Good to meet you, Jack." I feel the blood rush back into my hand as he releases his gorilla grip.

"Guess we'd better shake down and settle in. I hear we'll be on this boat for a couple weeks," he says.

All of a sudden, the tight quarters feel even tighter. At least I share this space with a guy who seems to be in the know. Kind of like Hank. I hope I can find Hank on this bucket of bolts. Locating him will be much harder here than at Fort Dix. Seems as though they put all our names in a Sunbeam mixer and whipped us up like eggs for Sunday ice cream.

"Where you from, Erv?"

"A farm in Nebraska. Born and raised in a little Podunk place called Grafton. How about you?"

"Me? I'm from Pittsburgh. And I didn't get this big from pushing a pencil. Been lugging steel since I was fifteen."

"Glad to hear it. I hope they put you right behind me carrying extra ammo."

Jack laughs and gives me a pat on the shoulder that almost knocks me over. I think I'm going to like bunking above this guy.

"Lights out at 2100 and reveille at 0530," the low voice over the loudspeaker announces. A unified moan spreads through the cabin.

"Early to bed, early to rise, makes a man pissed off," Jack says as if reciting from the *Farmer's Almanac*.

His joke makes me laugh. "You'd think we'd be used to the schedule by now."

"Maybe some dumbass thought this trip would be a luxury cruise," Jack mutters.

The low, gravelly voice on the loudspeaker continues with the kind of authority you'd never think of questioning. "Stand to on A Deck at 0530 with your life jackets on. Black marks will be given to anyone who's tardy."

"Stand to?" Jack says, searching for an explanation.

"In other words, get your ass on deck and make it snappy," a soldier with a definite Jersey accent and a mermaid tattooed on his forearm responds.

I don't like Mr. Jersey's attitude much. Seems as though he has a big chip on his broad shoulders. Oh well, not going to worry my head over him. The night will be short enough and tomorrow will be more of the same routine.

The military has a regimen for almost everything—lights out at a certain time, portholes closed at a specific time, sleeping and rising with the chickens, drills scheduled on the dot, and standing around waiting. Hurry up and wait. It seems as if the waiting never ends and the lines go on forever.

Long before day breaks through the dark sky, a buzzer goes off with three ear-piercing sounds that jolt us upright from our sling beds. The cracking sound of heads hitting iron pipes follows.

The Master Sergeant, decked out in his usual crisp uniform, with creases sharp enough to slice salami, switches on every light bulb along the narrow hallway. "Drop your cocks and grab your socks!" he booms, quickly moving to the next compartment bellowing more of his alarm-clock quips.

Scrambling to dress by the one dome light screwed to the ceiling, we put on pants, shirts, boots, and our life jackets. Because of close quarters, we look like teeter-totters on a school playground—one man bending down as the one next to him stands up. I make a note to lay out my clothes for the next day before I hit the sack so they'll be easier to find in the morning.

"Fists are going to fly the first time a guy gets an elbow in the eye," Jack says.

He hadn't any more than made the prediction when Mr. Jersey pinned a young soldier against a bed post and yelled, "Listen, you little prick."

Jack stands straight, puffs out his chest, and gives a stern warning in a steady tone, "If you want to fight, save it to kick some Nazi's ass. Can't battle no Jerries from the brig."

Jersey lets go of the kid.

I have a feeling we won't have any other skirmishes, at least not as long as Jack's minding our store. Without another word, we finish dressing and head above deck.

After everyone stands shoulder to shoulder, counts off, and the deck is inspected, we begin physical drills, life boat drills, abandon ship drills, and drills to remember the drills. Doing exercises with life jackets on makes us look like sausages dancing a ballet.

"You look like Mae West in that thing, Jack."

"Don't get any funny ideas, Erv. This voyage won't be that long."

By the time the sun peeks over the horizon, we're sweating, starving, and ready to hit the chow lines. For breakfast we have oatmeal, pineapple juice, and black coffee—just enough to keep us alive. The mess steward dumps food on my tray and I continue to a trough-like table where I stand and eat. Once at the chest-high plank, I move along, eating as I go. The huge stoves on the chow deck pour out a stifling heat that makes sweat run down my face and into my food. At the end of the course, I rinse my tray and then look for a place to hang out until it's time to line up for the next meal.

Everyone has to clean their own stuff and, of course, any mess they make. Personal hygiene, known as taking care of the three S's—shit, shower, and shave—leaves much to be desired. Bars of soap have the words "white float-ing" in raised block letters but are rock hard and produce a pitiful amount of lather. The salt water for bathing isn't fit for man or beast and makes me feel as dry as beef jerky. When I towel off, the salt dries on my skin and I feel dirtier and stickier than when I started. There's plenty of the brine for cleaning, but fresh water is strictly rationed.

"Salty showers? What the hell? If the cold doesn't shrivel something, the salt sure will," declares a man with hair covering every square inch of his stout body and furry eyebrows that look like caterpillars crawling across his forehead.

I've seen more naked men in the last two years than I care to think about, but I've never seen a man with hair covering all of his front and back. But just when

I think I've seen it all, I catch a man standing in line to use the head when suddenly nature cuts loose. I watch him convert his helmet to a portable john. The challenges of living in crowded quarters with five thousand men are many.

The biggest issue of the day becomes what to do between meals. Most guys make their own entertainment by reading books, writing letters, or playing craps and poker with cards worn thin from constant shuffling. We get news over the squawk box every day and supplement our boredom with talk about women, where we might be going, the latest rumors, if we're headed to England or France, and last but not least, more about women.

Because of our precious cargo, the prospect of a submarine attack always lurks as a threat, so we turn this way and that across the Atlantic in slow unison with a huge convoy of other troop transports, supply ships, aircraft carriers with partly assembled planes, an oil tanker, destroyers, and submarine chasers. There are times when we change course every seven minutes just to keep the U-boats off our tail.

Soldiers crowd every inch of the ship and lean against the rails, watching the ocean drift by. But the crisscrossing of the ship and occasional bad weather makes some men so miserable from seasickness that if they'd been able to make it to the outside rail, I do believe they would have jumped overboard just to end their suffering. I feel sorry for them, but nothing you can do when your stomach flips and flops like the waves.

Lights go out on ship at 2100 as if synchronized with the captain's wristwatch, and portholes are opened for ventilation. Darkness comes and our daily cycle ends, and the captain repeats the day's announcements when he has everyone's full attention.

"Smoking is allowed during daylight hours and only on open decks. Smoking at night is strictly prohibited," the captain warns with slow, perfectly spoken words. "It is a well-known fact that the glow of a cigarette can be seen at a distance of one-half mile. Anything calling attention to the whereabouts of the ship makes her a target for the first submarine that happens along," he continues. "Anyone who disobeys, be he officer or enlisted man, will be dealt with summarily and will finish the voyage under guard. The entire safety of this ship depends on your watchfulness."

"Wow! Can you believe that, Erv? The Jerries can spot a guy lighting up from half a mile away."

"Yeah, and they're probably listening to us flapping our gums right now," I say, as if I could spook Jack into keeping quiet. At this point, I see the similarities between sitting in the middle of the ocean waiting to be blown out of the water and being a duck on a Nebraska pond about to get blasted.

The captain continues in his deep, smooth tone. "The enemy has proven to be a master of detail, and we must exercise every effort to outwit him. What may seem insignificant can pose a deadly threat to every man on this vessel. The path of this ship can also be traced by anything thrown overboard. A captain of a sub can tell a ship's location by examining the condition of the refuse in its wake. Receptacles are provided for disposing of rubbish, and guards have orders to arrest anyone who does not comply. Carry on," the commander finishes, abruptly ending his lecture.

After the sobering warnings, a strange silence penetrates the cabin. I stretch out on my bunk and imagine a gust of wind ripping an ace of spades out of a guy's poker hand as it floats down to a German sub. I picture it being snatched up like a minnow in front of a hungry carp. I'll feel more comfortable when I can see the enemy face-to-face and not have to deal with his chicken-shit hiding.

"You know what they say?" Jack says.

I can't wait to hear his clever take on the subject. "What's that?"

"The man who relaxes is helping the Axis."

"Yeah, and loose lips sink ships, Jack. So let's get some shut-eye." Good thing he hasn't figured out that I think he's funny; it would only encourage him, and I need some rest.

I eventually find Hank, and we arrange for a daily meeting to shoot the bull on A Deck after lunch. If the line doesn't snake around too far, we go into the

Exchange and buy some Baby Ruths. We talk about what we think might be going on back home and how we'd rather be there than floating in the middle of the Atlantic with thousands of sweaty men. In a situation like this, there are new bonds forged and others that are wound tighter than an eight-day clock. I feel sure the brig is full to the brim by now. Thinking about the spats in my quarters, I tell Hank about Jersey, or Guido as Jack refers to him—of course, not to his face.

"I don't trust him any farther than I can throw him," I say, giving Hank my personal take on Jersey's character. "One of the guys caught him sneaking to the upper deck."

"What's the douche bag doing up there?"

"Sleeping and hanging out. He ought to know upper decks are for the poor devils who work in the boiler room. Down there, they sweat like a whore in church."

"I can't believe they haven't thrown the book at him and kicked his sorry ass out."

"Yeah. Selfish guys only watch their own backs, if you ask me. I'll be watching mine to make sure he's not anywhere around." I say, tossing caution out like a net on the water.

After fifteen days, our long voyage comes to an end. We dock at Liverpool, England, on the fifth day of April. A huge sense of relief sweeps over me as the ship stops and I feel something steady under my feet. Living in cramped quarters with all these men has made me crave a little privacy. For two weeks, I didn't have enough room to even change my mind.

Being Easter weekend, there's a mixed crowd of British soldiers, American MPs, and a small group of ATS girls—English counterparts to America's WACS—gathered around the dock. Everyone lines the rails and starts heaving cigarettes, candy bars, and various personal items to the eager audience.

A soldier flings a pack of rubbers into the waving hands of a cute little thing. "Hubba-hubba, doll. How about we meet up for some horizontal refreshments?"

Nothing like skirts to bring out the little boy in a grown man. We haven't even touched land and we already love the Brits.

We drop anchor and gather on the forward deck and wait for landing craft to take us to shore. Once the cargo is offloaded, we're allowed to disembark.

"About time we got off this canoe," Jack says.

I smile at his comment. "Yeah, let's find Hank. I'm ready to check out one of those English pubs everybody's been talking about."

"Yeah, that's what I'm thinking. With a couple of brewskis in us, those Krauts won't know what hit 'em."

Chapter 9

They whisk us away in the dark of night to board English cattle trains for the two-day trip from Liverpool to Wales. The coffee has mysteriously turned to tea. It seems as if the British had never heard of the drink. We can't get a cup of java to save our souls, and constant grumbling about their fried and tasteless food becomes the topic of almost everyone's conversation. Guys are thrown for a loop when they see sweetbreads on a Limey menu. They have no idea it isn't sweet and it ain't bread. None of it bothers me. On the farm, we ate everything except the squeal, so all this fuss about the local food kind of gets my goat. I imagine soon enough we'll be eating K-ration biscuits, tuna, and chocolate bars, and the current menu will resemble a feast on Thanksgiving Day. I'm almost sure there's a whole lot worse coming our way than tasteless grub.

Small boxcars called "forty and eights" for the number of men or horses they can hold sluggishly carry us across the neatly tended rolling hills of England into Cardiff. I'm not sure how they'd get forty men in one of the cars; there are sixteen of us squeezing into a place you might be able to fit ten outhouses. They even smell like the one-holers. The cars aren't equipped with seats, so we sit on our bags and equipment. If you're lucky, you find something to lean against. Occasionally, we see towels and handkerchiefs being waved from the windows of houses next to the rail line. The locals want to wish us well.

All in all, the emerald landscape of Wales looks like something out of a storybook—that is, if you ignore the deep scars from the countless bombing raids. Of course, the luxury of sightseeing doesn't exist, so we either sleep or play cards on the splintery floor. We will soon have bigger fish to fry.

When we finally arrive, we begin intense training on the beaches. "I never saw this much sand in my life," I say to a couple of young boys crawling on their bellies beside me.

"Yeah. I'm from Iowa," one of the young soldiers says. "All I know about is black dirt. Never seen this kind of land before."

"From what I've heard, Iowa has the richest farm land anywhere. Well, whatever you do, keep the muzzle out of this grit. If your gun gets clogged, it'll come apart at the seams and blow up in your hands," I warn. "Your M1 is your bread and butter. Take care of it and it'll take care of you."

Despite the rain that blows in almost every day, we spend hours at firing ranges. When we aren't practicing boarding and exiting different types of landing craft, we learn how to detect mines or are drilled on the finer points of hedgerow fighting.

The hedgerows on the farm where I grew up are a far cry from the century-old, dense thickets separating planted fields they say we're going to come up against. It feels like a lifetime ago when my dad and I flushed pheasants from those Nebraska windbreaks on cold, crisp winter mornings with the sound of dry weeds and brush crunching under our feet. You never knew when a critter would fly out with a startling whirr and a flutter of feathers. There I had been the predator, not the prey. Now the tables are turned. The Nazis will be taking cover and waiting for us on the other side.

In between all of the training and inspections, we march, and march, and march some more. "Pick 'em up and put 'em down," the sergeant chants as we cover five miles in an hour with full packs. You can't travel that far by just walking—you have to double-time it at least part of the way. Pissing and moaning usually follows, along with a guy who'll pass out or throw up his innards. In a few weeks, we might be running for our lives. But no matter what kind of shape you're in, you're not going to out run a bullet.

When I have time off from the constant drills and forced marching, I write to Betty using the Army's V-mail system—a cross between airmail and a telegram. It arrives much faster than ordinary mail, which goes by ship, plus I don't have to pay for it with my own dough. To save shipping space, a desk jockey snaps pictures of the letters, and the reels of photos are flown back to the States. At least, that's how Jack explained it. I don't care if it's one step above a carrier pigeon or how it works, just as long as it gets there and Betty knows I'm still alive and kicking. Whenever I have a chance, I snag a form with its red lines and print in the small spaces.

> *Dear Betty,*
>
> *Wanted to drop a line to let you know I'm safe. There isn't a lot to tell so this will be short. We're pretty much training and marching all the time. Sometimes I think I could sleep on a clothesline. Let me know if you hear anything from Ed in the Philippines. Say hi to everyone and give little Bonnie a kiss for me.*
>
> *I love you Sweetie.*
>
> *Ervin*

I never had much privacy growing up, but it feels strange handing personal letters to a fellow soldier to send to my wife. Like Miss Stanton, my grade-school teacher, the corporal scans my letter and clicks his tongue. I half expect him to hand it back with corrections. Instead, he turns and places the form on the stack behind him. His grunt acknowledges my thanks.

I bump into Jack on my way out of the field post office. He had been concentrating on his own V-mail and leaning against one of the tent posts when I'd ducked inside.

"Hey, Jack."

He looks up from his form with what appears more like chicken scratches than actual writing. "Say, Erv, you speak German, don't you?"

"Yeah, but I'm a little rusty. Haven't kept up with it since I've been in the Army. Why?"

"Well, I heard from a guy that they're looking for German interpreters. Said all you have to do is get permission from your sergeant to apply and then get yourself over to HQ."

"I'll check it out. Thanks." My mind races when I think about being able to do something to help the cause—something besides looking down the barrel of a gun. Any chance I have to stay out of enemy fire is a chance I'm more than happy to take. I hurriedly set out to find Sergeant Kingman.

Given it's almost noon, I figure I'll find him in the mess tent and make tracks over there.

"Sergeant Kingman," I gasp, taking a breath between his rank and name and then wait for him to finish his last bite of boiled potato.

"Where's the fire, private?"

"No fire, Sarge. I just need your permission to go to headquarters."

He lays down his fork. His dark brown eyebrows arch toward the widow's peak at his hairline. "Your lid, Ackerman."

"Oh, right. Sorry. I forgot," I say as I remove my hat and stick it in my back pocket.

Sergeant Kingman has a burly build, a bulldog face, and a short fuse. "Headquarters? What for?"

"I heard the Army's looking for soldiers to serve as German interpreters. I'd like to apply." I hoped I didn't sound desperate.

"Is that right? Well, go ahead. Give it a go. I suppose if I had that kind of chance, I'd sure snap it up. Who knows? Probably save your skin being with headquarters instead of with the infantry."

Sure glad I caught him on one of his good days. As I turn and take off in the direction of the motor pool, I call out, "Thanks, Sarge!" Thinking my life might have been spared on this soggy day in May, I pull my dog tags out from under my shirt and point them skyward; sealing them with a quick kiss for the good fortune I've been given. I would have done the same with a cross if the Army allowed us to wear them.

I drive the borrowed Jeep nine miles to HQ. The city of pyramid-shaped tents with some tarpaper shacks sprinkled in hums with activity. I find an officer standing still long enough to ask about the German translator position. He flips through some papers on his clipboard and gives me directions to the tent of Colonel Russell Williams. I slog through ankle-deep mud to the well-worn path leading to his tent. A young corporal standing outside his door listens as I give my name and explain what business I have with the colonel.

"Wait here. I'll check if he can see you." The corporal disappears behind the canvas flap.

Within minutes, a colonel who looks about my age comes out from his field office. He's a beefy man with a square face and a thick head of black hair.

"Are you the soldier who's interested in being an interpreter?" Colonel Williams asks, looking me over.

"Yes, sir."

"What's your name and rank?"

"Private Ackerman, sir. Private First Class Ervin H. Ackerman, colonel, sir," I quickly repeat, giving him a more formal reply with a salute at the end.

"Where you from, Ackerman?"

"The 359th, Company D, sir."

"No, I mean where in the States?"

"I'm from Nebraska."

"And how much German do you know?"

"*Ich spreche Deutsches sehr gut.* It's all we spoke at home. My mother and father both came to the U.S. from Germany, so I didn't even speak English until I went to grade school."

"Well, I need someone to translate—talk to the locals, interrogate German prisoners, read road signs and the like. Someone who can navigate where the hell we're supposed to go. Better to be with me than looking through a rifle site all the time," he says, pausing for a moment to let his remark sink in. "I'll need a driver too. What do you know about vehicles?"

"Being raised on a farm, there isn't any machinery I can't drive or fix. That's for sure. Even had to help repair a side arm on a train one time when I had leave from Fort Dix."

"Good. You'll have to keep a Jeep running and make sure we don't get stuck on these crappy, godforsaken roads."

I stand a little straighter in hopes of giving Colonel Williams no doubt about my ability to do the job. "That won't be a problem."

"We've got a mission to complete on our way to Berlin, and I don't plan on getting my ass shot either. You and me, we'll have to work together to come out of this war in one piece. Think you can handle it, private?"

"You can bet on it. I mean, yes. Yes, sir, I can."

"All right. Go back to your unit and pack your things." He signs a piece of paper and hands it to me. "Give this to your captain and report here tomorrow at 0700 for briefing."

"Yes, sir." I salute him once again before leaving. To my way of thinking, the colonel seems really sharp, with a lot on the ball. This is a hell of an opportunity to serve my country and maybe come home alive.

I can't wait to get back to base and turn my orders over to the captain. Afterward, I plan to find Hank and tell him the good news, but I'll also have to let him know we probably won't be seeing each other for a while. I'll miss him and Jack and all the other guys who are like brothers to me, but for now I have to take care of myself so I can live to tell about it. Hopefully, we'll all have a big party in the States when this whole damn thing comes to an end.

I drive like a striped-ass ape in order to return the Jeep and make it to the chow line before they close shop. Right now, my guts are growling and I have a shitload of stuff to do to get ready to leave.

After feeding my face, I hike over to Hank's tent before packing my gear. "Have you seen Hank?" I ask one of the men who bunks in his tent.

"Nope, haven't seen him."

"If you do, tell him Erv's looking for him. I'm shipping out at dark ugly in the morning, so he'll have to catch me tonight."

"Sure thing. I'll tell him."

A voice from the back of the tent breaks through the darkness. "How you gettin' out of this hell hole?"

"Gonna translate for a colonel at HQ," I say before realizing who the voice belongs to. Wouldn't you know it? Of all the guys I have to run into, it has to be Mr. Jersey. What the hell is that numskull doing in Hank's tent?

"Don't seem fair. Just because you're a Kraut you get a fat cat job at the back of the line."

The blood in my veins goes from simmer to boil in a matter of seconds. A flood of anger rises to the surface and makes my fists clench in rage. Fortunately for Jersey, I quickly decide he isn't worth the uniform the Army issued him, let alone my ending up in the brig.

"Yeah, well, too bad they don't need a translator for assholes because you'd be sure to get the job."

Jersey stands and bolts from his cot.

"Hold it right there, Joysey," one of the other soldiers in the tent cautions. "You've given a black eye to this squad more times than I can count, so put a fuckin' cork in it."

I turn and walk away. If I never see him again, it will be too soon.

When I finish getting squared away, I search high and low for a good part of the evening for Hank. Eventually, I catch another guy from his tent. "Hey, did you ever see Hank?"

"No, he didn't come back. Some guy came by and scooped up his gear. Said the Army was sending him stateside because of a medical condition."

"A medical condition?"

"Yep, that's what he said."

"He didn't say what kind of condition?"

"Not a word. Just got his things and left."

"Okay. Thanks."

Because I won't get to see Hank before I leave for HQ, I decide to write to Florence. One way or the other I'll let him know where I am. I hope I can find out why he got sent out.

That night I lay on my cot, starring at the stiches in the tent's canvas ceiling. It's tough to sleep. I keep thinking about what the colonel will be like and wonder whether he'll think I'm worth my salt. He seems like a good egg—straight down to business. That's okay with me. Don't want anyone who soft-soaps or beats around the bush.

The next morning when I arrive at headquarters, I pull in front of the biggest tent near the front gate, park the Jeep I'd borrowed from motor pool, and report for duty. I follow a young soldier, trying to dodge as many puddles as I can on the way to my living quarters. So many tents fill this Welsh countryside, you can't even tell we're stationed in a field. It looks like a small city. More than likely, the headquarters provides support to thousands of men—everything from chow halls to first aid stations.

The soldier points to my tent in the sea of green canvas. "Here you go. Make yourself at home. We're all confined to base. By the way, make sure you remember which tent you belong in. It can get dicey if you accidently end up in another man's quarters."

"Thanks. I'll keep that in mind." Nothing new here except there aren't numbers like there were at Fort Dix or Camp Barkeley, for that matter.

After I quickly get settled in, I report to Colonel Williams and go through orientation. He gives me the rundown on what he expects and what our mission will be.

"How good are you with a rifle?"

"I ranked expert with firearms. I can shoot the balls off a gnat at two hundred yards." I pause and add, "sir," waiting for the fallout from my smart remark.

"That's exactly what I wanted to hear. You and I are going to be a good team. Now, go over to motor pool and find us a decent Jeep. We've got to get this show on the road. They'll probably try to give you an old beater, but let them know why you need it. If you run into any trouble, give me a holler."

I do as he orders and pick the best of the bunch. I name her Betsy. The sergeant at motor pool makes a note on his paper and tells me it will be ready when we ship out. Whenever that turns out to be.

I hustle back to my tent to get out of the pouring rain. The tents where we sleep are equipped to house men on double-decker bunks. Between the rows of beds, guys form a circle around a small cup with a pair of rattling cubes inside. A guy who had just lost a big pile of money he'd been hoarding on his lap shouts, "Shut up and roll the bones." The crap game begins again, and a lucky schmuck will rake in more than his fair share. The cycle repeats itself with Army regularity. Surprisingly, there aren't many fights over the winning score or the amount of money won or lost. Most of the players don't really seem to care about the loot. Where are they going to spend it anyway?

Other than games of chance, there isn't much else to do. I don't sleep much; none of us do. Tensely sweating it out and waiting for the signal to go ahead with the assault, we listen to the radio every night with its constant crackling static in the background. During one broadcast, General Eisenhower describes the "beginning of the crusade" and says, "The eyes of the world are upon you." Those are the only two things I remember. I prayed more than I listened.

We spend a lot of time with our ears tuned to the radio, even to broadcasts the Army doesn't want us to hear, like Lord Hee-Haw and other bullcrap. Being restricted to the base, we're desperate for the sound of a female, and it comes to us over the radio waves in a mesmerizing, sultry voice known as Axis Sally.

She begins her nightly program with, "Well, fellas, this is Axis Sally. Talking to you Yanks in England. Why are you over here? We know. You know it, too. You're fighting for those Jewish bankers and stockbrokers on Wall Street. They just want to make some money with your life." A bunch of men verbally lash out at her, calling her Berlin Bitch and other, less flattering names. There's bitter bad-mouthing, as if Sally can actually hear them. She goes on for a while longer and then says, "Let's take a break and listen to some Glenn Miller now." Listening to the band play *Moonlight Serenade,* I think of Betty at home sitting in the front room, the radio playing as she holds the baby on her lap. It makes me feel good when I imagine her listening to the same song—sharing something common in an uncommon place. And it takes me home, if only for a little while.

Finally, on the fourth of June, after endless waiting and under a full moon, we ready for the invasion of France. We board LSTs—huge ships capable of floating men, equipment, and cargo directly onto shore.

The sky moves fast and the clouds whip around like cotton candy in a funnel storm. For twenty-four hours, we circle off the coast awaiting orders to cross the English Channel, but are sealed in because of bad weather and rough seas. The Navy made sure we had a hearty breakfast before heading into battle which, along with the rocking waves, makes so many men seasick that you have to grab onto something to keep from sliding in the puke. Sometimes, all it takes for a man to spew is to see or hear someone else doing it. Sure glad I didn't feel like eating all that much for breakfast this morning.

My attention quickly turns to what sounds like thousands of airplane engines throbbing over our heads, crossing the gloomy sky toward France. "Looks like flies headed for a butcher shop," I say to the colonel. "I sure hope the poor bastards make it."

"Those C-47s will drop our paratroopers behind the coast to capture and secure bridges and disrupt enemy communications."

I realize they're probably as scared as I am, but at least I don't have to jump out of an airplane in the dark. "Sounds good. I hope they get in and out quick."

"We can only hope they'll take care of business. It will make it a whole hell of a lot easier on the rest of us."

From my position on the upper deck, I see so many ships in the Channel that it seems as if you could step from one vessel to the next without ever touching the water. We crowd together as we wait it out, shivering in the salty air that blows in from the sea.

Probably in an effort to stave off the boredom and anxiety that's building, Colonel Williams shouts above the sound of the waves crashing against our ship. "An invading army hasn't crossed the English Channel since 1688."

I cup my hand around my ear, trying to hear over the roar. "Really? Why's that?" Or maybe I don't want to know.

"Always considered dangerous and unpredictable. But modern ships have rendered her as safe as a kitten," he explains, probably trying to squash any misgivings we might have been toying with.

"Do you think the Jerries will see it coming?"

"Oh, they'll see us all right, like an elephant in a bird cage. But there's not a damn thing they can do about a hundred and thirty thousand Allied personnel headed straight at 'em."

We are about to find out because H-Hour is less than sixty minutes away. At 0630 the invasion unfolds in the armada as flashes reflect off the clouds from the naval and air bombardment. I feel confident the mission has been well-planned and that we are highly trained, but witnessing three injured men from another damaged craft being loaded on our deck gives us all a chance to make peace with our Maker. Guys vomit, pray out loud, wring their hands, or stare at nothing in particular. The tension, dread, and a desire to get this thing done holds us together like glue.

God, will you watch over my family if I don't make it back home?

The colonel puts his hands on his hips and surveys the men huddled on the deck. "After the first wave secures the beach, we'll follow with supplies and equipment. Brigadier General Theodore Roosevelt himself is leading the 4th Infantry. If he's anything like the stories I've heard, he'll do everything he can to be one of the first on Utah. We're in good hands, if you catch my drift."

"Theodore Roosevelt himself?" I repeat the name as a way to convince myself instead of asking a real question.

"That's right. Oldest son of President Teddy Roosevelt. He served in the last war, too."

Being with the colonel provides an education I'd never imagined. I wonder how he knows so much. Guess he got a lot of facts from officer training at that college he went to somewhere back East. Everyone else seems to get information after shit happens.

The 915th Field Artillery Battalion releases its men to the smaller Higgins boats for the first landings. Close to shore, several vessels hit mines, with explosions lifting them completely out of the water. Pieces of men fly in the air and splash into the water alongside fragments of metal.

Shit! A fucking foot lands right in front of me.

I start to shake so bad my teeth clack against each other. I hope Hank makes it home in one piece. Wish I'd had a chance to talk to him before I got assigned to HQ. Florence was counting on us sticking together. Hope I don't have to face her with any kind of rotten news. I just want to have the chance to see her face again.

Shelling from the *Nevada*'s fourteen-inch guns blasts the beach, sending thick clouds of dust and hot shrapnel into the damp, cool air. The smell of gunpowder hangs low and drifts across the bow of our ship. Quarter-ton rounds are aimed at the front doors of the German pillboxes. We can only hope they're home and answering the doorbell.

Other units of soldiers follow in Rhino Ferries, large pontoon boats with two huge outboard engines, carrying troops and trucks. Officers have to bark out orders to be heard over the blare of guns and the drone of nearby engines.

After unloading cargo from our ship, we transfer the remaining infantry soldiers to smaller boats headed for shore. They climb down ropes dangling over the water and jump into small barges that lick the sides of our massive ship. The small crafts take on water from the drizzling rain and crashing waves.

Men bail water as fast as it comes in. Soldiers who don't have Pliofilm covers to keep their rifles from getting sopped slip Army-issue condoms over the barrels—good ole Yankee ingenuity, to my way of thinking. They sure as hell aren't going to need rubbers for anything else right now.

Near the beach, soldiers under heavy fire leap into chest-deep, choppy water with their rifles held high overhead and seventy-five pounds of combat gear on their backs. They are loaded with TNT, ammunition, a gas mask bag, food rations, t-handles, and extra clothing. They have to fight like the devil to keep from drowning in the icy water. Bouncing like bobbers at the end of fishing lines, most manage to stay upright and make slow progress toward land. Others inflate the inner tubes around them exactly as they've been told to do. I watch through binoculars with my heart sinking into my gut as things go sour and men struggle to turn right-side up with their heavy packs pulling them backwards into unmarked graves.

A man's no good to anyone if he gets all choked up over things he can't do anything about, so I concentrate on my job, which means reinforcing the guys who make it to shore. The colonel and I gather maps and light equipment while heavy artillery hisses over our heads and the smell of diesel fuel mixes with a thick fog of gunpowder. As the team from headquarters, we're tasked with unloading vehicles and supplies. Without these things, none of us will get very far.

After reaching the sands of Utah Beach, I put the Jeep in granny gear, then give her the gas and roll past shell holes big enough to swallow a car. I skirt the charred remains of equipment and men caught in vicious barrages. My stomach rolls and I gag from a mouthful of what tastes like acid. Thank God I'm not with the infantry. Just a few days ago, I was a dogface with a Nazi target on my back.

On the pebbly beach, posts are wrapped in barbed wire and dug into the sand and pointed out to sea—a present from the Germans. They have been laid to keep our boats from landing. Many men seek refuge underneath, but some never make it any farther. Whenever possible, two spent rifles are used to make crosses over their dead bodies. I quickly learn how to look without seeing. It strikes me that this might be what Hell is like. If it is, I sure don't want to end up there.

What had, only hours before, been a scene of chaos with men running, turning, and dodging bullets, has turned into a landing zone where boats are now safely docked and unloaded. Bulldozers come ashore and level sand against the seawall. Half-tracks and tanks drive off carrier ships to join the surviving infantry and paratroopers.

Colonel Williams scans the area. "A supply line for future battles has been chiseled with blood from the veins of our men, and a small piece of France has been returned to the French people. The way I see it, our boys and some Limey soldiers seized and held the beaches of Normandy and probably changed the way things are going to go from here on out. Maybe even change the course of history."

The colonel was in a windy mood, sounding more like a politician than a soldier, but from my farm-boy perspective, those damned Jerries had started this mess. Now we'd have to finish it.

Chapter 10

Even more challenges face us beyond the beachhead that was held by the Nazis. Next our plan is to drive our troops to the Cotentine Peninsula and capture the port city of Cherbourg, which will eventually be used to bring in much-needed men and materials. But first we need to join up with the paratroopers from the 82nd who survived the drop the night before. French villagers covered the flyboys who didn't make it with their own chutes. They left the dead Germans to bake in the sun—a fitting end for the rotten bastards.

To choke our progress, the Nazis flooded everything within two miles of Utah Beach in order to defend their concrete bunkers. The soaked fields are a swampy soup and make for slow going for me and the colonel. These slimy, muddy, one-lane ruts remind me of slipping and sliding on Nebraska country roads during a spring thaw. Somewhere along the line, I need to cabbage on to a few feet of chain that I can make fit on the tires of this jalopy.

Beyond this drenched mess, an entire division of men with rifles and machine guns slung over their shoulders hikes the high dunes where the remaining Germans shoot American soldiers like ringed targets at a carnival booth. We have to squelch this sniper shit, so the Signal Corps works up ahead, laying communication lines to keep pace with the division's advance movements. With radio connections finally operational, Colonel Williams gets through for updates and much-needed tactical intelligence.

He pounds a roll of papers into his open hand. "The First took a hit on Omaha. A lot worse than we had it here."

"How many KIAs at Utah?" I instantly wished I hadn't asked the question. Knowing a number doesn't change anything, but it seems as though the colonel wants to talk. Maybe I can shut off my feelings if I think about numbers instead of bodies. I have a hunch he deals with it the same way.

"Hundred and ninety-seven so far. We were the fortunate ones, if you want to look at it that way. The tide swept us about fifteen hundred yards farther south than our planned landing. It was probably the German's weakest position. Otherwise, you and I might be dead in this muck instead of stuck in it with this Jeep."

For the second time in as many weeks, good fortune had handed me a lucky break and smiled on my scruffy soul.

When our soldiers finally capture and clear the top of the dunes above the beach, they find a heavily fortified observation post with periscopes looking out over both Utah and Omaha. Those of us who have the chance peer through the long, powerful lenses toward the Channel. The water appears as if it has been painted red with sloppy brush strokes. Of course, it's blood that makes the water the color of brick, but I'd much rather think of the reddish tint as a reflection of the sun setting on the still water.

As daylight surrenders on this first night after the invasion, I make a slit trench deep enough to keep out of a sniper's gun sight while I sleep. When the shelling whizzes within a whisker, I scramble to dig a little deeper. Bedcheck Charlie—low-flying, German reconnaissance planes with an unmistakable whirring sound—fly overhead, trying to determine Allied strength. They introduce themselves to our American artillery, who in turn greet them with a less than friendly reception. Like the glow from lightning bugs buzzing by on a warm August night, the streak of tracer bullets and anti-aircraft flak shine on the horizon.

At oh-dark-thirty, under the drizzle of overcast skies, we learn of our next mission from the commanding officer. "All right, men. Listen up. We're set to take the bridge at Chef du Pont. There's a shitload of jumpers who need backup. German reinforcements have to be stopped before Picauville. So let's get there before they do."

The colonel and I roll out and travel eastward. The French countryside is fairly level, with an occasional gentle slope. A crazy quilt of fields separated by mounds covered with bushes about eight to ten feet wide and four to six feet high break the landscape into small plots. They would have been great places to hunt quail, but we're looking to flush out Nazis instead.

The fields have grain growing in them, or apple trees, but most of the land is pastures of green grass full of grazing cows. Cows are a welcome sight. Wherever livestock feed, there probably aren't land mines. Densely planted trees grow along the top of the dirt banks, with ditches running on one or both sides. These so-called fortresses used by the French to save the soil, now serve yet another line of defense for the Germans. The roads, narrow and winding, also provide one hell of a position for the defenders to ambush our advancing foot soldiers.

Despite the beauty of this strategic terrain, an unforgettable dank odor rises from the dark French dirt. It's as if the ancient, rich earth resents being a battlefield and oozes out a foul smell to ward off invaders like a cornered animal discouraging a predator with a nasty snarl.

We've been knocking around these mounds for a few hours when I decide to take a short break. As I slow down, the hair on the back of my neck stands on end. I bring the Jeep to a sudden stop.

The colonel sits up as if called to attention. "What is it?"

"I don't know. Something's not right. I saw a flicker of light behind us."

"We need to get going. We've got to make it to P'ville before noon."

I look around but don't see anything. "I'm telling you, sir, something's not right." I turn off the ignition so I can hear a little better.

He looks around, his head rotating in a half-circle. "There's not supposed to be anybody anywhere around here."

I raise my hand. "I hear something. It sounds like we have tanks on our tail. It could be ones with a star or a swastika. Who knows?"

"Holy shit. Well, no matter what, we need to get out of their way. If it's Krauts, we'll hope they go on by, and then we'll wait it out until we're out of harm's way."

After a minute or so, I hear the definite rumble of tanks in the distance. I drive like hell down a farm lane and pull over to a grove of trees where we'll be well-hidden. Again, I shut off the motor, and we wait as the sound grows closer. We watch as two German tanks clatter by with men spilling out of its hatches, slinging a boatload of mud in their wake. Trucks trail behind with soldiers scoping out the area in all directions.

As soon as they pass, I let out the pent-up air from my lungs. The colonel gives me a quick salute. I know now I've proven myself. After that, bouncing along in Betsy leaves me feeling more exposed, but I decide from here on out I'll definitely rely on the hairs on the back of my neck.

As we approach a small valley, I turn to him. "I can't see much of anything. It's thicker than fleas on a dog."

"I know. As soon as we can, we need to get to a high spot and figure out where they're located."

"I hope the Germans aren't thinking the same thing," I grumble. We have been trained not to fire until we see something to fire at, but that doesn't work in this country because I can hardly see any farther than the end of my nose in places. Honing my senses, I prepare to shoot anything that moves and ask questions later.

After reaching P'ville, we're ordered to Pont-l'Abbé, which is three-quarters of a mile up the road and most likely heavily defended. We know the Germans are masters at using the land to their advantage, and with 88-mm guns and a range of up to two thousand yards, it will probably be tough and deadly to clear out the bloodsuckers.

When we make it to higher ground, we don't see hide nor hair of them, not even those two gray tanks that rolled by earlier. I draw a deep breath before we move on.

The colonel radios coordinates and recon to our regiment. We wait for them to catch up. I smile as I feel the thundering waves of our approaching vehicles through my grip on the steering wheel.

At the front of the formation, our Stuart and Sherman tanks, jury-rigged with dozer blades, manage to plow through the brush, cutting openings for other equipment to go through and providing access for us to fan out across the next field and the one after that. The engineers place two charges with fifty pounds of explosives to breach the hedge during the infantry advance, and detonate them with a display of firepower. The team will then move forward to the next row to do it all over again.

The colonel and I, along with some officers, set up temporary headquarters in an abandoned building on the outskirts of Périers. Because we can only have small fires during the day, I make a mug of bootleg coffee over an open pit. As I sip my drink, the color of dishwater, I realize once again not being on the front lines has definite advantages. Those poor guys on the front can't have fires because their large numbers and the blazes that would be necessary might increase their risk of detection. And a gob of men hunkered around one pissy campfire would surely set off a knock-down-drag-out. Warm food never makes it on their menu. As the saying goes, "Rank has its privileges."

After breaking from our make-do headquarters, the colonel and I head out for the boondocks once again. I hope there aren't any mines buried or any Krauts hanging around in a Panzer tank waiting for us on the other side of the clearing while we gather what information we need.

The colonel swings his arm to the right. "Erv, let's head that way. The Germans are going to kick our ass and hand it to us if we don't figure out where the hell they're at and how they know every move we make."

I prepare to put my German-speaking skills to the test to gather intelligence about enemy troop movements, along with their supply and equipment locations. Traveling into the small villages and talking to the locals proves to be the only way we can get needed information. In the meantime, I make it my personal mission to keep our butts from being shot at. We have to think like the enemy every inch of the way.

He points up ahead. "Pull in at that farm."

"You sure about that? I mean, it would be a bum deal to drive right into an ambush."

"We'll see, but my gut tells me we'll be in the clear. If not, we still have to take a chance to figure out what's going on."

"Yes, sir."

An overgrown road that looks like it hasn't seen tire tread since the beginning of spring leads us to a small stone farmhouse. In the distance, an old man tends a couple of hay burners.

We watch for Germans or any kind of movement. A U.S. military Jeep painted pea-green with a star on top means we aren't stopping by for a cup of tea, so I jump out of the Jeep, grab a handful of mud, and toss it at the hood of the vehicle.

"We'll look a whole lot better covered up a bit." The star and its white stripes disappear under the muck.

We drive close to the farm yard, staying out of open view. A couple of chickens cackle and strut around. Unsure of what else we might find, I glass the area.

"You see anything?"

"No, sir. Just the old farmer."

"Let's get out and move in between those two buildings."

The old man stands inside the corral feeding his horses. I walk toward him with my helmet tucked under my arm, carefully stepping around the slop and manure. He looks at me and plants his hands at his waist. I extend my hand, and the old man shrugs without extending his.

"Nice farm." I point to the black, block letters on my shirt. "U.S. Army."

"*Oui*," he says, reluctantly shaking my hand.

I hope he speaks English or German. If not, I might be sunk, because my French includes not much more than the few phrases we were taught on the ship a little more than a couple of months ago.

The colonel approaches the two of us. "Ask him if he can tell us where the Nazis are holed up."

I ask if he speaks any German. He answers me with a nod. In my slowest German, I suggest we get out of sight and head into the barn. Luckily, the farmer understands and moves in that direction. The colonel follows, but stays back to survey for any suspicious movement.

On our way to the old building, I find out the Germans were here two days ago but moved east. The old farmer feels sure there are others around. But more importantly, he tells me they had twenty to twenty-five tanks and big artillery. I tell him it seems as if they know what we're going to do before we even think of it. He isn't surprised they can see our every move. Apparently, they are sitting tight on top of a hill called Mont Castre.

Artillery shells scream over our heads. "Jesus Christ!" I shout, turning to check on the colonel several feet behind, his eyes as wide as a hoot owl's. I grab the farmer by his elbow. He doesn't move, as if he's nailed to the ground, so I throw my arm around his shoulders and half carry him. A shell slams into the far corner of the barn in an explosion of fire and steel. I fly through the air, heat racing across my back, and hit face first, taking the old coot with me. We land at the nearest wall of the barn. When I come to on a layer of straw, I give him a nudge. With him not much bigger around than a couple of branches from a weeping willow, I figure he broke a few of his brittle old bones when we slammed down. He opens his eyes and spits out a mouthful of dirt and hay.

The colonel gets up and dusts himself off as I help the old man to his feet. "We'd better get the hell out of here, Erv."

"I couldn't agree with you more." The artillery that gets you is the one you never hear.

I check the old farmer. He's a little shaken but no worse for the wear, so we abruptly end our visit and leave him in the settling smoke and rubble.

When we hook up with the rest of our men, we set out straight toward the German outpost on top of Mont Castre, which has been nicknamed Hill 122. Until we can take 122, we have to strong-arm the Nazis with pulverizing fire. Right now, they're positioned on top of a knoll with a perfect vantage point and unlimited visibility. They can count the lug nuts on the wheels of Betsy. We have to sneak through and do away with them in swift fashion.

A church, a sturdy sandstone monument with a well-kept cemetery surrounded by two small buildings, stands just beyond the knoll. Resting fifty feet above the roof's peak sits a bell tower. The beauty of this safe haven doesn't deter the Jerries from converting it into a military fortress. It pops with firepower as a German machine-gun nest controls access to the area.

Beyond the church sits Hill 122, a steep, smooth crest poking out from a clearing. It overlooks the Cherbourg peninsula and will likely be the key to our entire southward drive. When we break from these stubby shrubs, we'll hopefully get out of this stinking hedgerow country. Unfortunately, an airstrike is out of the question right now because of low cloud cover.

One of our two assault battalions moves toward the hill. From the view behind my field glasses, our guys make it across no-man's-land without much of a problem, but near the enemy's line they run into anti-personnel mines. The explosions expose their location and the Germans cut loose on them. Some men buy the farm, some are wounded, and a few make it back to tell the story of taking Hill 122. It was goddamn bad news, that's for sure.

By the time we seize 122, we're cooking with gas again. We're destroying the German's main line of opposition in the area and bringing friendly forces to the best observation point possible. For the rest of July, we battle our way out of the Normandy peninsula and onto the plains of western France.

Leaving behind the tomb-like hedgerows for open, green rolling hills, the coming days bring hell-bent-for-leather maneuvers as we race across the heart of France. For me, each farm we come to stirs a memory of life back home.

As the German front in Normandy collapses, their soldiers flee east by any means they can. With our air power bombing roads, bridges, and railways, we seriously reduce their ability to move. By mid-August, the Germans are trapped at Falaise.

The area between the four cities of Trun, Argentan, Vimoutiers, and Chambois becomes the valley of death. The Nazis, caught helplessly in our net, run around like chickens with their heads cut off. They are hightailing it on horses, on foot, and by any way possible, trying to escape the tanks and machine guns spraying bullets into the valley. Now and then, a commander calls a temporary truce and large numbers of Krauts surrender. Hundreds are herded to POW bands at the rear. I predict the hardcore Nazis will eventually regroup, dig in their heels, and make another stand. When the smoke clears from the valley, junk and debris is strewn for miles alongside the charred remains of those who refused to surrender.

By late August, we are once again moving east toward Berlin. "Somewhere out there, the Krauts will be waiting and they won't be running away," I say.

The colonel nods in agreement.

Unfortunately, we've suddenly hit what we in the Army call a SNAFU—Situation Normal, All Fucked Up—and are running out of fuel. To keep trucks, tanks, and equipment humming, we need gasoline and diesel, and lots of it. This delay will give the Nazis plenty of opportunity to work out a new battle plan and rearm their men. It couldn't come at a worse time, but with three months of fighting under our belts, we welcome the break caused by the shortage and wait for the biscuit bombers to deliver supplies. After cleaning our rifles and using a rag with water sloshed in our helmets to remove the top layer of dirt from our faces, boredom sets in. It doesn't take much to get a game of poker started— four guys and a little spare time. I decide to write a letter home.

> *Dear Betty,*
>
> *How are you Hon? I know it's been a while since you've heard from me but I think of you every day and hope you and the baby are doing fine. It's been rough here off and on but we just keep going at it and hope each day brings us closer to the end. I got an assignment translating for a colonel. He's a really good guy and we get along great. Being with him is a pretty good deal. You wouldn't believe it but sometimes they even have a parade for us when we go through town. It does make a guy feel good for a while. Keep us in your prayers. I'll write again soon.*
>
> *Love,*
>
> *Erv*

In some places we're met with hardly any German resistance and are treated like heroes in French towns with names like Saint-Hilaire, Landivy, and Mayenne. Little girls dressed in their Sunday best, tightly holding bunches of daisies, toss their bouquets and smile at us with their mamas' encouragement. Most of the other kids run up and shout, "Gum? Gum?" What we have, we hand out to them. And almost always a village mayor in a fancy jacket, striped trousers, and a perfectly trimmed moustache waves his hands frantically, pleading for quiet, so he can attempt a grand welcoming speech. But more often than not, the reception committee ends up peeved because a commander can't take time to formally accept a key to their village.

What I never mention to Betty in my letters is the flowing wine, the flowers, and smiles a mile wide—and how the *mademoiselles* look better and better, mostly because there are more of them at each place we come to. From what I gather, the local gals think of us Americans as their saviors. There are times when temptation for a love-starved soldier proves too much. I ought to know. Not long ago, Paris dangled temptation in front of me like a crawdad to a catfish.

When fighting had boiled to the temperature of a blast furnace, those of us with the most combat time got R&R in places with baths, a clean bed, and some decent food. Colonel Williams put the two of us in for a short furlough, and we left the area around Fontainebleau and set out thirty-five miles north to Paris. A few good Joes chipped in cigarettes so I could sell them on the French Black Market and have a little extra moola to spend. Some of them had already been to Paris, or they'd heard stories from their fathers who were in the Great War. They all had colorful tales of loose women. To most of them, France was one big party, with hot and bothered French girls simply there for the taking. Unfortunately, there were some soldiers who took up with unwilling partners. Guess those guys thought they had a right to it. That wasn't for me. I was just looking forward to a bath and that clean bed. Real food wouldn't be too bad either.

We'd driven about half an hour in the flatland under a hot September sun when we came to the outskirts of Paris. A French captain, standing at his crossroads-post checking the comings and goings into the city, decided to give us the third degree before reluctantly waving us on. He seemed to take his job very seriously, even though every other Frenchman wanted to kiss the boots us Americans walked in. The Liberation had been a short two weeks before, but the party was still in full swing. There was a feeling in the air that it was only a matter of time before we took Berlin. We all knew there was fighting left to do, but it felt as if the end was near. Maybe it was because here in Paris the people looked well fed, there were green trees up and down wide streets, and fancy buildings without pieces missing like everywhere else I'd seen. It was almost as if the city had missed out on the war. Well, at least it seemed that way.

Driving Betsy would have been easier if I hadn't had to dodge bicycles darting out from every nook and cranny. A close call with a two-wheeler forced me to take it a little slower—which gave the women in brightly colored shirts a chance to hop on board so they could plant big smooches on us. I didn't mind, and the colonel didn't seem to, either. The *thank you*s didn't stop with the women. Men slapped our backs or shook our hands. I couldn't imagine what it would be like to be here when the war was officially over.

We decided to drive around the city and take it all in. I'd never seen anything like it. The colonel pointed out places like the huge arch that was a war memorial for French soldiers. Based on the size of the thing, it looked like they really appreciated their service.

As the sun began to set, the street corners lit up and so did the houses with their blue and red lights. According to the colonel, officers frequented the blue ones and everyone else was supposed to check out the red. I didn't ask what the difference was and didn't care how he knew. But like a lot of other times, he seemed to know stuff, and most of the time it came in handy.

With the bread and cheese we'd collected and eaten as we cruised around, we decided something to drink was in order. A bar seemed the perfect choice. We found an okay joint with a hotel next door. We went in and grabbed a table. There were men parked on tall stools at the bar and two young women sitting at a booth in the corner. We'd hardly had a chance to think about what we wanted when beers were delivered to our table. We raised our glasses to the other patrons and smiled. They smiled back.

"Here's egg in your beer," I said.

The colonel and I clinked our glasses together and took long swigs. I couldn't remember anything tasting better.

"The dark-haired brunette's giving you the eye, Erv."

"Nah, probably has a gut ache."

He laughed and downed another long draw, practically draining his tall glass. "You'd better get ready to say something because both of them are sashaying in our direction."

"Well, as Betty's mother always said, 'there's a lid for every pot'."

The colonel laughed again. One beer seemed to fire both of us up.

Other than the girls at the port in Liverpool, I couldn't recall when I'd last been this close to a skirt. The one with dark pin-curls hugging her face approached our table first. I didn't expect her to speak any English, but she did. Or at least I think it was English. I got lost in those brown eyes and long eyelashes, and her words kind of melted into what sounded pretty damned good. The next thing I knew, the colonel and I were tossing back beers, and then wine, and then a few more beers. Now the *mademoiselle* with pin-curls became Monique. Last names weren't important. In fact, I don't know if she even knew mine. It didn't matter. Every red-blooded soldier wanted to have one last fling before the war got him. The colonel and I quickly exchanged plans on where to meet up, and Monique and I went next door to the hotel. For one glorious night, the war seemed as if it was a lifetime ago. By morning, I had a headache and a bad case of regrets. I guess I could have blamed my sins on the liquor, but like most guys, I just needed the sweet love a woman. The colonel and I never brought up the subject after that, and I never mentioned it to anyone, especially not Betty.

Now, with each town's freedom we push the German forces across France and Belgium and closer to their own border. On September 10, 1944, we liberate the Grand Duchy of Luxembourg. Rolling in on a Sunday under clear skies, the leaves are as golden as the sun and practically sparkle on the branches. In the distance, bells ring as we approach the capital, Luxembourg City, with our stream of men on foot and our tanks and Jeeps clattering.

Moving along the dusty road leading to the city, one of the lead Jeeps with the windshield folded down onto its hood makes a quick U-turn from the convoy and pulls next to me and the colonel.

"Can you translate up ahead?" the corporal asks, coming within inches of the side of Betsy. "We found a young civilian walking on the road, but all we can get out of him is that he's from Luxembourg. It sounds like he's speaking German, but it's kind of different."

"It's probably High German. Yeah, I can talk to him." I swerve out of line and follow the corporal to the front of the caravan.

The young man stands with his hands in his pockets and grins from ear to ear. He looks about eighteen years old, but then, all of the locals look older than they really are. His shirt and pants hang on him like they were draped over a pair of crossed posts used to keep crows away from a cornfield. His dirty blond hair hasn't seen a decent pair of scissors in a coon's age.

The corporal says, "Okay, ask him where he's from and why the bells are ringing. Nobody rings church bells around here. The general thinks they're trying to warn the Germans."

"*Woher kommst, du?*"

He explains that he lives in Luxembourg City and points up the road.

I ask him why the church bells are ringing and he tells me it's a celebration. His words are a mixture of German and Dutch. "You are here to set us free." He explodes with his story as I repeat the gist of it to those around me.

"He's telling me his people have been waiting to be saved by the Americans for years. They've lived in fear, and hundreds were moved to work camps or forced to fight with the *Wehrmacht*."

"Sure making a helluva racket with those bells," the general says, using a gruff tone to show his disapproval of anything that might give our location to the Germans. The general speaks directly to his corporal as if he can't ask me the question without going through someone else. "Have him find out if any Nazis are hiding in town."

If you wear almost as many stars on your shoulder as the Big Dipper, I guess you get to use someone else to ask your questions. There sure are a lot of differences between Colonel Williams and the general. The colonel has never asked me, or any of the other men under his command for that matter, to do anything he wouldn't or couldn't do himself. I make a mental note to tell him how much I respect him the next time I have the chance.

I wait until the corporal relays the general's instructions before I ask the kid if he thinks there are any Germans still around.

"The Germans left days ago," I report to the men huddled close by. "He says they left with the collaborators."

Colonel Williams clears a place for the young fellow to sit in the back seat. "Tell him we'll give him a ride into town. But keep your eyes peeled in case any Nazi stragglers are staying behind."

When we arrive in town, everyone spills out onto the streets. Crowds, young and old, surround us, hand out flowers, and try to serve us wine as we file through.

Chapter 11

German soldiers pulling back from their losses scurry like cockroaches under a bright light. They disappear into miles and miles of bunkers, tunnels, and tank traps along the country's fortified boundary. We call it the Siegfried Line—the Nazis' safe haven from the Allied Forces who hunt them.

As usual, Colonel Williams seems to know the score and be on top of what lies ahead. "Hitler ordered his troops to withdraw. Had thousands of prisoners building concrete barriers for protection. Fucking bastards."

Intelligence proves the colonel's right on the money. Land mines lie between what looks like huge teeth thrusting through the gums of the earth—tangled bridgework in a giant's mouth. The cement bumps are about three feet high, staggered, and spaced in such a way that tanks will get hung up if they attempt to go over the top—German resourcefulness at its finest.

"I'd guess the snakes want to funnel us into areas where their Panzers can pick us off one by one," I say. "We can penetrate the Line if we ball-bust our way through the back door and then yank those blocks out."

The colonel squints, crinkles forming at the corner of his eyes as if giving my idea some serious thought. "The problem is it takes time and men to wind cable and chain around those concrete barriers. That would leave us open to snipers and ambush. Not sure we could do it anyway. God only knows how deep they buried them."

He's right, but I just want to get in there and tear the place apart. Unfortunately, our Shermans are no match for the more heavily armored German Panzers. When we go head-to-head with their Tigers, they kick the shit out of us. But with the recent arrival of a new wrinkle in armor-piercing rounds, our tanks might be on more of a level playing field. I hope the boys at R&D have hatched a winner.

The Chief of Staff sends word over the wire that the colonel and I are supposed to chart our progress in finding space between those teeth so our equipment can go through. This will call for more recon and getting friendly with some of the local residents. Speaking German has come in handy a number of times and also allows me and the colonel to break from the front line. Being on your own isn't a good idea unless you can talk your way out of a tight situation.

On occasions when we leave the regiment, we try to travel the Line mostly at night, taking turns sleeping and eating during the day and keeping a lookout for trouble. Whenever I can't turn on the Jeep's headlights for fear of being spotted by the enemy, I maneuver by the moonlight through the dry, crackling brush. When the moon shines not much wider than the curved needle my ma used for darning socks, I make my way by a sixth sense I developed while driving threshing machines on dark farm roads from one harvesting job to the next. Wondering about what's out there in the dense brush, I slow down and then come to a complete stop.

"I don't think we should go any farther for now," the colonel says.

"Yeah. Seems really quiet. Too quiet. Kind of makes my hair stand on end. I'm all for sticking here for a while."

"Stop in that grove of trees. We'll wait it out there."

I offer to start a fire in the middle of the thickets while he checks for enemy activity. Like so many times before when the coast was clear, I make a small campfire with gas siphoned from abandoned machinery and rustle up something for me and the colonel to eat. Gas makes for a fast fire with very little smoke, which gives us less chance of being spotted. Over the open flame, I roast vegetables I've found decaying in the dirt near farm plots scattered along the countryside. The crackling of the fire and an occasional chirping bird breaks the silence of the late afternoon air. Waiting for the screen of darkness, as the warmth from the autumn sun turns into the coolness of dusk, we talk as if there were no war to fight and no killing to be done.

"You know, Erv, I've never asked you about your family. You're from Nebraska and you've got a wife and baby girl. That much I know, but I don't know much else."

"Ask away. I'm an open book."

"You've got a big family. I figured out that much, but just how many brothers and sisters do you have?" His question takes on an easy tone as if we're playing a parlor game.

"Brothers and sisters? Oh, hell. I've almost got enough in my family for two baseball teams. Six brothers and five sisters. I'm fourth in line."

The colonel throws back his head and laughs. "Holy mackerel!"

"Yeah, there's a pack of us. Two of my brothers are fighting in the war. My older brother Jacob is a mechanic in the Army, and my younger brother Ed is fighting in the Pacific. The rest are home working the farm. How about you?"

"Just a twin brother. Didn't think much of me going into the military. Guess he figured it would be a worry for our mother. Dad always wanted me to work a more civilized job when I got out of college. He was an insurance man and hoped I'd wear a white shirt and a nice tie instead of a uniform."

"My dad never wore a white shirt or a tie unless he was going to a funeral. And me, I never set foot in a college."

"Yeah, well, you've got common sense that going to college doesn't give you. You know how to do things, Erv. You've kept Betsy running through hundreds of miles of this miserable backcountry without getting us lost once." He flings several twigs into the fire. "You've kept us from getting our butts shot at. And we're eating better than most, too. Who would've imagined you could mud wrap a potato and bake it in hot ash?"

"We might as well dine on something besides these tasty K-rations," I joke.

He smiles. "That's what I mean. You know what to do without somebody telling you how."

"I guess so." I feel embarrassed from his compliment. "Never really thought about it before. On the farm we had to make do—had no choice. We didn't have extras, if you know what I mean. Seemed as though we were always working. And if we weren't working, we were in church. We had Bible study on Wednesday nights, and every Sunday after church service we'd eat supper at my grandma and grandpa's place. They lived just up the road."

"Those were your dad's folks?"

"Yeah, you might say that. My dad's mother, but not his real father." I wasn't sure how much he wanted to know, but I continued on. "My grandma's family settled in the Volga region of Russia when Catherine the Great granted German immigrants a chance to work their own farm land. Things weren't very good in Germany back then, so they packed up and settled there. Everything went along pretty smooth for a while. But by the time my grandma was a young girl, the Russian government went to hell in a handbasket—like wanting the Germans to give up being Lutherans."

"Is that why they left?"

"That was part of it. The government decided they didn't want Germans there anymore if they didn't pledge to be Russian. They didn't even want them to keep their German ways. They outlawed anyone from speaking their mother tongue. It got really bad, I guess. The government suspected anyone who wasn't pure Russian of being sympathizers. Then a bastard in their army raped my grandmother when she was fourteen."

The colonel glances away from the red coals of the fire and looks at me with surprise, his brows pinching together. Then he chucks another piece of kindling into the flames, this time with extra force, as if to show his disgust.

"There's no love lost between my family and the Russians, that's for sure. It ought to be interesting when we meet those Bolsheviks in Berlin. I know they're supposed to be on our side of the fight, but I don't trust them. Anyway, to make a long story short, after my grandma had her baby, the family scraped up enough money to board a ship and came to the U.S. They gave up everything but the clothes on their backs and the teeth in their mouths."

He almost smiles and then takes a serious tone, "So that baby was your father, and he's half Russian?"

"Yeah, but no one ever talks about it. You're probably the only person outside my family who knows the story."

"Sounds like a tough deal. My military schooling tells me I should be more suspicious of them. Your story backs it up."

"I just don't trust 'em. They'll sell you down the river, if you ask me."

He sits quietly and uses a broken twig with its dried leaves to draw circles in the ash. "The fire's about out. Maybe we ought to try to go on down the road. We've got a lot of ground to cover before daylight."

Our talk gives me a good feeling. In another place and time, the two of us would have never met, let alone shared the stories of our lives. But when we hitch up with our battalion, I have to remember that even though we talked like two men shooting the breeze about the weather outside the Fremont County Courthouse, he's in command and will probably be kicked up to a higher rank before it's all said and done.

When the day breaks with hardly enough light to see, we discover scattered pillboxes, the concrete dug-out bunkers with holes for the Nazis to shoot through. Now we know we've made it to the Line once again. At dawn, we go on foot and low-crawl to the crest of a ridge where we can get a better look. With a recent frost, the drying vines and weeds provide some camouflage. Through my field glasses, I see no activity—no movement, no smoke, and no Nazis. As I lay there for fifteen minutes or so, glassing the pillboxes, and as the sun gradually warms my face, I catch a glint of reflected light.

"Shit. There are Germans here," I say. "I was beginning to wonder if they'd cleared out."

"How many?"

"I only count two, but I'd guess the other half dozen boxes are loaded with 'em."

"We need to get back right away and brief the CO, Erv."

We crawl on our bellies down the rim and then make a mad dash to the Jeep. Although the Jerries hadn't heard us when we arrived earlier, we quietly push Betsy about a quarter mile before revving her up and taking off like a house on fire. It's a good thing the weather has stayed warm enough to drive with the top down, because we bounce so high from the rocky terrain we probably would have poked holes in the canvas with our heads.

Based on earlier reconnaissance, we'd also found a small opening in a steep ravine where those giant teeth hadn't been laid. It will scarcely be enough room to get our tanks through, but it should work.

Back at base, the colonel gives the commanding officer the lowdown, and the two of them plan the attack. Our columns are to advance and run heavy tanks over the area, exploding the land mines underneath.

When we make it back to the ravine, the Nazis pelt us with heavy fire, which gives away their locations and allows our artillery to zero in. Engineers and infantrymen then cut the barbed wire and pull sections out for our vehicles to go through. Even though the tanks make it, we can't be sure there aren't mines still lying there waiting for us.

So, because of incoming heavy machine-gun fire, we lie flat against the ground on our bellies and slowly inch forward, shoulder to shoulder, probing the earth at an angle with a bayonet until we meet something. Once we find a mine, we get underneath it, carefully lift the sod, and set it aside. Next, a charge gets laid over it. We stand back and they let it blow. That's when we all start breathing again.

Besides the actual mines, there's always the risk of trip wires, spread out like an underground spider's web, to detonate the explosive. If a man shoves his knife too far or with too much force and snags one of the webs, it sets off an explosion, deadly to him and anyone else close by.

After a blast, a brief silence always follows, sometimes replaced by the agonizing moans of wounded men.

"Fuck!" a soldier shouts after one such silence. "There ain't nothin' left of 'em."

Several men lie scattered in the path of a tripped wire. One man's head, split down the middle, oozes out his brains.

"Oh, Mama. Help me, Mama," another man cries out, holding what's left of his insides.

A medic darts to where arms and legs litter the field like cuts of meat. Men's limbs land yards away from their bodies and spill their life. Nothing the medic or anyone else can do except bury the pieces. I've gotten numb to it just like everybody else. If you allow your fear to get the best of you, you're as good as dead yourself. When and if a soldier's dog tags are found, the commander collects the second tag and leaves the first one with the body.

I cross myself with my tags and say a prayer in hopes of keeping them together around my scrawny neck.

Dear God, don't make Betty have to claim chunks of my body. Dead or alive, just get me home in one piece.

By mid-October, after a lot more recon and progress measured in what seems more like yards than miles, the colonel and I rejoin our division. And by November, we have moved closer to the banks of the Moselle River, zeroing in on Thionville in France. The hilly terrain with deep-cut gorges and slippery slopes is defended like a polecat watching over its young. We continue our advance, taking the small towns west of the Moselle one by one.

In the north, the advancing V Corps, or Blood Buckets as they are affectionately known, join us on our right flank. In Thionville, we fight in frantic house-to-house combat and then clear the section of the city that lies on the near side of the river. We plan to bridge the Moselle at Thionville, despite Intelligence telling us that the enemy is defending it from numerous strategic positions. To the south, the 5th Division makes little or no progress with its bridgehead over the river. Apparently, the chokehold around Metz has not yet been squeezed tightly enough.

Scheduled for some time between November 6 and November 9, H-hour looms. The plan includes ripping the province of Lorraine from the Krauts' grasp while exposing the Siegfried Line to total assault.

But now, a new enemy strikes, an enemy dangerous and unpredictable—the weather. Rain, cold and piercing, soaks us to the bone, changing foxholes into pools of icy water and making dirt roads nearly impossible to travel. Even Betsy struggles to make her way. Day after day it rains cats and dogs. Trucks bringing necessary supplies by night sink to their axles in a gripping sea of sludge. Miserable and soaked, we wait for H-hour.

"Let's get this show on the road," a young soldier calls out. "This waiting is driving me nuts."

"Don't you know three-quarters of a soldier's life is spent hurrying up and waiting for crap to happen?" another soldier responds.

The commanding officer waves his hand over his head. "Hold your horses, men. We'll be in the thick of it again very soon. Just wait and see."

He's right. It doesn't take long until the assault boats make the first cross-ings. After establishing the bridgehead, the engineers build bridges to allow half-tracks and vehicles to cross. They watch the rain and study the river carefully, but grow increasingly worried when the current flows northward and races up the Moselle's banks. Normally, spanning a river three hundred and fifty feet wide would present few challenges. But this river flows in an angry rage and splatters itself against the shore. And still the rain comes down in sheets.

The engineers struggle to guide boats to landing points, discharge their loads of men and guns, and then return to begin the operation all over again.

The Moselle fights us every inch of the way, swelling above its banks and tossing our overloaded boats like corks on rolling waves.

The other enemy, the Krauts, seem temporarily stunned by the sheer boldness of our movements. Lulled into a sense of security by weeks of relative quiet and by the hope the river will stop us from crossing, the German outposts are quickly overrun. But the surprise is short-lived. Enemy reaction, when it comes, proves violent and deadly. The Jerries' artillery, aided by excellent observation posts across the river, shells the crossing sites with deadeye accuracy, kind of like shooting fish in a barrel.

At day's end, the situation looks critical. The river has swollen to about a mile and a half wide. Our infantry fights without a break. Men are numbed by the cold and totally exhausted. With no extra blankets available, rations skimpy, and ammunition close to running out, our guys paddle up shit creek. Difficult to say which we fear more, the Germans to the front or the river to the rear. We hope the Nazis don't take the offensive and push our asses back into the river. They have us between a rock and a hard place, and I think they know it.

Even without a bridge, enough supplies, armor, rest, warmth, or sufficient rations, we double the seized area in a single day. By about six in the evening, the Moselle also surrenders. The crest of the flood reaches its peak and the waters slowly begin to recede. With the bridge secured, we finally reach the other side.

On day six, supplies arrive. We score luxuries in the form of dry blankets, overcoats, clean socks, and, for some, their first hot meal in weeks. Wet socks on cold feet have produced a bumper crop of trench foot where the foot first turns red and then looks like a ghastly piece of raw, blue meat. It has to get pretty bad before most men will even think about taking off their boots, for fear of peeling them off and never being able to get them back on again. Brave men limped into battle while others had to be carried to their weapons. Whenever I find pieces of a parachute, I use the silk to cover my feet and hands and then put my gloves and socks over. I carry the only extra pair of socks I own in my helmet liner—letting the heat from my head dry them and giving my melon a little extra padding. Having been raised on a farm, I've had my share of the bitter cold, but this has really tested me.

The situation has grown shittier by the time the Air Force joins our fight, though not with guns or bombs. C-130s now swoop in low over the area at treetop level and drop their payload of medical supplies—an early Christmas present.

Unfortunately for us, the picture constantly changes. To the north in Luxembourg and Belgium, the German general Von Rundstedt hurls his best division into a counterattack. Facing the fury of his assault, we wince as if we've come across a pit of snakes. We turn to the west bank of the Saar River. At this point, we have our first experience with reversing a position. We feel like dogs that sniffed too close to the supper table and got their slats kicked. Amazingly, with only one ferry, one footbridge, and just a few assault boats, we manage to maneuver the entire division back across the Saar under the enemy's nose. Crews working on the bridge and ferry sites perform miracles to move vehicles and armor across. For days, the operation continues while the Germans remain completely ignorant of what is going on. With the crossing of the Saar also successfully completed and the Siegfried Line cracked, another triumph dangles within the grasp of the 90th Division. Now we know the Line can be broken. We also know we did it once and we can do it again.

The withdrawal begins and we get the hell out of there. As we retreat, or advance from the rear as we like to joke, we destroy any piece of equipment that might aid the enemy and search the areas they abandoned for anything usable. We even field-strip cigarette butts so they can't be smoked by the Krauts.

December finds us in the area between the Moselle and Saar rivers. The German border sits about twenty-five miles to the east, and everyone looks forward to the day when we can write "inside Germany" on letters home—even if it gets cut out of the paper by censors.

The 90th Division's next mission becomes how to prevent the German forces in that zone from reinforcing Von Rundstedt's position in the north. New replacements, like long-lost relatives, arrive to fill in our badly depleted ranks.

—

About the time our mood starts to sour, we receive another Christmas present. This one comes a little early, too.

"Good news. Have Waldron and Mackenzie round up all available men," Colonel Williams says.

"You bet. What's up?" I ask.

"There's a special show. It's what they're calling the Cow Pasture Circuit—a group of folks coming to entertain us troops."

I can't believe my ears. "Here? On the front lines?" Maybe the colonel's been dreaming.

"It's no joke. I'm serious, Erv. Have them send everyone over to the slope by the road. They'll know it by the USO truck that's parked there. Guys will probably have to sit on their helmets, but I don't think they'll mind. Going to hear the Crooner himself."

"The Crooner? All right. If you say so." I can't imagine what he has up his sleeve, but I quickly find Waldron and Mackenzie sitting with a group of men and get them moving.

"Make the rounds and announce that there's a surprise visit. Have the men beat it over to the road and wait there," I say.

"You mean like a big general?" Waldron asks.

"No. Not that kind of surprise visit. It's good, though. The colonel's sure excited about it."

As I leave, I overhear the usual snickers erupt with guys speculating about beautiful women being on display or something equally delicious.

"They're getting the word out," I report to the colonel.

"Good. Let's get going. We want to be as close as we can. Not every day you get to see the likes of Bing Crosby."

"Bing Crosby? When you said the Crooner, I didn't know you meant the real Bing Crosby. Man, oh man! Bing Crosby right here on the front lines!"

We practically run, but we aren't the first ones. Men have already filled in and are sitting in a half-circle surrounding the flatbed truck with an upright piano on it. A Jeep with a machine gun jutting out of the backseat is parked next to a truck with a USO flag tied to its windshield. The colonel gets called to the makeshift stage. He steps on the truck bumper and grabs the hand of none other than Mr. Crosby himself.

There he is, as big as anything, standing on the tailgate of a truck wearing an Army jacket and dungarees with a pipe dangling out the side of his mouth. All of us whoop and holler as Mr. Crosby shakes hands with the bigwigs.

Colonel Reid holds out his hands to quiet the crowd of men, which is about ten rows deep with guys standing along the edge. "Gentlemen, this man doesn't really need an introduction, but I gratefully present to you an entertainer with world-wide popularity, Mr. Bing Crosby." Colonel Williams shakes his hand again and then stands to the side with a smile as wide as the Moselle River we'd crossed.

The entertainer winks and takes the pipe with its dark bowl out of his mouth and stashes it in the pocket of his jacket. You could have heard a pin drop if there'd been a place besides the cold, hard ground to drop one.

"As I've said before, I feel guilty not serving alongside you men, but they told me I didn't qualify because of my age and my family," Mr. Crosby begins. "I guess that's why I signed on to entertain you fine men in uniform. I hope this song brings you good memories of home."

His low, smooth voice could have lulled a soldier to sleep in a foxhole. He starts out singing "White Christmas" and ends with "I'll Be Home for Christmas"—if only in my dreams. I never imagined a song could get to me like that, but it was as if I were a little boy again, digging into my Christmas sock for a prized apple and the handful of walnuts bulging at the toe. As long as I live, I'll never forget the day or the man.

Our short concert is followed by sharp, freezing winds that shift the snow from one place to the other, buries the roads, and turns them into sheets of ice. More often than not, I can barely see the end of Betsy's hood. None of us knows our destination, our mission, or the trouble that might lie ahead. Our orders are brief and to the point: "Be prepared for movement."

As we wait to roll into the area near Luxembourg, we receive another directive: "Round up women, children, and old men from the farms and villages and evacuate them to Luxembourg City. We need to get them away from the front lines." Things are probably going to get real bloody. As we travel slowly along the frozen roads, we check for boundary markers. Germany doesn't look any different from France or Belgium. The people don't look any different either. They have been pushed between countries for so long that switching languages comes naturally, and they all have the same look of loss on their faces. Except one old man who runs to an American soldier and kisses him on each cheek.

"Don't think I've ever seen a man kiss another man before," I whisper to the colonel.

"A lot of things you probably haven't seen before, Erv. Chalk this one up to the way they do things."

"I guess so. Surprises me, that's all."

By the time we successfully move the refugees to safer ground, the German border waits ahead. As we move closer to the boundary line, my instincts tell me the Germans won't roll over and play dead even though Intelligence thinks we have them whipped. News comes that we'll have a chance to get ready before the next offensive. Spare time becomes a new luxury, at least for a while. Given this breathing spell, I write another letter to Betty.

Hi Honey

I have a little extra time on my hands so I thought I'd write a book to catch you up on things. Sure wish I could be home with you for the holidays. Christmas will probably be long over by the time you get this. At least last Christmas I was in the states. You're not going to believe this but Bing Crosby himself sang Christmas songs for us troops. I'm not talking about some recording. I'm talking about the real thing. I still can't believe it. Even with that present, Christmas time over here still feels nothing like Christmas. I can tell you that for sure. We're all thinking about our families right about now. *A lot of the guys have youngsters or want to someday and I hope our kids learn that the Tough Ombres cleaned this up. I feel real bad for these little tikes though. They might never forget the terrible things they've seen. So many of them have been through hell and back.*

A few days ago we evacuated villagers from the front lines and moved them to Luxembourg City. It was colder than blue blazes and we had to load them in Army trucks the kind with canvas sides. Better than walking I guess. We divided them in groups by who could stand the weather better. We put mothers with their babies toward the front of the trucks where it was warmer and not as windy. Women with older kids filled in wherever they could. The old men crowded around the tail end where the canvas flaps are tied to the tailgate. Most were as light as a feather. Don't think they've had much to eat lately. It was a three hour ride behind our lines and the colonel and I made it to HQ when a truck came rolling in with a couple of refugees. A woman ran in screaming that she lost her daughter. Somewhere along the way she had fallen asleep and her little girl slid out of her arms and out the back of the truck. She didn't realize it until she woke up. I never saw a woman so crazy. She was crying and screaming and kept saying we had to help her find her daughter. I felt so bad Sweetie. I thought of our baby Bonnie and how I'd want someone to help you if something terrible happened. I told the Colonel I needed to find the little girl even if I had to go behind the German line. He said if anyone could find his way it was me. He asked me if I was sure I wanted to go and I said I was. He gave me the okay so I took a Jeep and drove with no headlights. You know me I'm a Cracker Jack at finding my way around in the dark! Every time I came to some GIs I asked if anyone had seen a little girl. Nobody had seen a thing. Finally I saw something that looked out of place. I flashed my light and there she sat on a pile of pine boughs hugging her knees. She had a gray coat with a plaid frock and fit the description to a T. She was scared and cold but not hurt that bad.

Sure was a cute little thing—maybe four or five. She settled down a little when I told her in German that I was taking her to her mama. She never talked—just looked at me with those big eyes. I plopped her in the Jeep and covered her up and away we went. After about an hour I wanted to stop and get some shut-eye but she wasn't having any part of it so I kept going. She finally fell asleep in the backseat. I didn't think anyone could snooze in an Army Jeep but she sure did. I got her back not long before daylight. The Colonel put me in for a Bronze Star. He said it was outside the line of duty. Can you believe that? Anyway the look on that mama's face that morning was worth more than any star. So saving that little girl is my Christmas present to you Honey. I love you more than anything in this world.

Erv

BOOK III:
CATHERINE REVAUX

LABOR CAMP 1944–1945

Chapter 12

The Nazi guard with a rifle balanced across his knees drifts off to sleep. I recognize him as one of the jackals who combed the linen factory hunting for Renier. He still has the look of a dog waiting for his master to issue a command. Perhaps he failed his previous mission and has now been assigned the simple task of guarding helpless women.

We bounce from side to side in the truck, and it feels as though the driver deliberately swerves to hit every rough place in the road. There is no give. There is no cushion. The only sounds are the whine of the engine and the dull thump of our bottoms against cold, wooden planks.

My mouth is dry, but even so I'm thankful we haven't had anything to drink. Squatting to relieve ourselves in front of leering eyes is an experience I don't wish to repeat. Even as I wallow in self-pity, I wonder what will happen to Maman. I picture her with tears running down her cheeks, staring at the Christmas box I wrapped only days before being taken from the factory. She must be sick with dread. *Find strength in your faith, Maman. I will come home.*

"Where do you think they're taking us?" I whisper to Nina.

Nina looks at me with her porcelain-doll eyes and shrugs. Her eyes betray the fear.

127

The eight of us sit facing each other on benches lining the sides of the truck. Dark brown canvas fastened over a wire frame blocks our view to the outside. It resembles a cage. The freezing, sharp wind whistles through the cracks.

Even though I have no idea where we're going, I am certain we have been chosen mostly because of our age. Those who the Nazis didn't pick at the linen factory were mostly older and more visibly frail.

I imagine myself escaping through the spaces in the metal framework, but decide I wouldn't last long without decent boots or an adequate coat. I place my hand protectively on my belly and the bump that is forming. I have more to worry about than myself. This baby I carry inside, Renier's child, needs me. I will do whatever it takes to keep her safe.

As I watch the other women crowded together, I'm not sure their will matches mine. Claire and Sylvie slump against each other as though their souls have left their bodies and nothing remains to keep them upright. Rosa, the youngest of us at fifteen, cries softly through a bloody lip that she makes no effort to treat. The guard had roared at her to stop her sniveling, but even a punch to her face with the end of his gun didn't contain her anguish. The rest have spent all their tears, with only hollowness and darkness left in their eyes. They stare at a distant scene only they can see. It's as if their minds have died but their bodies hang on.

I will not give up. I will not let the Nazis break me and cast off the pieces.

The flap tied to the truck's back gate occasionally whips open. A triangle-shaped gap gives me a glimpse of the tire tracks making parallel ruts through the snow. With what little there is of the moon's light, I search for a marker that might indicate where we are, but eventually quit looking and lean on Nina. I fall into a dream that takes me to a safer, warmer place.

The truck stops abruptly and I'm awake. Muffled German voices break the silence. I am paralyzed with fear. From the words I piece together, the driver is merely given directions. As much as I want this dreadful journey to end, a shadow of terror creeps into the pit of my stomach as I imagine what we might face when we get out.

We move again and the truck makes a laborious turn. The guard stiffens and stands his rifle on its end, using both hands to hold it upright. After another twenty minutes or so, we make another stop. This time, men bark orders strong and sharp with authority. The truck's gate opens and our guard jumps to his feet. His head touches the canvas top as he steps forward. He cringes as if trying to avoid something unclean. Using the tip of his rifle to prop open the flap, he watches as an old woman struggles to climb into the truck and take the next available place to sit. Each new face looks the same as the others—scared and hopeless. There are three men with graying hair. All the rest are women, mostly my age, except one girl who looks about thirteen and one even younger girl, about six or seven. Stinging tears pool in my eyes as I think about my own child and wonder what this world will be like for her.

Those who can't squeeze into a space on the benches fill the area on the floor and curl their arms around their bent legs in an effort to stay warm and allow room for the others. The little girl burrows between the legs of one of the women. Cramped as the truck has become, I welcome the warmth from their bodies.

Two of the women talk softly in what sounds like Polish. I scan their skimpy jackets but don't see yellow stars sewn on them. Relief surges over me when I realize we aren't slated for a place where people go just because they are Jews or undesirables. Immediately, my own naïve stupidity replaces any feeling of relief. Their gaunt faces and vacant eyes suggest they have already had the spirit and soul worked out of them. All of them look as though they would welcome a chunk of stale bread. The lack of a yellow star will likely make little difference in the Hell we're headed for.

Chapter 13

The canvas flap is pulled back. It's pitch-black outside, but spotlights blind us from all directions as we leap from the truck. With my right hand, I shield my face from the stabbing light until my eyes adjust. Nina stands next to me, her shivers ripple through my clothes. I stand silently, shocked by what I see and afraid to even breathe.

A tall fence surrounds a large dirt yard sprinkled with a dusting of snow. Fences are topped with dozens of wooden spools wound with barbed wire that sticks out like needles poking from a pincushion. Women's cries, children's screams, and the shouting of guards nearly drown out the beautiful, peaceful sounds of violins being played by three men standing on a rickety platform.

A whistle pierces the raw night air, and a train rumbles to a stop just outside the yard. It's not a train where passengers ride in seats in neatly arranged rows, one behind the other, but a train of boxcars, the kind used to move cattle or sheep.

Two men unlock a wire gate and approach the train. They struggle to lift long, wooden crossbars from their thick metal brackets and slide the doors open. The human cargo is packed so tightly, only the variation in height distinguishes them as individual people. They begin pushing their way out. Those who have the strength jump down. Others fall or are shoved out. Suitcases tumble, with most of their contents spilling on the ground. Their owners scramble to pick up clothes, menorahs, and other belongings before being struck by guards. They clutch their injuries and hurry away from their treasures.

Boys, and men with long beards, shuffle in one direction, following the soldiers' orders without protest. Women in shawls, some carrying babies or holding the hand of a child still in bedclothes, are pushed into a different line.

The small city of people cowers together in the cold, as close to each other as they might have stood inside the boxcar. The stench of human waste mixes with the smoke-filled air. I retch, but quickly swallow to keep myself from vomiting.

"*Mach schnell! Mach schnell!*" the guard yells.

We move forward, but the command is probably just meant to confuse us. No one knows what they want us to hurry for or to.

People who apparently do not move quickly enough are prodded with long sticks by men in striped nightshirts and flimsy trousers. Barking dogs on strained leashes, their pointed ears standing at attention, growl and bare their teeth. I blow into the sleeve of my jacket to warm my hands. Not one of us wears a coat heavy enough for this bitter cold.

Those of us from the truck are herded into an already long line winding into what might once have been a meeting hall of sorts. Exhausted, I lean into Nina and she leans into me. Somehow both of us stay on our feet. At the front of the line, we are stopped short by the end of a pencil-thin baton held by the outstretched arm of a Nazi officer. It is as if we have a sickness and must be kept at a safe distance. After a quick glance around, the officer uses his stick as a traffic signal. He directs us to the entrance on the right. I watch old people and the very young move to the left. Women, mostly old, but younger ones with a baby or child, also shuffle in the same direction. For an unknown reason, I am grateful to enter the door on the right even as I flush with guilt and horror at the thought of what the others might endure.

Behind me, an old woman cries out, "Good-bye, my sweet daughter. Remember me forever. I will see you in the next world." There is only wailing in reply.

Fearful of a strike to my head, I don't turn to look back.

Miraculously, those of us from Colmar have stayed together through the crush of bodies. Once inside the building, the men are marched through a doorway and out of our sight. Just like at the factory less than a day before, we are lined against a brick wall. Other women from the truck join us and are pressed to another wall—but not all of them. The two who spoke with Polish accents are absent, along with the woman who held the little girl between her legs.

My self-pity drains from me like water through a sieve as I watch the grotesque picture develop in front of me. In five rows of five, women and teenaged girls stand rigid as men in striped clothing chop at their hair with squeaky shears until there are only clumps sticking up on their heads in uneven patches. A guard scurries around with a burlap sack to carefully scoop the piles of hair. A girl cries for her dark curls lying on the cement floor.

We bear witness as the other women are ordered to undress and drop their clothes around their ankles. Those who hesitate are struck with clubs until they do as they are told.

"You are too good to be seen by men?" the Nazi commander says as he scans a woman from her toes to her chin. He runs his gloved hand up her belly like a knife. "You are nothing but a Jew pig." He spits the words out in a vile heap.

For a split second the room falls silent. As if waiting for the hateful words to soak through, the workers pause before they resume their chore of gathering and carting away clothes and personal belongings. When the women are completely naked, they are shaved with long-handled razors. Not only their heads are bald, but all their hair is cut—under their arms and their private areas. Some cry, some stand like statues staring straight ahead as if they could see through the thick walls. Others laugh hysterically until their laughter ends in sobs.

The skinny women are given clothes that would fit women twice their size while the larger ones are issued skimpy rags barely covering them. A few must wear coats and nothing else. None are given undergarments. We are witnessing the humiliation of these women for a reason. I am sure of little else.

Will this happen to me? To Nina? My knees bang against each other. If I have to undress, I doubt I'll be able to hide the fact I'm pregnant. If they find out, will they send me to the other side? I am too frightened and exhausted to reason. All I can do is stay close to the women from Colmar, stay with Nina. We must be a family. We need to belong to each other in order to protect ourselves.

A thin officer with lonely strands of hair slicked down across his scalp pulls three of us from our shabby formation. I stumble from his yanking force, but I will myself to stand straight. He brandishes a long silver dagger from a scabbard attached to his belt and brings it to my face. I stare at his dusty boots and smell the coffee he drank. He grabs my braid, saws it off and tosses it onto the pile of curls, twists, coils and waves. He proceeds to the other two girls and does the same, then turns on his heels and walks away. I fall back in line, my shoulders tight against the wall. I steal a glance at Nina and see tears in her eyes. I put my hand behind Francine who stands next to me and hold her hand. Her tight grip tells me she is thankful for something to cling to. With my other hand behind me, I clutch the hand of Lisette on the other side. A quiet rustling against the wall signifies a chain reaction that begins the silent pledge to support one another. The gentle touch from another human being gives me strength, at least for now.

"Put this on," another guard orders, shoving a long gray dress to a naked girl who appears to be about the same age as Rosa.

She looks more embarrassed than scared. The guard speaks with the hard edge of a man, but the voice is that of a woman. With their bald heads and gaunt faces, I have mistaken women for men. Nothing is as it appears.

The guard turns our way, her stare pins me to the wall. But she isn't really seeing me. I'm a specimen, a butterfly stuck to a board still fluttering uselessly. Disgust rolls across her face. I fear we may be in for a fate far worse than the degradation we have just seen.

The guard scribbles on a paper clamped to a board. Metal tags fastened to thin straps dangle from her arm. She fumbles to untangle them and examines one of the metal pieces. After making a check mark on the sheet of paper, she looks up and thrusts a tag at Rosa, the first one of us in line. She repeats this ritual until each of us has our new identity. I look at mine, 81314, and commit it to memory. To them, I may be nothing more than a number stamped on a flat piece of scrap tin, but it is not who I am.

After all the tags are handed out, the guard gestures to a tall, gangly woman who hurries over. Together they look at the paper. No words are exchanged.

The guard, who I decide is probably Polish because of her halting accent, moves to the front of our line and jerks her head, a signal for us to leave. We file outside, staying so close to one another we are unable to take normal sized steps. The long, wooden structures we pass look like dormitories, but there are no windows. Many of the outside boards fit together so poorly that large gaps are visible—gaps big enough to put my fingers through. A sign posted above the door of each gray building reads, "One louse, your death."

Nina looks at the sign and then glances at me, her eyes pleading for reassurance. I can give her none.

On the other side of this well-worn footpath, a building probably three times the size of our coal shed at home sits a fair distance away from the other weathered buildings. It has one greasy window and no sign above the door. A small shack that reeks of excrement sits by itself not far away; another worn path leads to its latched door.

The Polish woman climbs the two steps to the building's narrow opening. "You sleep here. Keep it clean," she commands. Her words are sharp and abrupt as if she might be punished for wasting extra syllables on us.

We file past her and find the room almost warm. Heat seems to be coming from huge, round pipes running along the ceiling. Beds with thin mattresses line the outside walls. The only thing unusual about the room is the covered bodies lying on four beds pushed against the wall. Hair poking out from skimpy blankets gives no clue whether they are men or women. They do not acknowledge we have disrupted their sleep. I wonder if they are all alive.

The Polish guard slams the door behind her. We are sealed in. Rosa collapses on the closest bed. One of the bodies rolls away from the wall and a pair of eyes open. I make out a woman's face. A look of disdain quickly disappears, and sleep returns her to a place where we cannot bother her.

Rosa sits with her knees pulled to her chin, rocking back and forth. Her eyes are tightly closed as if shutting out the world. Tears roll down her face.

Francine, the oldest of us, places her hands on Rosa's shoulders. She jerks when touched. Francine tries to stop her from rocking and says, "Rosa, look at me." She stops for a moment and then begins to cry again. "Listen to me," Francine cajoles. "Crying takes energy. It's the one thing we cannot afford to waste. We have to use our heads now. It will be what saves us."

I glance at each woman around the room. "Francine is right. We must save our strength and look out for each other. They expect us to be weak, but we must prove them wrong."

"But what do they want with us?" Rosa pleads between sniffles.

"Maybe they want us to work like we did at the linen factory," Nina answers, her sweet voice masking her fear.

"Then what do they want with the other women? And why did they treat them that way?" Rosa's voice trails off and she resumes rocking.

Francine looks down at her hands. "I don't know. Right now we need to get some rest. Morning will come soon enough."

As much as I hope Nina is right, the thought of what the future might hold makes my stomach ache. I lie down, my head spinning. The thin mattress is filled with straw packed so tightly it feels like stone. My body assumes the indentations left by others who have lain in this same place. I want to cry like Rosa.

I think of Maman and find comfort in recalling times when we simply sat at the kitchen table—times when it wasn't necessary to say anything. I lay my arm low across my middle trying to cradle and protect the child growing inside me. I feel a flutter of movement. My eyes close easily and I pray my child will not know this war, or any other.

Feeling as though I've slept only a few minutes instead of hours, I wake to a shrill sound that vibrates in my head and makes my teeth hurt. When I sit up, I feel queasy. I swallow hard to keep what's inside my throat from coming up. If I could have a piece of bread, I might feel better, but the thought of food makes my stomach turn. Living in this crowded room, I wonder how long I'll be able to keep my baby a secret—a secret I must keep. People who are afraid do and say strange things. I am terrified of being sent to the other side.

Those of us from the linen factory seem dazed, but the other four in the room move quickly. I am relieved they are all female. We follow their lead and get ourselves ready.

A short, dark-haired woman is the first to speak. "That was the signal for roll call. We all report to the yard. No exceptions."

From her stinging tone, I imagine she has given these instructions before. I wonder how many times. How many have come before us and where are they now?

"There's a pot in the corner. The last one has to dump it outside. Make sure you cover the pile with plenty of dirt. And hide it under the building so the guards won't find it," she adds.

With my insides rolling like batter being stirred in a bowl, I hurry to the corner before I am the one who has to empty a full chamber pot.

A tall woman with narrow-set eyes introduces herself as Ruth. She has a sweet, sing-song lilt in her voice. Listening to her reminds me of Maman, and I am overcome with a sense of grief. I have been so lost in my own troubles, I've barely thought about whether she's safe.

I am struck once again with the morning's reality as Ruth rattles off more instructions for the day. "We haven't much time before roll call. You must get in line by the number on your tag," she says, rubbing the metal between her fingers. "And make sure you never take it off."

"Thank you. I'm Catherine." I point to the rest of us from Colmar. "We don't even know what we're doing here."

"There isn't time to talk now. You'll be given assignments. For now, we have to go out for *appell* and be counted. If one of us is not there, the *kapos* will come back to find what's wrong and then we'll all be punished," Ruth warns. "We'll talk tonight."

Light begins to fill the sky. As we walk toward the center of camp, we arrange ourselves from the smallest to largest number, occasionally stumbling on a loose rock hidden under the dark soil. Our breath is suspended in the still air, and our footsteps the only sounds.

The yard is already filled with men and women lined in rows. "Stand next to me," Ruth whispers to Rosa, who has the lowest numbered tag. The rest of us quickly fall in place.

Many of the people in the rows are so thin I don't see how they are able to stand, let alone do anything else. One prisoner has his arm around the waist of an old man, trying to hold him up. When the guard sees this, he signals to a soldier to whack both of them with a rifle until their bond breaks. They fall to the ground, limp and lifeless.

Without thinking about the consequences, I gasp but quickly cover my mouth to muffle the sound. The guard concentrates on his victims and doesn't notice. I press my arms to my sides to keep my hands from shaking.

"The old man was already dead," another prisoner says, pleading for a small amount of mercy.

The guard stares at his papers. "Roll call is roll call. Get them out of here."

Two men in striped nightclothes quickly appear from the side. One maneuvers a cart while the other hoists the bodies and stacks them like logs onto the platform. Skeletal legs and arms dangle from the sides and bounce with each rough spot. I am stunned and no longer feel the biting cold. No one makes a sound. I stand as straight as I can manage.

Occasionally, the German officer makes note of a number on a prisoner's arm before placing a check on his paper. But most of the faces he seems to have memorized as he quickly matches them to the numbers on his chart. That is, until he comes to us, his eight new arrivals. He stops at Rosa. *Oh please, Rosa, don't cry.* He reaches for her tag. She doesn't move. He makes a mark on the paper and goes down the line. He stops at me. He's clean-shaven and smells of a flowery soap. I keep my head straight and my eyes downcast. He wears jodhpurs that flare out from the waist but fit tightly from his knees to the top of his knee-high boots, which have mud caked around the soles.

I watch from the corner of my eye as he continues his task, stopping in front of Nina. He lingers, first checking her tag, then writing something. He looks at her tag again, caressing it gently between his fingers. He swaggers on, proceeding until he reaches the end and is satisfied with the count. He then signals to a guard in a hut high above the yard, and the siren blasts. I'm sure in the days ahead even our bowel movements will be regulated by that bell.

People leave in all directions, but the eight of us follow Ruth. It's a relief to get out of the cold even though this so-called building with canvas sides provides little warmth. No one needs to tell us what to do. A single loaf of bread sits on the bare wooden surface of a long table, and a black pot rests on a stove in the corner with stacks of metal cups placed to the side. Hot coffee would go a long way in taking off the chill, but I'm disappointed when I tilt the pot to fill my cup and find only water streaming from the spout. A system for dividing the loaf of bread has already been established by the four women. We will each take turns divvying up the portions. Obviously, if you give yourself extra when it's your turn, you'll be shorted the next time around. For the first time since arriving here, I feel a sense of fairness.

We gobble our bread and quickly wash it down. The other four women seem to savor each crumb and sip their hot water as if enjoying refreshments at a sidewalk café in Paris. The rest of us are left to watch with envy. As soon as everyone finishes, we place our cups by the stove. There is no basin to wash. The short, dark-haired woman with the earlier, razor-sharp instructions sweeps tiny crumbs from the table into her hand, licking the meager leftovers from her palm. I make note of her survival skills.

"You are Elise?" I say, having heard Ruth call her by name earlier.

Her eyes open wide. She quickly puts a finger to her mouth. The message is clear. No socializing.

The siren blares again and the four, led by Ruth, leave the tent. On her way out, Ruth stops, looks around, and then turns to the eight of us huddled together and says in a low voice, "Come. Your work will be assigned. Whatever you do, never complain. If you do, we won't see you at the end of the day."

We walk single file behind Ruth and the other women. She points to a doorway and continues on ahead. We obey her silent directive and cautiously enter the building. A tall woman stands at the front of an open room and glares at each of us as we mechanically take seats in chairs assembled in rows so precise they must have been spaced by measures or a ruler.

"If you know German, raise your hand." The Polish woman's words hang in the air like the gray smoke drifting from the tall chimneys. She licks her lips as if to taste our fear. Understanding her words, I instinctively look up.

No one moves. I'm quite certain there are others who understand her. I search their faces, waiting for someone, anyone, to volunteer. In an attempt to go unnoticed, I hunch over, my shoulders curling forward. When I look up again, my gaze locks with the Polish woman's stare. Before I can glance away, she points at me. A sigh of relief from everyone else separates us like oil from water. I stand and silently plead to God this won't turn out badly.

She scribbles on a piece of paper and thrusts it at me. Written in German and signed at the bottom, I pick out the words I'm certain of—brick, building, gate. It's an order to report to a brick building near the main gate. I am only able to make out the first name of her signature—Lidia.

"*Schnell*," she says, looking toward the open door. The German word sounds odd on her Polish tongue.

I know exactly what that means and quickly turn, leaving the other women for the first time since being taken from the linen factory. I vowed to stay with

Nina, but I have no choice. I must do what is necessary to keep from being punished. The morning chill increases my feeling of dread. I wonder how much trouble I'll be in when they discover how little German I know, but the thought of being in a warmer place dilutes my fear.

The only brick building, a magnificent manor house, stands by itself on the perimeter of the compound as though embarrassed by its present company. Perhaps this was the home of a wealthy farmer, or maybe it belonged to royalty. Either way, its residents have been banished or possibly worse.

Inside the double front doors, an open staircase about two arm-lengths wide greets me from the foyer like an elegant lady. Carved wooden spindles lead to a second-floor landing where a chandelier glistens; its cut edges catch the small amount of sunlight from the slender windows on each side of the door. A portrait of Adolf Hitler rises over the landing like an approaching storm. Rooms line the first floor on both sides of the entrance. All are shut with dark, paneled wood doors except the first one on my left.

Men are talking inside. I don't want them to think I've overheard their conversation, so I open the door and shut it hard, making enough noise to be noticed. No need to post a guard here. Who would have the nerve to enter unless they were told to do so?

A young Nazi officer steps out from the open room. His boots click on the polished wooden floor.

"*Ihre papiere,*" he says, holding out his hand.

Keeping my head down, I fumble for the order. I unfold the paper and give it to him, remembering one of the warnings from this morning: *some of them you should never look straight in the eye, others will leave you alone if you meet their gaze.* I hate measuring the quirks of these bullies as if their nature could be predicted. I raise my chin enough to notice his cap cocked to one side. It hangs so low, it casts a shadow over his face. He reads the written command. I stare at his dark boots which reflect the light.

"*Wer bist du?*"

"81314." Each number catches on my tongue as if it doesn't fit in my mouth. I hoard my name, relieved I won't have to share it. To replenish the spit in my mouth, I imagine taking a bite of Maman's sweet brioche.

"Warum bist du heir?"

His question makes no sense. I'm asking myself the same thing. Why am I here? No one has explained anything since I was forced onto the truck in Colmar. Isn't he supposed to know? Should I answer? Should I try to pass his test? I glance at him briefly before looking away and shrugging.

He grabs my arm and drags me out the door as if I'm an animal that accidentally wandered in from a pen. I take two steps for each one of his long strides. When we get out in the open, he lets go and then shoves me toward a building across the yard. Blood rushes back to my arm. As I reach the tall building, he pushes me aside and stretches to open the door. I'm hindering his path and must catch the door before it slams against me. He rushes the entrance as I warily step inside. The stale air and my fear make me want to heave the hot water I drank a little while ago. I swallow hard.

We enter a cavernous warehouse filled with large bags stacked on shelves that climb to the ceiling. Suitcases of all types and sizes fill every possible gap.

My future, written on a piece of paper, is presented to a squatty man wearing a long, brown apron. Having delivered his recruit, the officer turns in place without lifting his foot and marches out. I feel the vibration from his boots striking the floor even after the door closes behind him.

I tower over the old man and stare at his balding head. Short, gray hair shoots from his scalp like sparsely planted crops peeking out of spring soil. His leather apron almost touches the floor. He reminds me of M'sieur Dubois, Renier's supervisor from the warehouse at the linen factory. The memory of Renier makes my legs feel as though they will buckle under me, depositing me on this dusty, wooden floor. I press back tears and bite my bottom lip. I say a prayer to steady myself.

"Ich bin Cath…," I say, but he stops me with the flat of his hand in front of my mouth.

"I know you speak German, otherwise they wouldn't have brought you here. I don't want to know who you are. It's no good to know too much," he says in nearly perfect French.

"How did you know I'm French?"

"It's not hard to tell these things when you see so many come through those gates. That you are French is all I want to know. Come. We have much work."

I follow him to an area where unopened cases and bags are stacked in corners. He pulls a bag from the closest pile and slings it onto a workbench made of wide wooden planks. Sturdy blue and orange cloth of paisley swirls covers both sides of the bag. Dark leather strips form a frame around its edges and stained corners. The hinges are a dirty brown color that might once have been shiny and golden. Near the broken handle, emblems telling of the owner's travels have been scratched beyond recognition. It doesn't matter now; this is its final destination. The little old man flips the locks, dumps the whole lot on the table in front of me and removes a record book from the shelf. It looks exactly like all the other books. The only thing distinguishing them are the dates etched onto their black spines: 1940, 1941, 1942, 1943 and 1944. He opens one marked 1944 and finds the last entry in the nearly-filled ledger. Categories of items, such as clothes and photographs, are written across the top, sitting over columns filled with tally marks—an inventory of life.

Pointing to an empty line on the page, he says, "Start here."

I am to sort each piece and make a mark under a fitting category—shoes, photographs, hats, books, dolls, food. Slowly, the clothes and the pictures become people; the dolls become tiny babies without their mothers; and the little shoes become children, barefoot and crying.

"Don't linger, girl. Just make the marks and put the pieces in the bins. And don't look at the faces in the photographs. They will keep you awake at night."

He resumes his work nearby, but I can't shake the loneliness I feel. I want him to stay and talk.

I try to engage him in conversation. "Are we the only ones sorting things from these cases?"

"Yes. Before, there were many of us. But now there are fewer coming on the trains, so the work is not as much. You should finish everything in that corner before lining up for *appell*. The more we get done, the less they watch."

The late afternoon siren blares, summoning us to the center of camp. I take my place with the others. *I am Catherine, not 81314.* I repeat it silently like a chant as I reach for the braid that no longer spills down my back. This time it takes much longer for the Nazis to count us, although our numbers seem fewer now. Several prisoners collapse during the tedious process and are carted away.

The eternal barbed wire frames our view of this bleak reality. Why did we end up here? How will we ever get away?

Now, with *appell* mercifully over, we are ordered to return to our barracks. Ruth, being the first in line, leads us to a tent where we collect a kettle containing our evening meal. Even after witnessing death, I am ashamed that I feel nothing besides hunger. But I am lucky and probably not as hungry as the others. The old man took a risk and gave me a piece of dried cake from one of the suitcases. I told him I wanted to hide it and share with the others, but he warned me I would be shot with no questions asked if they suspected I pilfered food. It wouldn't matter if it were only a crumb; the penalty would be the same. I will try to find another way to help the other women, especially Nina. She is so fragile, and I worry she will not survive this place.

Our meal, a watery mixture with a few potato skins and tiny pieces of cabbage floating in it, tastes like dirty rainwater. You would have to fish around in the pot to find a piece of potato. We sit on the beds, sipping our thin soup and cradling the tin for added warmth.

Nina sits silently and drinks until the bowl is dry. "Where were you today?" Without allowing me to answer, she continues, "I moved rocks, Catherine. I moved rocks all day from one pile to another. Others climbed up and down steps with bags of stones on their backs. Lisette was lucky and did laundry over boiling vats." She begins to weep, but I can think of nothing to say or do to make her feel better, so I merely clasp her hands. With her sickening report of today's assignments, I'm even more convinced we have been brought here for nothing more than to inflict punishment—the tasks we complete will merely grease their war engine.

Waiting for total darkness of night to come, the conversation turns to food.

"Tell us your recipe for cherry strudel, Judit," Elise begs. "That one's my favorite. When you tell it, I can almost taste the tart, red fruit—exactly like I remember."

Judit, one of the women we found in the sleeping quarters when we arrived, rests her elbows on her short legs crossed in front of her. "Let's talk of other things tonight." After a short pause, she tells us her dark hair is actually gray. She explains how she stains it with coal from the stove to make herself look younger, a healthy specimen more able to work. Years ago she worked with her mother to run a house for boarders and helped with the cooking.

"Tell us of the strudel," Elise pleads again.

Judit sighs, yields to the request, and begins to describe every step, every detail, including how she helped her mother stretch a single lump of strudel dough to cover an entire table—the dough thin enough to read newspaper through.

Elise seems much softer than she did this morning when she barked out instructions. Her eyes twinkle with pleasure by the time Judit finishes.

This shred of enjoyment feels stolen—a feeling ripped from a time I can barely remember, taken like a thief in the night.

Ruth breaks the stillness of our thoughts. "You said you were from Colmar. What did you do there?" She inquires of no one in particular.

"We worked in a linen factory," Francine begins. "Late one afternoon when it was almost time to go home, the SS soldiers came. They didn't take everyone from the factory, only the eight of us."

Hearing the story again forces me to remember. Now, I too wish we would talk of something else. There are things I'd like to ask the four women, but I'm not sure I want to know their answers.

What I do know is this is the end of the first day. I have survived.

Chapter 14

I measure time, not in weeks or days, but in people's lives destroyed. Picking through their belongings, I often find subtle references to the connections between them—a face in a photo in one bag reappears in a family portrait in another. I don't dare pause too long for fear the old man will scold me. Although he seems pleased with my progress during the past two months, he occasionally urges me to hurry along, reminding me the Nazis will use any excuse to punish those they believe don't work hard enough. For that matter, they torture some for no reason at all, at least none I can see.

When I complete a section in the book or finish sorting a large case, I pause and raise my hand until he notices. Reaching a good stopping place in his work, he approaches, leans over the pages, and reviews my work.

"Ah. Your penmanship is excellent, the tallies so perfect. I may confuse you with an accountant."

I lower my head and a rush of heat comes to my face. I never before knew such praise at school or the factory. It's not that I didn't do good work. I was expected to do a good job and it was supposed to be high caliber. Perhaps he treated all his students like this when he was a visiting professor at the University in Heidelberg—before the Nazis. He's always teaching, telling me what to watch out for, who I should trust and who I should not. He can even be lighthearted.

When he wants to let me know of an approaching guard, he quietly hums *La Marseillaise*, the French national anthem. It takes all my concentration to stifle a smile. For now, I am his only student and I pay close attention.

"Back to your work. I heard talk of an inspector coming soon. Maybe this afternoon."

"An inspector? Today?" My fingers tighten into fists at the idea of anyone invading our refuge.

He gives me a wry smile, the deep wrinkles on his face accentuated by his expression. "It's usually a high-ranking officer. Once there was a banker from Erfurt," he explains. "Whoever it is will probably only check to see that nothing has been moved or is missing. They never spend much time—never actually count anything. There's nothing to really worry about," he assures me. "But the German commanders take notice, of course, and there's no slouching or leaning against the walls by the guards when an inspector is here."

"What are they looking for?"

He points to a large iron door with a heavy lock. "The valuables, my dear. Pieces taken out of the cases during the first sorting—jewelry, silver candlesticks—anything worth money. Many people brought cash and coins. It's all in that room."

He turns to his work, indicating it's time for me to return to mine. As I catalog the contents of the satchel in front of me, my thoughts drift to the room with the iron door.

I had seen inside only once. It was a few days ago, when I had sorted through a sturdy brown suitcase with a belt around the outside to keep the large number of belongings from falling out. It contained mostly work trousers and shirts, along with a dark blue jacket rolled like a sausage. When I unrolled the jacket, one side felt heavier than the other. A gold watch was hooked on a pin inside the pocket. I carefully removed it. The watch case was etched with feathery scrolls, tiny leaves of ivy winding around the edge, and a smooth, green stone in the center. I pushed the button at the top and it sprang open. The hands on the face, holding a place in time, were as delicate as fine thread. The inscription on the inside of the cover read, "From this day, August 7, 1913. Love, Miriam." Closing the watch made a snapping sound that caught the professor's attention. He shuffled over to me and held out his hand. I placed it in his palm.

"This belongs in the vault. It must have been overlooked," he said, removing a leather strap from around his neck. From it dangled the piece of metal stamped with his camp number along with a large key. As he opened the vault, I leaned to the side of my chair and craned my neck to get a glimpse. I saw rows and rows of large metal boxes lining the shelves. The one that stood out was labeled, "Gold Teeth." I crossed my arms across my chest to ward off the chill I suddenly felt. He closed the door and twisted the key. I settled back in my chair while he retrieved a brown ledger unlike the other books on the shelf, and wrote in it.

With a start, I realize I have finished sorting everything in the buckled case. Columns of neat numbers in my own handwriting prove I have marked each item with care despite my wandering thoughts. Guilt washes over me when I become aware I have held the most personal possessions of the unnamed woman who owned it, but have shown no respect or regard for her memory. I had vowed to testify to the brutality surrounding me, but this day, I fail to even do that.

I consider re-sorting the items in the case as atonement for my callousness, but the old man notices I am finished and wakes me from my fogginess when he speaks.

"There is something unusual about the way things are now. It's very different than several months ago." He has talked more today than ever before. Anticipating the inspector seems to have loosened his tongue. I am grateful for the break from routine. I tilt my head toward him, keeping my hands still and concentrating on his every word.

"The oven chimneys no longer spew their mortal ash." He pauses, as though considering his own words, and then continues, "The soldiers are less sure of themselves now. Maybe we are nearing the end of the fight…or maybe they too are tired of death."

I try to navigate the weight of his words and gain my bearing as if guided by some inner compass. I feel woozy. I sit up straight and smooth my hand over these baggy clothes outlining my growing belly as a gesture to reassure this baby the end might be close. But the knowledge of so many people dying the way he suggests, something we all suspect, is difficult to comprehend. I feel sick. Everything Renier told me about these camps is true. Or worse. I hope the professor is right. Liberation is near for those who have made it this far. God rest the souls of those who didn't.

All of a sudden, I hear voices outside. Louder and louder, the sound echoing off the building. Could this be the inspector?

"Quick! Get back to work!" he orders with an urgency I have never heard before.

Three men, a German officer, the young guard who brought me to this building weeks ago, and a civilian in a long brown coat, barge though the door. The civilian's heavy wool overcoat looks as if its weight would make it difficult to wear, especially for such a small man. Upon entering the warehouse, he removes his hat, exposing his shiny, bald head. Dark, round spectacles rest on his beak-like nose. The only things he shares with the two Nazi officers are piercing eyes and the ugly mark on his sleeve—a black spider, like the ones Maman had to sew on red armbands. His right arm is cocked at his hip; his left hand grips a brown leather attaché case and a silver walking stick.

The professor hurries to greet our visitors, his right palm outstretched in the expected salute. He knows the civilian and addresses him by name. I stand behind my chair, holding on to it to steady myself, unsure I should say or do anything.

"*Hinsetzen, Witrowski!*" the officer thunders, spitting the professor's last name as if it were acid in his mouth.

Keeping his sight on the Germans, the professor backs up to his chair, rests his hand on its tall back for support, and sits as directed. "What can I do for you, Herr Vieck?"

"I have studied the balances from all the camps that have been submitted, and there is a discrepancy," he says with a deliberate and menacing air. "What is being reported here has far less value than any of the others, despite the fact you have almost twice the number of laborers."

"I report everything. Nothing has been unusual," Herr Witrowski stammers.

"I don't believe you."

The two officers surround him and force the old man down, pressing his shoulders against the back of the chair.

"I swear on my mother's grave that every gold ring, every piece of jewelry, every gold filling, every gem is in the vault. Nothing is missing. I swear to you."

"You are the same as the other academics. So high and mighty. The Fuhrer warned about the likes of your kind years ago. I don't know why I trusted you." With a glance to the nearest officer, a silent order is issued, and the professor is struck in his groin with a rifle.

I slap my hand to my mouth to smother my impulsive gasp. The blow is so fierce, the other guard lets go of the professor's shoulders. The old man doubles over and topples from the chair. He curls at the feet of his persecutors. This patient man, this kind man, has been reduced to a shriveled lump no larger than a child.

Tears of frustration and anger leak from my eyes. I carefully move my hand from my mouth to wipe away the wetness. My small movement captures the attention of Herr Vieck. I shudder as he fixes his eyes over my right shoulder. He doesn't acknowledge seeing me but is clearly addressing me.

"*Sprecht!*" he shouts.

I have no idea what he wants me to say. His hand moves, but before he can gesture to the swine he commands, I interrupt in desperation. "*Wir haben…*" I wet my lips and start over, praying my German is clear. "We have made much progress." The mountains of bags still filling the warehouse make this statement laughable, but I have caught the greedy man's attention. His hand drops to his side. He sets his case on the floor, and his eyes briefly flicker to my face.

"Go on."

I have not planned anything, but the words seem to stream from my mouth on their own accord. "The workers from Verdacht were very wealthy."

My gaze falls on the brown ledger I had noticed a few days ago. I sense, even as the name leaves my lips, that what I say is true. The professor lies on the floor with bloody mucus dripping from his nose and mouth, probably listening for anything that might save him. Trying to trigger the professor's memory, I continue. "Of course, as you are already aware, Verdacht is well known for its jewel dealers. The precious gems, too valuable to be kept where someone might happen upon them, are recorded without appraisal." I stop, and the professor slowly lifts himself on one elbow, still nearly bent in half.

"She's right. Gemstones are cataloged, but no value written. No way to determine their worth." The words struggle out from the professor's mouth. Pearls of perspiration bead on his forehead.

"You, young girl, are a smart one. And you, old man, had better have each and every piece accounted for and ready for shipment by tomorrow morning," Herr Vieck demands. He storms out the same way he came, with the Nazi officers following on his coattail like obedient house dogs.

With the door securely closed, I rush to the professor and use my thin shirt to wipe the blood from his face.

"When you save a life, your bonds are for life. You are truly my child, Catherine."

I manage a rueful smile and press his hand against my cheek.

BOOK IV:
ERVIN ACKERMAN

DEAD OF WINTER

Chapter 15

We're slam-bang in the middle of an assault with our men badly shot up, trying to hold a line against the Nazis with a limited number of infantry soldiers. Fortunately, each day brings a trickle of raw recruits to replenish the ranks of our regiment. Today, we get Hanes, Hauck, Hays, and Hoback. Companies are usually alphabetical by last name, so it's the H's lucky day. Hoback looks about nineteen, not long out of high school. I'd say he's a city boy with only seventeen weeks of basic training to his name—which isn't nearly enough. I can usually tell whether a new guy will crack under fire just by looking at him, and this baby-face sure looks like he will. As my mama used to say, "He's still wet behind the ears." His uniform is almost spotless. I'd guess he's been eating hot C-rations and sleeping under cover until now. When the occasional German mortar shell falls, Hoback jumps like a drop of water on a hot griddle.

Colonel Williams shouts orders to Private Hoback, pointing to an open area in the line. "Start digging."

"Yes, sir," Hoback replies. He makes his way to a clearing and leans his M1 against a tree. For almost twenty minutes, he chops and hacks at the frozen Belgian dirt. Twice he slips and falls into his unfinished hole. Looking around as though hoping no one saw his clumsiness, he lays down his t-handle. With his shallow foxhole ready, he grabs his rifle, gets in, and takes a position.

The high-pitched whistle of an incoming mortar screams out of the sky. "Hit the dirt, Hoback!" I yell, making myself as small as possible inside my hole.

The earth erupts with a thunderous roar, the explosion shaking and scattering fragments through the air. A brief silence follows along with the smell of burned cordite and singed flesh. Smoke billows out of Hoback's foxhole. When the fog clears, tattered pieces of his newly issued uniform hang from nearby tree limbs. Bloody parts of his body stain the snow.

I rest my head on my forearm. Jesus H Christ. That's it. One minute a guy's alive, the next he's in pieces. Nobody had a chance to find out anything about him, not even where he called home. When the dust settles, some men from his unit gather what body parts they can find, lay them in the hole, and cover them up. After some simple words he'd probably heard from a sermon somewhere along the line, Colonel Williams pockets one of Hoback's tags. Another kid who came in with him kneels on the ground and cries, his forehead planted in the snow. Everyone else looks the other way, pretending they don't see him breaking down. One young recruit sits there with a gooney-bird stare, looking at something no one else can see.

I try not to think about it. I need to keep going, pay attention to what I have to do. I don't want to be the next one to bite the dust. Bullets have a way of picking out those who aren't paying attention. It's called short-timers' jinx.

The battles heat up as we storm across the European countryside. Supplies can't keep pace and good combat boots are more in demand than a hefty steer on sale day. Even so, the loose heel on my boot is as annoying as a burr under a horse's saddle. It's ridiculous that something so piddling could cause such irritation when we're under the constant threat of sniper attacks, but it still rankles me. The colonel tells me the Army's trying to find something to take the place of leather. Probably aren't enough cows in all of Nebraska to stay ahead of the need for boot leather over here. Most of us have watched a man's leg rot from trench foot, and we know full well the value of the cracked cowhide protecting our feet. So more than one American soldier tromps around in German footgear lifted from the dead. But I can't bring myself to rob anyone, even the corpse of my worst enemy, because of my ma's disapproving look flashing through my head. Instead of stealing, I make do, like killing a pig for the fat to grease my boots. Right now I'm hanging my second pair of socks under my shirt and around my neck to dry. Taking care of my feet will keep me alive, especially in this nasty cold with deep snow that sucks me down to my knees.

When the Nazis counterattack, we load the wounded onto trucks and cover their numb feet in blankets. As long as they can fire their rifles, they will prop each other up and defend their posts. Cooks and bakers also fight under orders to hold their positions at all costs.

A few weeks ago, almost everybody thought the war was about over with the Nazis withdrawing from the Ardennes, but they came back at us full force. With the kind of fighting we had today, we'll be lucky to get any shut-eye tonight. We don't dare use our bed rolls, or "Purple Heart" bags as we call them. If the Germans sneak in during the night, they could bayonet us before we had a chance to struggle free and reach for our weapons. So I lie in the frozen earth and shiver until I'm spent. It's December 24, 1944. I'm filthy, hungry, exhausted, and frozen. I not only wonder if I'll survive until next Christmas, I wonder if I'll even see this one. Back home, choirs are probably singing of Peace on Earth and Good Will to Men. I hope they remember us. Eventually I drift off. But it's a fitful sleep filled with thoughts of those men who will sleep forever.

At daylight, two German medics wave a white flag and signal they want to remove their wounded and dead. We let them do it. There are a few moments of peace that seem unnatural, but welcome.

Then bullets pummel the dirt right outside our trenches, breaking the morning calm.

"Goddamn it! Where did that come from, Erv?"

"I don't see anything, Colonel. Must be a sniper in the trees." This guy has every possible advantage. He's above us with plenty of cover. His weapon fires so fast it sounds like cloth tearing. Moving is suicidal.

The colonel quickly lays out a plan. "Erv, you fire a clip into the trees and then move to the left. Then Hanes, you do the same and back up Ackerman. I'll fire a third round. Hopefully, we'll hit whatever's out there."

If the sniper figures we have a colonel in our midst, he'll shoot him first. An officer has a short life span. I make it my job to cover his rear.

We get lucky. The sniper falls to the ground with a thud. The next minute we hear someone running through the trees.

"*Hände hoch!*" I yell. "And throw down your weapons."

The Nazi stops, drops a knife, and puts his hands above his head exactly as I ordered. He's young and scared as all get out. He doesn't have a rifle, but I search him all the same. Once I know he's unarmed, I question our prisoner to find out what he knows. Turns out, not very much. He's one of the inexperienced *Volkssturm* troopers, not a combat-hardened veteran. We're lucky for a second time today. Only a greenhorn would get disoriented and run right toward the enemy. He was lucky too. Lucky one of us didn't take him out with a lead vitamin. Snipers are despised by everyone. They're cheating fuckers, and we'd rather shoot 'em than look at 'em.

A back and forth exchange of artillery goes on most of the day. Dusk, and the chill that comes with it, swallows me whole. I sit in my foxhole, this icy pit of misery, and think about Betty. A warm tingle rushes through me as I imagine her arms hugging my neck, but a minute later, I'm back in the war, in this miserable cold, freezing my ass off. As the blackness of the night meets the blackness of my thoughts, I thank God I've survived this far. If I do get hit, I hope it'll be enough to send me home. If it's my fate to die on foreign soil, I pray the end will be quick and clean, not slow and agonizing like so many others. As I look at the night sky right before I doze off, I wonder if God is listening to American or German prayers tonight—or if God is listening at all.

Chapter 16

"Prepare for movement at 0500," Colonel Williams orders, reading from a small piece of smudged paper. The responsibility of overseeing this unit of the Third Army has tilled lines in his forehead that are almost deep enough to plant seeds in. "We're heading for an assembly area near Luxembourg. Hide anything that might identify your vehicles and remove the TO insignias from your sleeves."

Shit. This Tough Ombre patch has seen me through a lot—kind of like an old Army buddy. I sewed it on pretty damned good. Hope it's not bad luck to rip it off.

A message from the field radio interrupts my daydreaming. "Headquarters? Intelligence and Recon of the 357th here. Lieutenant Thorngren and me…we saw smoke coming from the side of the hill," the soldier says. "It's spewing out like a volcano."

Colonel Williams speaks into the handset and grins. "What's your name, soldier?"

"Joseph Walker. Private Joseph Walker, sir," he sputters.

"Private Walker, where are you?"

"West side of Mt. Siersburg, sir."

"Well, Walker, I doubt you saw a volcano. You and your lieutenant find out what's going on. The Nazis wouldn't be fool enough to burn anything. A lot of smoke's a sure-fire way to have uninvited visitors."

"Roger that." Walker assures the colonel that he and Lieutenant Thorngren will get to the bottom of it and radio a report.

Within an hour, the radio squawks again. Walker's on the line. "Colonel? The smoke, it's coming from a hollowed-out entrance or something. We heard voices inside, but it ain't soldiers. There's kids squealing and carrying on. We couldn't believe our ears," Walker says, describing the scene with the excitement of a six-year-old.

"Is Lieutenant Thorngren with you?"

"He's glassing the area. I'll get him if you want, sir."

"You do that, son," Colonel Williams says.

A minute later the lieutenant responds. "Yes, sir. Lieutenant Thorngren here."

"Are you sure you heard children?" the colonel asks.

"Definitely. Yes, sir."

"Then take Walker and some other men and see if you can find an entrance where people are getting in. Let me know what you find." The colonel switches off the radio. "Damn. That's all we need is civilians to deal with right now. If they're German, you'll have to talk to them, Erv. Find out why they're out here in this God-awful winter and so close to enemy fire."

"Not a problem, sir."

A while later, the radio whines again. "Colonel Williams. Captain McMurray, I&R with the 357th. Lieutenant Thorngren and a couple of my men found over a thousand men, women, and children holed up in a cave. We'll need headquarters to help us out."

"A thousand?" the colonel says, disbelief in his tone.

"Probably more like fifteen hundred, sir."

"Okay. Give me your coordinates and the 90th will come in."

"If you've got anyone who can speak German, we could really use them. There's not a one we've found who understands any English. Oh, and one more thing. If you can find some DDT that would be good. I think we may have a lice situation."

"Will do. Over and out, Captain." The colonel shakes his head. "Lice."

My skin is already crawling.

We set out and find the tunnel to the cave. It's a half-mile long, dark and damp. Men, women and children gather in small clusters inside the huge cavern. A large fire smolders in the center, filling the air with a smoky haze that sticks to the rock ceiling. Beds, chairs, and tables form temporary rooms along the walls, while broken dishes and trash are piled in sooty corners. Scrawny animals—cattle, goats, and chickens—nose the hard floor searching for grass they will never find. An old woman sits propped up in a bed staring at the wall. A young mother nurses a baby while older kids run wild, occasionally stopping to cling to the leg of a soldier. I thought I'd smelled every kind of crap on the farm, but the smell of this cave makes cleaning out the chicken coop seem like tending a rose bed.

A priest weaves his way through the crowd and approaches me and the colonel. "*Sie sind Amerikanische Armee?*" the priest says, double-checking his hunch.

"*Ja, Vater,*" I assure him.

"Ask him how long they've been in this place," the colonel instructs me.

"Forty days or so," the priest says, and continues in his thick German accent. "The Gestapo ordered these people to move farther into the interior of Germany. They didn't want to leave their villages so they came here to hide, defying the orders. When the *Volkssturm* found them, they threatened to block the entrance and bury them all alive." The priest crosses himself as if the symbolism will protect his flock. "The German soldiers charged me with getting them out immediately, but I begged them for more time. I explained it would be impossible to move everyone so quickly. Many are sick and almost all are covered with lice."

"You're still here. Why did the Germans leave you alone?" I ask, finding it strange they would let anyone live who defied their orders.

"I persuaded them to let me talk to von Richter. He intervened, and they were permitted to stay."

"Who's von Richter?"

"Franz von Richter. Very high up with German connections," the priest says, pointing upward. "These caves are part of his family's estate, where they used to grow prized mushrooms. There are at least two thousand more refugees in other caves nearby."

I translate to the colonel as the men from I&R huddle around, hanging on every word. They move in closer when I repeat the word "lice."

"We've got to get this situation under control. Find the powder and have them line up for dousing and get rations for them while you're at it," the colonel orders. "It won't be enough food, but we can spread around what extra we have until we can get additional supplies here."

I return to the truck and find the canister of DDT. I give it a couple of good pumps to get it primed and ready to go. Who knows what kind of job you'll land in the Army? Maybe even blowing lice powder up old ladies' skirts.

BOOK V:
CATHERINE REVAUX

HEADED TO THE MINE

Chapter 17

"Catherine, over there. The little bird perched on that post." Professor Witrowski points out the filmy infirmary window, hardly able to lift his hand. "I tell you this is a sign of life—a sign to live. With God's help, you will get out of here before your baby comes. I know it now."

I stroke his hand. "You must not talk of such things." I fear someone will hear him, and the lie I've lived for months will be revealed, but quickly realize anyone in this place who might overhear us is probably too weak to speak of it. Many are merely skin covering bones.

Sitting on his crude bed, I marvel at the old man for being optimistic, unsure if it's real or a case of delirium. His mind has not been right since the inspector and his yes-men came to the warehouse yesterday and accused him of stealing and then interrogated him with the ends of their guns. He's far too old and feeble to withstand such treatment. Maybe his near-death experience has given him the ability to foresee the future.

I readjust the thin paper bandage on his forearm. "Rest. I'll come back later."

"I pray that you..." He closes his eyes, weak and spent, unable to finish his thought.

I pat his shoulder. "Don't talk. I'll be back."

It feels as though I'm losing all that's important, but I must keep my wits about me and get the shipment of jewelry and gems ready for the inspector.

Nina was assigned to work in the infirmary a month ago, but the similarities of moving rocks from one pile to another and the task of taking care of prisoners with no hope are clearly evident. She does what she can to tend to her patients. "I'm going to the warehouse, Nina. If you find anything for his pain, please give it to him."

She looks at me and shrugs. She probably has no supplies to help anyone. It shows in the way she shuffles from cot to cot, searching for life in some and helping others let go. I can still see the beauty in her face, but her hair, which once glimmered in the sun, now looks brittle and thinning. Her eyes expose the toll this place has taken.

"I'll be back later on," I assure her.

She uses a pair of striped pants to cover a body. "They don't remove the dead for at least a day or so." The lost look in her eyes makes me wonder if she is talking to me or to herself.

"Why do they leave them here when they're already dead?" The words stick in my throat as the sickening realization comes over me. I glance at the bodies lying on the floor. How many are dead and not sleeping?

Nina confirms my suspicion. "The trustees who keep count for their block want the bread ration, so they say nothing."

Her statement, simple and matter-of-fact, pierces me like a hot needle. I grab her shoulder, bringing her close. Her bony arm and shoulder against me reveal another horrible reality. "I'm so sorry you have to take care of others. You need someone to take care of you."

"Go. There is nothing you can do."

Is the resignation in her voice for Herr Witrowski or for herself? It doesn't matter. Either way, she's right. But I can do something to survive. I have to believe Renier will find me when this is all over—if it's ever over. But now, survival means pacifying the inspector.

I hurry outside, drawing in the bitter cold and emptying my lungs of death until it makes my chest hurt. I pull up the collar of my coat, the scant cloth hugging my ears. I try to block out the guilt along with the chill. The snow covering the ground, a greasy gray, matches everything I see and feel.

When I reach the warehouse, I pull at the large wooden door. It doesn't budge. The door wasn't locked when I left. I must get inside. Think, Catherine, think! Maybe there's a window to pry open. I try the windows and another door. Nothing.

A guard rounds the corner of the building. "Are you looking for something, *fraulein?*"

I tug on the door again and try to conceal my fear.

"I need to get inside. I must have locked the door by accident. If you'll kindly unlock it, I'll go about my work. Herr Vieck will be here any moment. We don't want to disappoint him, do we?" I look him straight in the eyes, hoping he will fall for my boldness.

He fishes in his pocket and pulls out a ring of keys, dangling them like a piece of cheese in front of a starving mouse. His repulsive grin demonstrates the true character of a man without concern for consequences.

"Maybe you could introduce me to your good-looking friend."

For a moment I'm taken back to school days in Colmar. All the young boys wanted to sit with Nina at the socials. If this had happened at home, I would laugh at his approach. Does he think this hell is some sort of social club? The silence between us confirms his determination, and I feel as cold as a graveyard stone.

He licks the corner of his mouth. "I would treat her better than the other men she services in the officers' quarters."

I bite my lip and pretend his words mean nothing to me. My mind flashes to the dead look in Nina's eyes, and I digest the ugly truth.

"Unlock the door. If this shipment isn't ready we'll both pay for it."

"Bah." he says, apparently annoyed that I'm right. "Introductions aren't necessary. I'll have my turn." He forces the key into the lock and turns it between his fingers.

I quickly duck through the door and collapse against it on the other side. I wipe tears from my face and hurry to inventory the precious stones and jewelry from the vault before the inspector returns. The contents of the leather sacks must match the notes in the ledger. I separate the stones by color and compare them to the descriptions as best I can. Finally, the number of stones agrees with the tally at the bottom of the page, and I sigh with relief. I haven't any idea about the value, but no one else does either. As far as I can tell, everything appears to be in order, exactly as Herr Witrowski said it would be. Who knows whether the inspector and his pack of wolves will see it the same way?

"Here you are, my little Jew counter."

I hadn't heard Herr Vieck's footsteps, his voice startling me from my concentration. As he slowly approaches, I hold myself still and continue to study the ledger. His gloved fingers pinch my chin. The smell of leather polish from his boots reaches my nose. Bile rises in my throat. I say nothing.

"You look like a Jew," he snorts. "And you count like a Jew."

"I'm French."

"Much better."

He grips my chin and forces me to look at him. I focus on his hideous smile, more a baring of teeth than a show of friendliness or warmth, and notice his yellowing teeth and the small v-shaped scar between his nose and lip. I keep my expression blank, emotionless.

He releases his fingers from my face and frowns, then removes a piece of paper from his pocket, unfolds it, and lets it drop on the table. "New orders."

I stare down without touching it. I search for names, anything that might offer a clue. Nothing.

"Maybe my little Jew counter isn't as smart as she seems."

"I know you need someone who has experience with these ledgers. The old man is no good to you now."

"Humph." He picks up the paper and neatly creases it before sliding it inside his coat. "You and some others will leave tomorrow morning for a different camp. With your head for numbers, you'll track shipments arriving from Berlin. It seems some think your memory could make ledgers unnecessary. Only time will tell how valuable you are to them." He points his walking stick between my breasts. "And don't think you're fooling anyone about that bump under your flimsy blouse."

Chapter 18

"*Halten,*" the guard snaps, blocking my entrance to the infirmary with his rifle.

"I've come to see Herr Witrowski."

He swings his gun and points the barrel at my head.

My jaw tightens and I close my eyes for a few seconds to calm myself. "Please, let me inside. I promised Nina I'd come."

A faint smile drifts across his face, but a scowl quickly replaces it. "She's not here. Go. No one allowed." His clipped words are a clear signal not to press further.

I back away. It's late, with an eerie, foggy haze hiding most of the moonlight. Still, there are signs of spring. Evidence of the earth's renewal spreads beyond reach, outside the tall wire fence where a hint of green colors the ground. Sadly, I am trapped within these gates where everything reeks of death.

My steps are quick, easing the evening chill. The barrack sits at the outside edge, and I follow the dirt path hugging the fenced boundary. Most of the women should already be inside. I hope Nina will be there with the others. I pray she'll be able to leave with me tomorrow.

Each breath I let out hovers in the cool air, dissolving in front of me. I concentrate on the trail in an effort to clear my head, but the idea of the old man with no one to care for him haunts me. If it weren't for him, I doubt my baby and I would have made it this long. There won't be anyone like him at the next camp. I'm sure of that.

I recall Herr Vieck's spiteful words at the warehouse. *"Don't think you're fooling anyone about that bump under your flimsy blouse,"* he had said, as he jabbed at me with his shiny walking stick. I promise myself I'll cleanse my shirt when I get back even if all I can find is a soiled rag.

Again, my thoughts turn to Nina. I'm reminded of what she has been through; the image of the impertinent soldier's smirk and his crude language brings it into focus. I wonder if she will ever know the love of a man when so many have taken what they want from her. I feel heartless and stupid for brooding about something as petty as a poke. What they've done to Nina swallows me whole and spits me into the darkness.

Up ahead, light seeps through a slit in the boarded window of the barracks. Decaying steps leading to the door creak under the thin soles of my slippers.

All eyes are on me as I enter. I'm intensely aware of my pregnancy now. Do all the women know what I've tried to hide? Surely Nina does, although she's never let on. If it's so obvious to the inspector, whom I've seen only twice, then everyone else must suspect. I've betrayed Nina's friendship by not telling her. She should have my confidence above all else. I'll tell her tonight. A sense of relief removes some of the weight I've carried.

"Evening, Catherine," Ruth says, her greeting spoken for the women huddled in a tight circle. A candle melting to a tin plate sits in the center.

I glance at the others around the room and am relieved to see Nina. "Evening." Nina looks up, but her face seems blank and empty.

I approach the women and sit down. "I brought bread from the warehouse. It's not much." I hope the smell on my breath from the bite I already took will go unnoticed. My guilt holds me in a tight grip and feels more burdensome to endure than the hunger.

"You are taking unnecessary risks. They kill for less," Frieda admonishes, her tone quite harsh.

I wave off her concern. "There are bits and pieces stashed in places they are too lazy or don't care to search. No one pays much attention now. The Nazis are more worried about shipping their valuables. They've been stacking and loading all day. Almost everything has been stowed on the train."

Frieda peels small pieces from the bread to give to those who still have strength to eat. "You've been lucky to go unnoticed." She continues while chewing a small piece, "You have promising news? The furnaces have stopped, and you tell us the Nazis are shipping their loot. What are we to make of it?"

"I know nothing except about the shipment." I hesitate for a moment before continuing, "Some of us will leave in the morning for another camp." A gasp fills the room.

"What kind of camp? A work camp worse than this?" Rosa asks, dread overtaking her usual softness.

I shrug. "I'm not sure. A place where things are counted. Shipments will arrive from Berlin. Could it be worse than this? I don't know. It doesn't matter. We'll do what we have to."

"Who's going? Will the old man go with you?" The optimism in Rosa's tone is clear.

I half-smile at her suggestion. I'm the only one who really knows what happened to him at the warehouse. "I don't think so, but no one…"

"He's dead. Died this afternoon." The lifeless look in Nina's eyes matches the lack of expression in her voice. It is as if she's reporting the weather.

The news catches me off guard like nothing else I've experienced here. Not the dead bodies, not the suffering, not the brutality. Nothing. I collapse and drop my face in my hands. Nina comes to sit next to me. For the first time since leaving the factory, I sob like a child. I wrap my arms around her, my tears soaking her shirt. I'm thankful for the comfort, and we embrace until we're exhausted and can no longer sit upright. Sleep takes me to a place where sadness temporarily fades.

—

The quiet stirring of a few women beginning their day wakes me. Nina stands in the corner, adjusting her scarf to cover her unruly wisps of hair.

I gently approach her. "Nina."

She stands stock-still. I'm not sure she hears me.

I put my hand on her shoulder, and she turns to face me. "Nina, I'm so sorry for what has happened. I know my words can't help, but I will always cherish our friendship no matter how far apart we might be." I hug her, and she rests her head on my shoulder. "I'm going to have Renier's child," I whisper. "I should have told you before." The words spill out, knowing I'm running out of time to say everything.

"I know. We all know. We didn't want you to worry that one of us might say something." A tender smile brightens her beautiful face.

I look at her and see only the person I knew before. "I've missed your smile. I've missed everything we used to do."

She manages to nod. With her smile now gone, she stares at the floor.

"I was afraid to speak of it. The longer I said nothing, the harder it was. I hope you understand, Nina. Please forgive me."

She puts her thin arms around me and tries to hug me, but I can tell her strength is nearly drained.

The sun is not yet up. Soon the blare from the camp's horns will pull the rest of the women from their nightly escape. Daily rituals will begin, with routine making sense of chaos. When the siren goes off, everyone shuffles in different directions as if precisely choreographed to never cross paths.

Before the second signal pierces the air, I'm out of the barracks and filing into the yard. Places in the formation are systematically filled. The officer goes back and forth between the rows, stopping at new gaps—probably created from yesterday's deaths—and draws a simple line through the numbers on his list. There is no acknowledgement as the guard moves without expression to the next person. His scrawny mustache, which looks as though he drew it on his face this morning, twitches as he goes along the rows, striking out some numbers and noting others with check marks. He stops in front of two young men. Although I can't hear exactly what he says, he must be giving them instructions because they leave roll call and approach another guard holding a dog by a short leather strap.

The bright sun casts a new spring warmth on my skin, making the wait more tolerable than usual. Are the two men going to the new camp? I close my eyes and let the sun thaw my soul and pray the only prayer I permit myself. *Mon dieu,* let Nina come with me. What will happen to her if she stays? Will I ever see her again? I want to take her away from here. She is all I have. *Please, please.*

The guard stops at me, studying the numbers that are my identity.

"Over there," the guard commands, his chin and pencil pointing to the two men standing near the guard with the dog. Another guard in the lookout tower high above aims his rifle at me, following each step I take. I'll be leaving through that gate and getting onto the train. I see no need to foolishly attempt an escape. The end of this suffering is close. I can feel it.

Chapter 19

The men turn their backs while I relieve myself over the hole in the center of the dusty floor. I hold up my skirt with one hand; the other I use as a brace to keep from toppling over. The train sways from a bend in the tracks, and I temporarily lose my balance. At the commotion, a man with a gaunt face and tinge of pink at the tip of his nose twists around. I meet his stare and he turns back to the corner. I chastise myself for waiting until daylight to use the primitive toilet. Even though we were segregated at camp, men from women, we still valued privacy and fashioned a curtain from flour sacks to shield ourselves when we used the bucket at night. Just because we were treated like animals didn't mean we had to act like animals.

With as much dignity as I can summon, I finish and return to my small pile of loose straw at the end of the boxcar. I'm thankful for the meager cushion and the limited amount of separation I'm afforded by the nine men traveling with me. We've been traveling less than two days and already my legs are covered in flea bites. I want to claw at them, but I know it will only make the itching worse. I choose to ignore this misery and focus on the occasional movement in my belly—and what the men are saying. As usual, the conversation turns to food. Each man has a favorite dish and recollects it with painstaking detail. Remembering the swill the guards passed off as dinner last night only serves to make their stories more vivid. My stomach aches for something better to eat this morning.

"I was in Camp Three for about six weeks," one man says, speaking to the group. "Then the Nazis sent us up north to an armament factory. When they realized the Russians were closing in, they put us on a small fishing boat scarcely big enough to hold the crew, let alone twenty-three of us prisoners. One day we were out on deck and I spotted a cabbage floating in the water. I grabbed for it. It was soaked with engine oil from a passing freighter, but I tore it apart and we each had a piece of it."

The thin man with the pink on his nose clears his throat and begins to recite.

"'The time has come,' the Walrus said,

'To talk of many things:

Of shoes—and ships—and sealing-wax—

Of cabbages—and kings—

And why the sea is boiling hot—

And whether pigs have wings.'"

The poetic interruption transforms into a stillness that sinks us into the current reality. I close my eyes and lean back, resting against the wooden frame. The train's rocking motion moves my head from side to side. Silence settles over us like a blanket. The only sound is the incessant clicking of the rails. This tiny reprieve from the ugliness of the journey takes me to a comforting place; I am at home with Maman and the memory of her baking bread, which soothes me to my soul.

"You are with child?"

My eyes fly open.

A man with a stubble of dark brown hair crouches in front of me, his weight shifting from one knee to the other to keep his balance. Sunken eyes belie his youthful voice.

"Yes." My answer bounces through my body with a sense of freedom. I want to shout it as loudly as I can.

"When?" he asks.

"It's not supposed to be for a few more months, but it feels like it will be soon."

"I see. How long were you in a work camp?"

"Since last year, right around Christmas. I worked in a warehouse and cataloged belongings from prisoners."

He sits and locks his eyes on me. Nervousness makes me run off at the mouth. "It was comfortable enough—much better than what others had to do—and my supervisor found scraps of food for me to eat. I tried to take food to the women, but it was always dangerous. There wasn't much to share."

"You were indeed a fortunate one."

"Yes, that's true." I have said enough for now.

"One day as we waited for roll call, one of the women gave birth to a baby. None of us knew she was pregnant. Well, at least none of us men knew it. Anyway," he continues, "it came out as we stood there. She made a hole in the dirt with her foot and buried it."

I bite my bottom lip to keep it from quivering. The inhumanity that has been endured fills me with disgust, and I lower my head in a silent prayer.

"I'm sorry I told you," he says. "I shouldn't have said anything."

I look directly into his eyes. "No. The stories are all we have. Silence is the devil's brother. If we share with others, the stories will live on for someone else to tell."

"You're right. Yes, you're right. What's your name? I am Godek."

"I'm Catherine."

"You are French, no?"

"Yes, but I don't feel French or anything anymore."

"Ah, but you must always have pride for your country," he chides.

"I've seen people from my country do bad things. I've seen them silent when they should have spoken."

"We all have. But there is good, too."

"I know. It's true. Even I have stood silent. So, yes, there's good, but far too little of it to go around." He doesn't argue the point. With little interest in discussing philosophy, I change the subject. "Do you know where this train is taking us?"

"No, only that we are to unload it and maybe other trains as well," Godek offers. "You'd better rest. The work will be waiting for us."

The sound of metal grinding on metal screeches through the rails. I am propelled forward by the sudden stop. Without air passing through the cracks in the sides, stink settles into the boxcar like an unwanted guest. I pull my collar to cover my nose and mouth.

With a squealing sound, the large wooden door opens.

"Out! Out!" the Nazi guard orders. "To the front of the train."

The men let me out first. There's a fair distance from the opening to the ground. I hesitate to jump.

"*Mach schnell, fraulein!*" The guard demands, spittle leaking from his mouth. The barrel of his rifle rests in the palm of his outstretched hand, ready to shoot or use it for striking.

I hold my belly with one hand and the opening of the boxcar with the other. The jolt from hitting the ground sends pain down my back, but it's a relief to touch something solid. It feels as though I'm still moving, and I'm unsteady on my feet. Godek walks beside me and props his arm around my shoulder.

"Leave her be," the guard bellows, cracking his rifle across Godek's tall frame. He drops to his knees, and I land on top of him.

The guard's mouth twists into a snarl. "That's what you get for not minding your own business. To the front like the rest."

I pick myself up and try not to touch Godek for fear I might also meet with the end of the guard's rifle. Godek rises from his knees, dusts his clothes, and walks behind me.

From the side of the train, a Nazi officer strides toward us, his cohorts practically running to keep pace. He wears a brimmed hat instead of an upturned helmet like the lower-ranking soldiers. His tail black boots come to his knees and his britches fan out at his waist. I lower my head as he passes and stare at the dirty snow.

I look over my shoulder as he stomps past and watch him stop at the guard who struck Godek.

"You didn't follow orders. The woman is to be treated better than the others. Get her food to eat and then bring her to me. *Verstehst du mich?*"

"*Ja, wohl.*"

The officer speaks privately to one of his other comrades.

"This way," the guard says, his head down and his shoulders slumped. If he were an animal, his tail would be between his legs.

What could they possibly want with me? My worry is tempered with the prospect of eating more than watery soup. The guard and I walk toward a red brick spire and stop at a cottage surrounded by larger, much taller buildings. He unlocks the door and we step inside. It's warm, but if there is food, I detect no sign of it. Detailed maps of different sections of a city hang on the walls. The words "*Schacht II*" and "*Schacht III*" are written in bold letters. What kind of place is this? Then I realize these are not maps of a city, but of a mine. And the numbers designate specific tunnels. Instantly my heart sinks. Are they disposing of the dead down mineshafts? I say a silent prayer for an end to this butchery.

He clicks the door lock. His icy glove rests on the back of my neck. I turn to face my opponent, realizing very quickly I'm no match for his size and strength. I want to confront him face-to-face, instead of cowering like the lowly person he thinks I am, but the look on his face challenges my resolve, and I back up until I'm against a wall.

He eases toward me, his fingers tracing the opening of my shirt and stopping just above my breast. He positions his knee between my thighs until it touches the wall and removes his coat. "Too bad you're pregnant. There should be more German children, even if they are only half-blood."

The door swings open. "Get away from her!" yells the officer who chastised him earlier. "I gave you orders to get this woman food. You are a disgrace and not worth a bullet from this gun." He unsnaps the cover to his holster, exposing the black handle of his revolver.

The soldier slowly slinks away from me and the wall he'd pinned me against. "It's not the way you think. She wanted it." He glances at me and sneers.

"I don't care about your illusions. This is the second time you've disobeyed orders. Clearly you cannot be trusted. My suspicions about you were correct."

"She's a little whore. You can see the proof."

"Whore or not, the general values her. Do I make myself understood?"

The soldier snatches his jacket from the floor. "The war is over for the Reich." A look of scorn sweeps across his face as he hurries out the door.

The officer watches him from the open doorway and draws his pistol. "*Korporal,*" he calls out. A single shot pierces the air followed by a dull thump.

A small gasp is the only sound I can make. My shock quickly turns to a sense of relief.

The officer calmly replaces his gun in the holster. "*Ja*, the war is over for some."

I turn to peer out from the corner of the small window. Two soldiers run from a nearby building and stop to inspect the body.

"Bury him and see that his family is notified," the officer orders from the doorway. "Cause of death—altercation with the enemy."

"*Ja, wohl,*" the two soldiers reply in unison.

The officer steps outside to oversee the removal. I take the opportunity to look at the maps more closely, carefully watching for the officer's return.

After several minutes, he comes back into the room and closes the door. "Come. You need to eat. There is work to be done."

I follow him to the rear of the building, to a small but warm kitchen. The officer gestures for me to sit at the table and fills a glass with water. I sip it slowly. He rummages in the cabinet and finds a loaf of bread and a block of white cheese. He tears a piece from the loaf and cuts slices from the creamy block. Its pungent aroma fills the tiny room. I swallow the saliva pooling in my mouth.

"Here. Eat this but nothing else. Too much food will kill you. Go slowly."

I give him a look as if I understand. I haven't had enough to eat in months, and I want to eat the rest of the bread he has carefully wrapped in muslin cloth. The cheese has a fruity taste along with spices I can't identify—something I've never tasted before. After a few bites, I have the sensation of being full but continue to savor each mouthful. It feels strange to sit in a warm room, eating clean food, and drinking water from a glass instead of a dirty, rusting tin cup. He stands against the wall with his arms crossed and observes me as I eat.

Two days ago, I drank soup with paltry slices of vegetable floating in it and was then herded onto a train as if I were livestock. Now I am treated like a special guest. Images of Nina flood my mind and guilt overtakes me. Nausea rises in my throat, and I push the plate away.

"That's enough for now. You're right. I don't want to make myself sick."

"You're a smart girl. I have a niece about your age, maybe a little younger. How old are you?"

"Eighteen."

"Are you married?"

"No." I watch the officer's eyes and see him focus on my bulging belly. "This baby is half German—a guard at the factory where I worked." I stutter, trying my best to be a convincing liar.

He looks away and then stares for a while at his polished boots. "Your accent sounds French."

"I'm from Colmar."

"Where did you learn to speak German?"

"Colmar is close to the border. People speak it there, but mostly I learned from others at camp. It's not hard to learn a language."

"Apparently not for you. From what the general told me, you have a reputation for numbers coming easily, too. It seems you also made an impression with the speed at which you completed your tasks."

"Maybe so. I worked in a warehouse and remembered things. It wasn't difficult."

"Good. You'll be working with two others who manage shipments coming to the mine. Come. Let us talk to General Krenek."

I suppose some Nazis are capable of kindness, but he is still a Nazi. Punishment will come to him in due time.

We make our way to another building and enter the general's office. Although it's daytime, heavy plush drapes block the sun so the only light in the room comes from a tall lamp in the corner.

A German shepherd poses at the general's side like an Egyptian sphinx. "Sit down," the general orders.

I pull an upholstered side chair from a long table. It scrapes along the floor as I move it to the front of his desk. The general sits very straight in his tufted-leather chair, as if a board is fastened to his spine. The creases in his uniform are razor-sharp. The captain stands at attention behind me.

The general presses his fingertips together to form a steeple as he talks. "New shipments of the Third Reich will be arriving by train. You will help inventory the contents. If I had a German to do the accounting, I wouldn't need you. So having this assignment makes you a very lucky girl. But if you don't do exactly as you're told, you might be mistaken for a Jew."

I nod, but the general doesn't look at me. He picks a paper from one of the piles on his desk, writes something on it, and then shuffles it to a different stack. The glow from the single lamp makes his ears an eerie translucent red. "And," he pauses and stares, his eyes looking through me instead of at me, "nothing you see is to be spoken of. Is this understood?"

I nod again, too shaken to speak.

"Take her down to the mine, Captain Mitschke. The others will show her what needs to be done."

"Yes, of course, General."

The captain puts the palm of his hand under my elbow and lifts me from the chair. I follow him out; the crisp air fills my lungs. We head toward the tall brick spire.

He holds open a metal gate. There are SS guards at each side. We go a little farther to an opening where a cage hangs suspended from a single cable. I gingerly step inside and it sways gently with the shift of my weight. Captain Mitschke steps in and pulls the door, snapping a pin to latch it in place.

"Go ahead, Herr Gorski," he says to the elevator operator, and we start down.

The dangling cube is pitch-dark except for a single bulb that illuminates our faces. The captain's strawberry-colored hair shines in the light. The wobbly elevator gains speed as it descends into the cool air. The longer this trip takes, the more time I have to think about what unknowns await at the bottom. I have always disliked being in places where I couldn't see outside, and the darkness of this shaft does even more to rattle me. After what seems like five or six minutes, Herr Gorski pulls a long steel handle and brings the elevator car to a gradual stop. He slides the door open.

I step into a large, hollowed-out hole probably ten meters square. The walls are striped layers of rock, with the rough surface resembling a newly tilled field. Light bulbs hang every meter or so from a thick black wire; a narrow track runs directly underneath. Rows of large brown sacks are tagged and stacked knee-high like headstones in an overcrowded cemetery, filling the room from one end to the other. My mind races. What's in these that is so important that a general in Hitler's Army and SS soldiers need to guard it?

"Come with me." Captain Mitschke leads me from one huge room to the next. It's a maze of interconnected chambers that seem to go on without end. Panic sets in, and I wonder how I will ever find my way out. Maybe I'm not supposed to. Maybe my baby will be born in this underground vault. Despite the even temperature, goosebumps raise on my arms.

We cross over tracks dissecting the middle of the cave on our way to yet another room where more suitcases are stacked waist high. I already know their contents. The familiar disheveled and worn bags look exactly like those I handled at camp. I shiver. Each step becomes more difficult. My feet feel heavy as if my shoes are filled with wet sand.

Two or three men work in each room, unloading handcarts and stacking crates in some and cases, trunks, and boxes in others. There are no other women. One room contains stacks of baled paper. An unusual odor circulates from the bales.

"Captain Mitschke," a tall, slender man calls out, acknowledging our approach. He walks quickly toward us.

"This is your new assistant. Show her what you need to have done. These shipments must be cataloged quickly," the captain orders.

"Yes, sir." The slender man with sandy-colored hair and pale green eyes like shimmery sea glass watches the captain until he walks out of sight before addressing me. "And you are?"

"I'm Catherine. Catherine Revaux." It is the first time I've freely given my last name since I left the factory.

"My name is Victor. I am the curator. That's Herr Steuben," he says, pointing to the man sitting at a sturdy wooden table. Herr Steuben reminds me of a mouse. His eyes are small and his nose long and pointed. "Come. I will show you the books."

The ledgers are also similar—leather bound and labeled on the spine. The difference only that there are many, many more of them. The valuables here are probably far greater than anything I could ever imagine.

Victor opens a book and takes out pages from a folder labeled *Amerikanisch 20$ Goldstücke* and clips the papers to a board. Even the lined paper appears the same as what I've seen before.

"For now, you'll jot down descriptions and serial numbers and make sure they agree with what's on the tag. Then go through the list and determine the total. This area is a good place to begin." He starts to leave and turns around, "Oh, by the way, you're not allowed to wear your wrap. I'll take it and put it over here. You'll need it tonight for a pillow."

"I'll stay down here?"

"Don't worry. The lights remain on."

"I'm not worried as much about the dark. What about the guards? Do they stay at night?"

"Not many do. Most of them leave after the townspeople bring supper."

"I see." Knowing only a few guards sleep here fails to ease my mind. There are surely others like the *korporal*.

Victor and Herr Steuben continue with their work, but Herr Steuben watches my every move. He can't possibly be afraid I'll try to escape. I don't have any idea where I'd find the elevator. Every room looks similar to the next one. I play a silly game in my head of mapping the mine by noting things I remember that distinguish one cavern from another. I remind myself to pay close attention to landmarks like the size of the carved openings and the types of things stored in each room.

With each entry, I carefully write information to match the tag. The lettering on the tags is so neat, it appears to have been done by a machine or possibly stamped. On occasion, one of the labels will vary in a minor way, but all contain the word "Melmer." Nothing on the sacks offers an explanation about where they came from.

I work for what seems like hours tallying and checking, but it's difficult to gauge the length of the day when nothing changes. There is no sunlight, only bulbs steadily burning without a flicker. Down here, it's as if the world is frozen in place and time non-existent. The only measure is the grumbling of my stomach telling me it's time to eat. The taste of the bread and cheese I ate earlier lingers in my mouth. To keep my mind off food, I focus on completing my assignment.

I finish the last description and return the board to Victor. "It's all recorded. There are seven hundred and eleven bags."

He lays the folder on the table. "Good. You can help me now."

We move to a much smaller area where different sized bins lean against the wall. Small crates are stacked to the ceiling.

"How long have you been here? You seem to know how things work."

"I came about a month ago. The Reichminister for Education decided I was needed here at the Kaiseroda Mine. Before that, I worked at the Kaiser Friedrich Museum in Berlin. After the war started, there wasn't much left at home in Poland to return to, even if I could have found a way. My assignment is to help Herr Steuben with the inventory."

"I would never have guessed you were from Poland. You don't have the accent."

"I spent much of my youth in Austria. Most of my family comes from Poland, so that's where I would have gone. But there was no easy way to leave, not unless I could find someone to forge papers for me. What about you, Catherine Revaux?"

"There's not much to tell. I lived with my maman and worked in a linen factory in France. It was all very dull until a worker went missing. The German soldiers searched everywhere but never found him. When they returned, they took eight of us in a truck. We were sent to a camp where prisoners were held. Those of us from the linen factory were there to keep their machine running." I hope I haven't said too much to the wrong person. I feel comfortable with Victor, but my instincts may fool me. It's hard to judge allegiances when people change sides as quickly as taking an eraser to a mark on paper.

"This is a much better place to be. The Nazis only care about hiding this loot. They don't pay much attention as long as we do our jobs. Let's hope everything is hidden before the Russians come. Once that happens, the Germans will panic. It will be every man for himself."

"They already seem like dogs chasing their own tails. Captain Mitschke shot one of his soldiers earlier today."

He shrugs. "I'm not surprised. The shipments are coming faster, and there's an urgency to get things done I haven't seen before. Come. It's almost time for the food to be brought in."

"That's good. I'm famished. But then, I seem to be hungry most of the time."

"The townspeople usually serve rumors with the meals. It's how we know what's happening above."

"Why would they take a chance and talk to us?"

"As I said, things are changing. I think people in town see the end coming. No one wants to be on the losing side."

I follow Victor to the table where Herr Steuben sits doing his work.

"Victor, the first inventory sheet for the American dollars is not in the folder," Herr Steuben says with exasperation.

"That can't be. It was…I…I just saw it," Victor says, tripping over his own words.

I put it with the other papers that were clipped to the writing board. Maybe I put it in the wrong place.

Victor takes the folder I was working from and quickly thumbs through the pages. "Here. I knew I'd find it. It was the last page. I must have inadvertently put it behind the others. I do apologize, Herr Steuben. It won't happen again."

"I've worked with you for quite a while, and I've never known you to make such a careless mistake, Victor. Maybe you should get some rest. I think it would be good for me as well." Herr Steuben waves his hand in an upward motion as if to dismiss what happened. "I'll be back in the morning. Be sure you have the gold room ready. A large shipment will arrive tomorrow." Maybe this is a day job for the old man and he can leave the mine whenever he wants.

"Yes. I'll work on it first thing tomorrow morning. The work will go much faster with someone else to help me."

"Keep watch on her." Herr Steuben eyes me from across the small area and talks as if I can't hear him. "I don't understand how a girl so young can possibly be a benefit to us—and one with child, at that." He swats the air with his hand. "Ah well, that is not my affair. I am in charge of the bank receipts. None of the art or any of the rest of this will be of use if the Reich can't pay to feed their army," he says, resignation in his tone. "Good evening, Victor. I will see you in the morning."

"Good evening, sir."

Herr Steuben puts on a dark overcoat and grabs his black satchel. I watch as he zigzags through the crates and boxes. I lose sight of him and turn to Victor. "I can't imagine why you took the blame for something you knew was my fault." I feel an uncommon bond with him.

"You didn't know how things were supposed to be filed. I didn't really think to explain it to you. He could have you sent away for any reason, even for something as insignificant as that. He probably has more power than General Krenek if he wants to use it. Besides," he says, "I need someone to help me."

"I'm grateful to you, Victor. I really am." I purposely look away and change the subject. "Herr Steuben reminds me of a mouse. A very shrewd mouse."

"That's funny. I never thought of him as anything other than Herr Steuben. But now that you mention it, I see the resemblance." He covers his mouth with his hand to stifle a chuckle.

"I'd ask you what he has against me, but I overheard his comment about my age and my baby."

"He's not as bad as he seems, just a little eccentric, I suppose."

"Why is he able to leave?"

"He's from the Reichsbank in Berlin. I have no idea where he goes when he leaves. I see him each morning with a pressed white shirt. He must have an entire closet of shirts squirreled away in the mouse hole he lives in."

I imagine Herr Steuben crawling through a hole in the woodwork in one of the buildings above the mine and let out a giggle. The sound seems strange and out of place.

"I haven't laughed in a long, long time." I feel guilty about my outburst and hope no one except Victor heard me.

"Your laugh makes me feel good inside."

Again, I turn away. A shrill whistle echoes off the walls and interrupts my uneasy feeling.

"Our day is done. The guards are bringing food. We should get in line."

I follow him, winding through rooms that look like half-domes chiseled in the earth. A long line of workers twists from one room into another. I look for Godek but don't see him in the horde of other men. Two tables are pushed together to hold tall pots of food. The wooden tables are similar to the one Herr Steuben uses for his bookwork. The strong aroma of cooked cabbage sears my senses and overpowers the dry, stuffy air. Few words are spoken, mostly *bitte* and *danke*. These *please* and *thank you*s demonstrate that civility still lives in the recesses of the earth. The only other sound is the tapping of large wooden spoons against metal plates. Workers who have already received their evening portion sit on the dusty floor and scoop food with their hands. Apparently, we are not to be trusted with eating utensils.

Victor leads the way to a cleared area where the other workers can see us, but far enough they can't hear what we're saying.

I steady my plate and try to sit on the floor. My extended belly throws me off balance, and I start to lose my footing. Victor grabs my arm before I fall and then moves a wooden crate closer. "Here, sit on this."

"Thank you. I'm grateful for your help, Victor. You've been very kind." His thoughtfulness is appreciated, but I don't want him to make any assumptions about me. Again, I feel a need to change the subject. "Are there no other women here?"

"There is one other. Her name is Beata. The men allow her to go first in line. She usually sits by herself and doesn't talk to anyone. Maybe she'll talk to another woman."

Victor and I eat our food with our fingers. The heat from the carrots warms my hands.

He points to a middle-aged worker in the far corner. "There she is."

With her short hair, I initially mistook her for one of the men. Her size stands out. She is a thick woman, not emaciated like so many of the men.

"You should talk to her."

"Now?"

"Yes, go ahead."

I finish what's on my plate and carry it to the table. The guard grabs it from me and sloshes it in a barrel of gray water. "Swine," he says, giving me a look that makes me sick to my stomach.

I smooth out my shirt as if I were a classy lady in a fancy restaurant and amble across the room.

"Hello."

Beata looks at me but says nothing.

"I thought maybe we could talk."

"Nothing to say." She stands and takes her empty plate to the table. She swishes it in the dirty water and then stacks it on top of the other plates.

I walk away and seek the comfort of Victor's friendship.

I sit on the crate next to him. "It seems there's very little talking after supper."

Victor almost laughs. "She works in one of the art rooms and re-packages crates. Without everyone around, she'll be more open. Anyway, we'll find her tomorrow after I show you the mine. We'll give ourselves plenty of time and start out before Herr Steuben arrives in the morning."

He makes it sound so simple. I'm not completely sure why I trust him. It's an unfamiliar feeling. Maybe the end is near.

Chapter 20

Victor nudges me. "Catherine, wake up. We need to get going in order to see the rest of the mine."

"What time is it?"

"It's early. We have to get back before Herr Steuben arrives."

"Are you sure there won't be a problem? What about the others?"

Victor sighs. "It's fine. They won't care. Even if they do rouse, they'll think we're working on the inventory."

I'm still not sure, but I'm relieved to leave and crawl out from under the thin blanket, slip on my wrap, and smooth my clothes before catching up to him. We walk through passageways and stop in front of a large metal door.

Victor unbolts a series of locks. The enormous door swings open, making an ominous sound as it bumps against the rock wall.

He is being reckless.

Facing the mammoth stone cave, he places his hands firmly on his hips. "This is the gold room. It's taken men centuries to hew the potash and form this great vault." He seems more proud of the carved stone than of the meticulously stacked bags.

"There's gold in the bags?"

He gives me a sly smile. "This is how gold is shipped so no one knows what's inside."

I return his smile to show I understand and hope he doesn't think me a fool. I want him to keep talking so I can gather my wits about me. It's difficult being in a place with such wealth. I feel as though I'm suffocating despite the cave's cool air.

The vastness of the cavern is breathtaking. It stretches far into the darkness, as if there's no end to it. The deep shadows slumber like hibernating bears. The stillness of the air chokes me. Naked bulbs strung on a single wire light the space with a pale yellow glow. What seems like thousands of lumpy burlap sacks are precisely placed in rows and stacked as closely as possible to one another. From a distance, they resemble a sea of people bent over in prayer with tags cinched around their thin necks.

"Each bag contains gold ingots. Long, slender bars of melted gold—very shiny."

"How many bars are in a bag?"

"Each contains as many as thirty-five. With a single gold bar weighing maybe twelve and a half kilos, well, the bags are quite heavy." He pauses as if trying to calculate the value in his head. "It depends on the number of bars in each sack, but if you were to sell one ingot, you and your mother could live comfortably for a very long time."

I imagine what life would be like if I had one single gold bar. Maman might never have to sew again.

The hush of the cavern is unnerving. "And there's more to be delivered?" The huge space seems to swallow my words even as I speak them. Victor hears me anyway, and his grin shows he is pleased with my curiosity.

"Yes, Herr Steuben said there will be a large shipment today."

The mention of Herr Steuben reminds me that we are in a dangerous situation. This tour is ill-advised. The idea, however, of returning to the sleeping room sends a flutter of panic through me. A night of lying still among all the sleeping bodies is a dreadful kind of torment. When I lay there, I half believe I'm already dead and buried. To keep him talking and the images of Herr Steuben and the others at bay, I attempt to create a lighter tone.

"I'm not sure where they'll find room."

Victor points to the top of the large opening which is at least three times his tall height. "They will make room even if they have to stack it to the ceiling."

He directs me to walk to the side of the tracks running through the center. "Follow me." The floor, uneven in places, forces me to tread carefully. Despite near starvation, my belly has grown to the point where it can be difficult to see where I'm stepping. One hand glides downward to cradle my baby as I weave through the nameless fortune. We go around an empty tram cart waiting silently for its next load. He unlocks another vault-type door and we enter a smaller room.

As we pass more bags like the ones containing gold, I notice the name "Melmer" in heavy black printing on one of the tags. The American gold coins I inventoried yesterday had the same label.

"What is Melmer?"

"Ah, Bruno Melmer, an SS officer. He made deliveries to the Reichsbank. The account is in his name so the bags are marked with "Melmer" to designate valuables belonging to that account."

"These are from the Reichsbank?"

"Yes, Berlin is no longer secure. The Nazis are clearing their vaults."

"I see." I can tell from the tinge of excitement in his voice, he thoroughly enjoys his role as expert. He quickly resumes the tour.

"Over there, the smaller sacks are filled with specie from—"

"Specie?" A number of things come to mind but none of them related to valuables.

"I'm sorry. It's a word for money in the form of coin. There are coins from different countries—Switzerland, France, and others. There are many different kinds of valuables in this vault."

He makes a sweeping gesture. "There are Arras tapestries, a Titian Venus, and original Goethe manuscripts from his library in Weimar."

I point to stacks on the left side of the rail standing opposite the gold. "What's in the boxes?"

"German paper money. It will eventually be used to pay their soldiers in Berlin and elsewhere. Even the lithographic plates to print the banknotes are stored here."

As I try to imagine a way to destroy the Reichsmarks and put an end to fueling this insanity, I quickly realize it would do no good. They would only print more.

I shake off my somber daydream and hear him talking about silver bars and old battered valises at the rear of the cave.

I ask what I already know the answer to. "What's in the cases?"

As if reciting a list of goods to buy in town, he replies, "Religious relics and family heirlooms hammered flat to fit inside—silver flatware, teapots, candelabras and the like."

His disregard feels like a slap to my face. Doesn't he care where these came from? To him, these family heirlooms are merely pieces of metal flattened to fit into a desired space. He hasn't witnessed the suffering. It makes me question whether I should trust him. I feel sure being the curator in an isolated museum, he's been told the Nazis' version and believes the lies he's been fed.

Having detailed most of the contents of the two rooms, Victor marches toward the enormous door where we entered. I follow him and wait on the other side while he fastens each lock—a succession of carefully orchestrated movements. I cringe when one of the mechanisms makes a loud clicking noise. I'm afraid the sound will carry to the others. He is either so involved in the task that he doesn't notice, or he's oblivious to the danger we might face if someone questions what we're up to and then snitches to a Nazi officer. I silently pray.

Leaving the vault, we turn left and proceed through a passageway lined on both sides with wooden crates. Each carton is labeled with its contents and a name or maybe a place; I can't be sure. There are different languages—French, German, and others I don't recognize. The names are swirling in my head, and I feel totally lost. If I were to be separated from Victor, I'd never find my way back before the morning's count.

He stops at the largest crate in the corridor. "This is a very unusual piece. It's the Painted Queen. Queen Nefertiti. It was removed a long time ago from her tomb in Egypt by German archeologists."

"But what is it doing here?"

"The belongings weren't safe in Berlin any longer with the bombing and all, so this mine is not only a safe haven, but a place with stable conditions for the pieces from the German museum."

"Stable conditions?"

"Yes, the humidity and air remain quite constant. Not too cold or too hot. And because this was a salt mine, the air is extremely dry, which is especially beneficial to the pieces that are fragile."

"Pieces?"

Victor points to the thin boxes leaning against one another. "Yes, art pieces. Paintings. Many of the great masters: Raphael, van Dyck, Monet, Renoir, Manet, Rubens, even Rembrandt." He reels off the names as if he knows the artists personally. "This one is *The Graces in the Gardens of the Hesperides.*"

It probably isn't crated because of its large size. He straightens the painting to show it in a better light. It depicts three women with an angelic child balanced on the branch of a large fruit tree. The women are bare-breasted, and I quickly look away, trying not to catch his gaze. *Don't act naïve, Catherine.* The women are standing under the tree. It reminds me of something you might see in a Bible, if there were pictures. It is so beautiful and dreamlike. It must have great value.

I don't know if I should be impressed, surprised, angry, or scared. I have my fears about where these things came from, but I say nothing. Some questions are better left unasked.

We continue walking. There's a fresh smell of wood from the shipping crates combined with a musty smell of things stored in an attic for a long time.

Victor points toward another uncrated painting equal in size to the one of the three women. "That's a Manet. It's titled *In the Winter Garden.*"

"It's beautiful." There's a certain calmness about it, with a proper lady sitting on a bench and a parasol in her lap. It looks as though she's waiting for an apology from the bearded man leaning against the bench. Her hat is the color of ripe lemons, and flowers are in bloom.

The painting's image of the world outside overwhelms me, and I imagine all the weight of the earth above crumbling down and trapping me. What use is a painting of a garden with greenery and blooming flowers in a place without sunshine or water?

Victor stops abruptly, and I'm shifted from my panic. We've gone perhaps fifteen meters when we stop at another large chamber unprotected by lock and key. He looks around and pokes at the boxes.

Not only does it seem like we've been gone too long, but I wonder if I've seen too much and know more than I should about the Germans' secrets. But for the moment, I am worried Herr Steuben will arrive at the mine before we return.

"Shouldn't we go?"

Victor goes on about the large cavern, shuffling and looking, as though he doesn't hear me. "There are hundreds of tons of records from the German patent office here. Unlocked. It could be worth more than the gold itself."

I don't care about these records. I pull on his arm to get his attention. "Victor, shouldn't we be getting back?"

"Oh, yes. Yes, of course. Don't worry."

I don't know how he can be so calm. I pray we aren't caught. We begin to walk quickly through the tunnels. I have no idea how far we are from the sleeping area. The fast pace hurts my belly.

He stops and looks to the left and then to the right. "This way, this way."

I'm not deceived by his self-assurance. I'm certain we've made a wrong turn and are doubling back. The terseness in his voice contradicts a spoken confidence.

After winding through more tunnels, we pass the elevator shaft. Things start to look familiar. I see Herr Steuben's table. No one's there. Relief overtakes me, and I release the air from my lungs. My heart settles and I swallow, attempting to clear the dryness in my mouth.

Victor hands me a ledger. "Here, take this." He pulls a paper from a file and pretends to study it as a sharp whistle pierces the stagnant air.

Our eyes meet. We made it.

Chapter 21

"I'm surprised Herr Steuben isn't here yet. You can always set your clock by him." Victor taps his watch to emphasize the tardiness.

I hear the click of boots and see Herr Steuben approaching. "Here he comes." I keep my voice just above a whisper. "It's a good thing he's late or we wouldn't have made it in time." My tone is harsher than I intended. Victor looks crestfallen.

Glad to have work to do, I review pages in the ledger and check entries as he approaches.

"*Guten morgen*, Herr Steuben," Victor says.

"*Morgen*," the old man mutters. He lifts his chin toward me and looks away, acknowledging me with a curt nod. I'm a non-person to him, but it doesn't matter. I know more about what's in this mine than he realizes. A sense of satisfaction flows through me.

"The situation has changed. The entire reserve must be returned to Berlin. General Krenek ordered railcars this morning."

Victor stares blankly and then holds his fists to his forehead, his arms covering his eyes as if to protect himself from this change of direction. Slowly, like a wave receding from a shoreline, he lowers his hands, his eyes practically boring through Herr Steuben. "Even the art?"

"*Ja*, everything must be returned." Steuben's hand trembles as he makes a sweeping motion. "Today's shipment will stay in the railcars. Decide what art will go first, but it must be sent after the currency and gold."

Color vanishes from Victor's face and his shoulders sag as if he's a marionette folded in half. "I see."

"*Ja, ja.* There's much work to be done. Much work to be done." Herr Steuben shuffles off, mumbling to himself.

I wait until The Mouse is out of earshot before quizzing Victor. "So what's the hurry?"

Victor looks dumbstruck. It seems an eternity before he answers. "I have no idea what's going on. It has taken weeks to store the gold and art here, and now they want to move it all back instantly. He can't be serious."

"He doesn't seem the type to joke about anything, let alone something as important as this. But why move everything? And why be in such a hurry?" I ask again.

He doesn't answer.

Excitement and fear course through my body at the same time. Could the Russians be getting close? Or is it the Americans?

Victor sits at the table, the one usually occupied by Herr Steuben, sifting through papers and straightening them.

"Victor, do you need help with the art pieces? You'll have to decide what should be moved first."

He continues riffling through the files. "Yes, yes, you're right."

"I'll help you. Tell me what you want done. It will be better if we just get started."

He looks intently at me as if a spark has finally caught hold. "We'll need those three." He points to the thin ledgers on a shelf behind him. "Bring them. They have the art listed by areas of the mine."

I grab the three ledgers. My pace is slowed by the books bobbing on my pregnant belly, but Victor seems preoccupied and offers no help. We make our way toward a room where art is stored, walking through tunnels, passing other workers. Occasionally one of the laborers stares but then quickly looks away and returns to his task.

A sharp pain squeezes my belly. "Wait. I have to stop." I hold my arms over my stomach and the pain subsides. "Where is Beata?"

"I didn't see her this morning. Are you all right?"

"Yes. It's nothing. Nothing really."

After a short rest, we continue at a slower pace and pause at a hollowed-out room—the one Victor had shown me with the two large, uncrated paintings. I hand him the first ledger.

"Here," he says, handing the book back to me. "You read and I'll match the title to the crate. Then I'll mark the crates that go in the first shipment." Victor's instructions focus me momentarily.

It seems as though we're adding an unnecessary step. I have no idea why I couldn't read the entries and mark them while he decides which pieces are most valuable and then move to the next collection. I keep the suggestion to myself. The longer this takes, the more time I'm away from Herr Steuben.

As we work, I hear men talking, but the sounds are muffled and far away. I can't tell who they are. The conversation gets closer, and the men stop in an adjoining tunnel.

It's Captain Mitschke's voice. "There's nothing that can be done. It's the Easter holiday and the rail system is shut down. We won't have time to get everything shipped before the Americans take Merkers."

Victor and I shouldn't be listening. We exchange nervous glances.

"Get Krenek to requisition trucks, for God's sake!" The words tremble from Herr Steuben's mouth. "We must get payment to the distribution points."

"Then the mine will have to be sealed off." Captain Mitschke's words dangle like a noose in the stale air.

My gaze meets Victor's. We both know what can't be spoken. I feel as if I'm walking on marbles. Do they plan to leave us here? Victor starts to speak, but I put my hand to his mouth. I stoop over and crouch behind a huge painting leaning against the wall and motion for him to join me. I sit on my heels in the tight triangular space. The three ledgers are closed but lay where we left them. It's too late to retrieve them now.

"We can't be concerned with the artwork." Herr Steuben's voice emanates from the opening to the hollowed-out room.

I hope I'm the only one who can hear my heart beating.

"Once the Americans move out, we'll be able to return." Captain Mitschke's words trail off down the corridor.

I let air escape from my mouth when I'm sure they've gone. We creep out from behind the painting.

I look at Victor. "We have to find a way out."

"I can't run, Catherine." He puts his hands on my shoulders as if he can shake sense into me. "This is my life—the art. It's everything I know. Besides, guards are everywhere."

I break from his grasp. "Didn't you hear what they said? They're going to seal the mine. You told me yourself you considered escaping if you could get documents. Why not now?"

"That was a long time ago. The war is almost over. I'm sure of it." Victor clutches my hand. "We can start a new life."

Victor's intentions surprise me and his tenderness a welcome reprieve, but I don't feel the same way about him. I have to find Renier—that much I know.

I shake my head. "They don't really care about anything but the gold and money, Victor."

"That's true, but they won't hurt you. I'll tell them I must have your help."

He hasn't seen what I've seen. They don't need him any more than they need me.

I try to regain my composure. I must find a way out of here. I look into Victor's eyes. I'm so close I can feel the warmth from his face. "No. You're right. We can do this together. But right now, I need to find out if Beata will help me when the time comes to have my baby."

"Yes, yes," the excitement in his voice palpable. "We'll find her. I'm certain she'll help."

I'm not so sure. She doesn't even seem interested in talking.

Victor grabs the ledgers and tucks them under his arm. "We'll find her."

We snake our way through the tunnels to where the records are kept. Victor replaces the books on the shelf.

"Finished with the art so soon?" Herr Steuben inquires with accusation in his tone.

Victor opens his mouth, but nothing comes out.

"He doesn't want to take credit, Herr Steuben," I begin. "But Victor worked out a clever plan. All of the art pieces have been grouped by numbers that correspond to what will fit most efficiently in a cart. It's all broken down in the ledger." I'm counting on him caring more about the Reichsmarks than the art and hope he doesn't decide to check further. *Please don't look in those books.*

"Fine. That will—"

A guard's heart-stopping whistle signals lunch. Herr Steuben looks like a mouse that's had its tail stepped on and stomps toward the elevator.

As the workers congregate for the noon meal, I scan the crowd, looking for Beata. I see only men.

The pungent, earthy smell of cabbage wafts through the air as the kettle lids are lifted.

Victor elbows me. "There. Over there. Standing in line. Go talk to her. I'll stay here."

I cross the room and get in line. Men step aside and let me to go ahead of them. No one fears there won't be enough food to go around.

I take a tin plate, and the guard slaps cabbage, carrots and a small chunk of bread on my dish. Once out of line, I follow Beata who has found a place along the back wall, and I approach her. "Do you mind if I sit here?"

Beata looks at me but continues eating vegetables with her fingers. "Up to you."

Despite her indifference, I set my plate down and lower myself to the floor.

She glances at me. "Looks like you're about due to have that baby."

"Yes, it's not far off." I take a bite. "I'm Catherine."

"I know. You're the French girl who came from a work camp."

"You know a lot for a person who never talks to anyone."

"God gave us two ears and only one mouth. You can learn more by listening than talking."

Her statement makes me laugh to myself. "How did you end up here?"

"You ask too many questions, but I've seen enough to know you'd be better off delivering down here than on one of the trucks."

"The trucks are already here?"

"We loaded Reichsmarks this morning. There are more trucks waiting. And with each load that goes up, a pallet of bricks comes down."

"They must be planning to wall off the entrances," I whisper, trying to keep alarm from my voice.

"I doubt they would take a chance and leave us unless they were sure they could barricade every entrance. But if they take us somewhere, it might be far worse than being trapped here."

"If they take us to another camp, we won't get out alive."

"Maybe your friend Victor can help."

A whistle pierces the air, ending our short break and conversation.

"I'll talk to him."

"It has to be soon. There isn't much time," she says.

I get in line to rinse my plate and stack it on the table for the guards to cart away.

If anyone is suspicious of me and Beata talking, they don't let on. There are no sheepish glances, no knowing looks.

The clanging sound of the arriving elevator echoes off the walls. Herr Steuben and Captain Mitschke appear and walk straight toward Victor. The captain gestures impatiently while Herr Steuben scribbles on a writing tablet. Victor's chest puffs out. Occasionally he nods, but he says nothing. I keep a safe distance, straightening papers at the table.

Victor calls out to me, "Bring that currency file, the one on top."

As I approach the three men, Herr Steuben takes a sheet of paper from his tablet, hands it to Victor, and turns toward the elevator. The captain follows, barely keeping pace with the old man.

"I'm to oversee loading the Reichsmarks—200 million." Victor almost chokes on the number.

The staggering amount makes me even more certain everything is held together by a loose thread that will easily unravel when given the slightest tug. Beata is right. There isn't much time.

"The trucks are here, Victor. They will only need one truck to move the Reichsmarks; the other trucks will most likely be used to transport some of the workers to unload trains at the other end. And they're already bringing down bricks. They must plan to hide what's most valuable and block the entrances."

"How did you hear about that?"

"Beata. She helped unload bricks this morning. Pallets of them were brought down on the elevator."

"We'll talk to her tonight. Do you think she'll help?"

"Yes, I think so."

"Good. You have to carry on as though you know nothing. I'll come up with a plan. I promise." Captain Mitschke returns and calls out to Victor. Victor dashes toward the elevator.

The tension in the air makes the time after our noon meal turn as slowly as a spoon in thick French porridge. I struggle to keep my mind focused and decide to circulate through the various rooms, pretending I'm examining shipments in an attempt to see what's going on. Masons are furiously laying brick like bees building a hive. With the adjoining cavern to the gold room almost sealed, they start laying a second wall in front of it. I haven't seen Beata since lunch, and Victor was summoned hours ago. The bricked walls make me feel as though everything is folding in on itself. Pain crosses my round belly. I try to think of something else until supper comes.

The guards are almost finished serving when Beata enters from a tunnel with several other workers. They quickly grab dishes from the table. She fills her plate and comes to the far corner and sits next to me. We eat in silence for a while before talking.

"Where's Victor?"

"Above. I'm worried. What if he doesn't come back tonight?"

"Then we'll have to make it out ourselves," Beata says.

"I hate it down here. I've been afraid of being underground since I was a child. I dreaded each time Maman asked me to gather things from deep inside the cellar."

"You get used to it."

"How long before you got used to it?"

"You have a certain way of getting the information you want. I have to admire that." A faint smile calls attention to the creases at the edge of her eyes. "You're a curious girl. I'm surprised it hasn't gotten you in trouble. Anyway, my story's not that interesting."

"We have to tell our stories. It's all we have." The distant sound of shovels mixing mortar in wheelbarrows and masons tapping bricks into place helps to muffle our conversation.

"I was brought here after my grandfather died. I worked with him on his farm outside Merkers. The Nazis took it over because it was close to the railroad. He was a foolish man. Now he's gone."

"I'm very sorry."

"No need to be sorry. There are other things to worry about. We have to find a way out of here."

"I've been thinking. There may be something other than the elevator, if they don't block it."

Beata's eyes lock onto something behind me, but her body stays unnaturally still. "Don't turn around. It's Victor with the captain and the general."

I'm relieved to know Victor's here, but why is General Krenek with them?

The captain blows his whistle. All the workers stand and stare at the three men, especially the general, who looks conspicuously out of place.

I stare at Victor. When he sees me, he glances away. He looks like a pet on the general's very short leash.

Now when the general speaks, he doesn't seem as fierce without his dog by his side. "Everyone leaves in the morning. Captain Mitschke will assign three men in the first truck to unload at Merkers. The rest of you will go on to another site."

Victor looks at the floor; his shoulders slumped as if air has leaked from his lungs. It will be up to me and Beata to find a way to escape.

General Krenek turns to leave, a tiny cloud of dust whirls around his black boots. The captain and Victor follow in his wake.

At the elevator's whine, a cacophony of chatter fills the air.

"*Halt!*" one of the Nazi guards commands, aiming his gun and fanning the barrel around the room. The other guards pull up their rifles, ready to fire. Abruptly, the room falls silent.

The soldier sweeps the leftover plates to the floor and sits on the table. "Not another word." Guards scatter around the room, each taking a strategic corner to occupy.

I stick close to Beata, but I'm afraid to talk until the guards are asleep or not paying attention. I fold my wrap and place it behind my head as a pillow.

The night drags on as if it has no end. I sleep very little.

"Catherine." Beata's voice is as soft as velvet compared to the usual morning whistle.

I focus my eyes and rise slowly. My tattered coat drapes across my arms, and a wad of rags rest under my head.

"The guards are milling around. Something's going on," she says. "Victor's talking to one of them."

Victor points in our direction and the guard nods.

The Nazi soldier roars orders for men to form groups of ten. Workers scramble in all directions.

Victor speaks to a small group and then makes his way toward me.

"I can't talk long. In less than an hour they'll start loading the trucks. Find a place where the guards won't discover you. I'll come back for you as soon as I can, Catherine. I promise." Victor gives me a quick smile before moving on to talk to others.

I give Beata a nudge. "I have an idea. We'll get those three ledgers. If anyone says anything, we'll tell them Victor told us to bring them along."

Beata pulls the books from the shelf.

"Stay close and don't look at anyone."

She trails behind me to the area near the elevator where some wooden crates are stacked. "On the first day I came, I saw maps of the mine; there were also diagrams in the paperwork I filed. If it's what I think, there's a shaft that runs next to the main elevator." I pull one of the crates. "Let's get these moved."

She heaves the heavy boxes two at a time. Each one I lift sends a pain darting across my back.

Moving the crates reveals a wobbly gate barely hanging on its frame.

"This must be the original shaft," I say.

Beata peers into the opening. "We'll hide in there. When everyone's gone, we can climb out. There's a sturdy ladder. Do you think you can make it? It's a long way to the top."

"Yes, I know. The diagram showed six hundred and forty meters, but I'll make it."

"Good."

I step inside. She scoots several crates up against the tight opening, squeezes in, closes the gate, and leaves the three books where they won't be discovered.

"We'll climb a short way for now. Sound carries up the shaft, and we will be able to hear what's going on. When it's safe, we can go all the way."

It's as black as soot, and I can't see my hands gripping the wooden rungs. Beata crawls behind me. My hand slips and I claw at the ladder to keep from tumbling. She pushes on my bottom to steady me.

"Sorry," I say.

"Don't worry. My arms are strong. When you need to, you can sit on my shoulders."

We climb about fifty steps. A small hollowed out area gives us a place to rest and hide from the possibility of a guard's probing light.

"This must have been used as a place to store provisions while they excavated the mine," she says.

"I hope this isn't the only one we'll find."

"We'll stop here," she says quietly.

Cables passing over pulleys in the main elevator shaft temporarily drown out the sound of chaos below. We wait as the elevator ascends with its cargo of men.

"Should we go farther?" I whisper.

"No. Not yet."

I feel at peace. It's as though the past months have disappeared in this total darkness. I imagine finding Renier. I know in my heart he's looking for me. My trance is shaken loose by the sudden whining of the cables as the elevator makes its way down again. At the end of its long journey, it stops, and the voices of Victor and Captain Mitschke carry up the shaft.

"Check this area, and I'll look over there," Captain Mitschke says.

We hear the two men rushing below.

"I don't see anyone. It looks clear."

"What about the two women?" the captain asks.

"I sent them on one of the first trucks," Victor says

"I didn't see them."

"I sent them on an earlier truck," he repeats.

"All right. Let's go. When we get to the top we'll cut the power."

She squeezes my hand. Freedom is within our reach. When the elevator reaches the top, we continue climbing.

My legs burn each time I lift them to the next rung.

"I've been counting the steps, and I think we're more than half way." Her voice echoes in the blackness.

A good feeling washes over me and gives me additional strength. To give myself needed stamina, I imagine Renier waiting at the top.

"I'm so thankful for you. Without your help, I wouldn't make it," I say.

"We're not there yet, but I have you to thank. You knew about this shaft, and it was because of you Victor lied for us. We could be on a truck to God knows where right now."

"Yes, and Captain Mitschke was nice to me the first day I arrived. He told me I reminded him of his niece. Perhaps there was some kindness and civility left in him."

"We all have faults, but I know one thing. You're a lucky girl."

I hope she's right. We come across other hollows, and she lets me rest on her whenever I need to. She even pushes my leg to the next step when I falter. I clasp the ladder until my hands feel as if they will permanently curl.

"I don't think it's very far now, Catherine. We'll make it provided they haven't blocked the entrance."

A sense of panic shoots through me, but I continue on, concentrating on one step at a time.

A fragment of light streams through a slit in some wooden slats. "Look. There's sunlight coming through those boards."

"I see it. If nothing else, we can chew our way out."

I smile at her fearlessness.

"Move over as far as you can. I'll climb above you and try to break through."

I appreciate her strength and endurance. I move toward the wall, wrapping my arms around the ladder's side rail. It terrifies me not to have her below to catch me if I fall, but I'd never be able to break through the boards. She straddles my crouched body and lifts herself to the top.

With a couple of solid strikes, she breaks out one of the planks. With sun shining through, I close my eyes from the piercing light as dust scatters on top of me. She uses a part of one slat to pry the other pieces loose. When she has a hole large enough, she pulls herself out. From the opening, she reaches down and grabs one of my wrists and then grasps the other, hoisting me through the gap. With little energy left, I hug her, our foreheads touching. She holds me the way Maman did when I was a child.

The trucks are long gone. We are alone, faced with the decision of what to do next.

The prior echo of Beata's strong voice is replaced by her hushed instructions. "Based on how quickly everyone left the mine, the Allies must be nearby. When we get close to them, we'll go our separate ways. There will be less suspicion if we don't stay together. You'll need to ask for their protection. I can make it to some people I know before nightfall."

Even though what she says makes sense, I feel a sense of loss.

"We'll find each other after the war."

A smile lights her face. "Of course."

The fresh smell of spring air fills my lungs. Green buds peek out from the branches. There is new life. Renewal and a sense of hope are everywhere.

BOOK VI: ERVIN ACKERMAN

OUTSIDE MERKERS

Chapter 22

The Krauts unleash a frantic push to destroy the bridge in front of us. With only a small patch of useable land along the river, our engineers decide we can't safely get tanks to the other side of the Rhine River, so they quickly throw together a pontoon bridge. The German effort is about as worthless as tits on a boar. Even after we cross, there isn't a single Nazi lying in wait. But just over the crest of a nearby hill, a couple of *Messerschmitts* buzz around. They must be low on fuel and ammo because they only take a few swipes at us. Guys near the bridge dive head-first into the water. Everyone else who has an M1 takes a pot shot at them, filling the air with the smell of gunpowder, like opening morning of deer season.

"Those yellow-nosed bombers are like pesky bumble bees," I say.

The colonel looks at the darkening sky. "I'd call them damn annoying. But we're on a roll, and they aren't about to stop us now."

We advance to the Main River, where we cross in assault boats. From there, we meet only scattered resistance as the race continues toward Berlin through Stockheim, Schlitz, and Vacha. God willing, we'll get to Berlin before the Russians.

Colonel Williams and I have been ordered to do recon for the umpteenth time. We set out again this morning to check things out. The rest of our regiment will follow based on intelligence we radio in. The early spring morning is cool, but by noon we're peeling off our jackets.

The colonel glasses the area. "Let's swing in here. There's a farmhouse up the road, Erv."

"Good idea. I've got to piss like a racehorse." I shut off Betsy so we won't make a racket as we near the farmyard. I relieve myself by the side of the dusty road while he studies the area.

"We can get a lot closer on foot," I say, looking over my shoulder to see if anything appears out of place. I don't hear anything except the squeak of a weather vane on the old barn's roof.

The colonel piles out of the Jeep. "Let's see if anyone's been living there. I'd sure enjoy finding something to eat besides K rations. That shit's getting old," he says, propping one foot on the channel iron that serves as Betsy's bumper.

I zip my pants. "You can say that again." The thought of having Mama's cooking fills my mouth with juice. "My ma could've put up a whole side of beef with the salt that's in one of the cans of dog food we cart around."

We walk about a hundred yards and stop short at a small grove of trees. Late afternoon shadows fall across the buildings. We watch and wait. Most of the windows in the house are broken or covered with dust. A small barn and shed, probably used as a chicken coop, sit a stone's throw away. No animals, no movement of any kind—except a lone chicken.

"Looks like dinner," I say.

"What's that?"

"Over there. She's a little scrawny, but she'd make a tasty supper."

"Boy oh boy. That'd be a treat."

"More than likely with only one chicken running around, there aren't any hungry German soldiers nearby," I add.

The colonel gestures to the left side. "Okay, go check that side of the house. I'll head around this way. We'll see about that hen later."

I dash over to a side window. Nothing. I creep around the back and check the door. It's unlocked and I stick my head inside. Fine dust coats everything. "Doesn't look like anyone's been here for a while," I shout.

"Nothing here either." No sooner than the colonel finishes his sentence, the poor hen makes her move. She flaps her wings and runs past him. He takes off after the poor old gal. It looks like a pillow fight as black-and-white feathers come loose and drift to the ground.

I'm of absolutely no help because I'm laughing so hard I can't stand up. Tears roll down my face as I sit and watch him chase the squawking bird. If a Kraut came out from the bushes right now, I'd probably shit my pants. But I wouldn't care—this is a sight for sore eyes. It doesn't appear either one is going to give up, so as soon as I catch my breath, I go into the farmhouse and look for a piece of wire. I find a small wardrobe. Lo and behold, there's a chicken hook ready to be rigged from a clothes hanger. I quickly fashion a snare and rush outside to join the chase.

"Let me show you how a farm boy does it." I flap my arms as a way to corner her against the fence. She makes a break for it. After a couple of passes around the yard, I snag the old broad's leg. There are almost as many feathers on the ground as there are on her. I grab her and tuck her under my arm so she doesn't flap her wings right off.

"She's as good as in the pot, Colonel."

"Okay. So now what?"

"There's a grain bag hanging on the side of the shed. I'll put her in that, and we'll take her to the cook."

He looks at me with a broad smile across his face. "We'll have the old hen over for dinner tonight."

We head back with an occasional squawk coming from the back seat. A sign tells us we're eight klicks outside the little town of Merkers. The rest of the battalion caught up with us yesterday. Colonel Reid orders in a few Shermans, but Colonel Williams and I are still a ways ahead of the advance column.

However, we won't be the first to go in; that's a job for the big guns. Hopefully we'll take this village without a single shot. But just in case things aren't that simple, we'll have to block all the roads, in and out, except one. One route stays open for the Nazis to escape. They'll funnel through like rain down a drainpipe. Besides, a trapped animal will fight to the bitter end. One that's out in the open is easier to polish off.

"I doubt there'll be much of a struggle from the town folks. Things are collapsing for the Germans, at least based on the young recruits we've seen lately. They're not even old enough to shave," Colonel Reid says. He pulls out a map and signals the tank commanders and platoon leaders to come in for a quick briefing. "Take a knee." He squats and points to landmarks on the map, identifying the location of the roads leading into Merkers. Whatever land mines might be out there, sweeps on the front of our tanks will take care of them. I appreciate that Colonel Williams and I aren't blazing that trail either.

"All right," Colonel Reid begins. "We'll split up when we get within half a mile of Merkers. Company A takes the main road. Company B to the south. C takes the north end. Assume there'll be a fight. Don't get sloppy now, and make sure your men have a good supply of grenades. Remember," he says, pointing a finger at his troops, "Don't go through doors or windows, in case they've been booby trapped. Your demolition guys might need to rig up explosives at about every fifth building or so. When you radio in, we'll coordinate our time to set things off, if need be. Maybe with a boom or two, they'll go running like rats from a sinking ship. Intelligence says there's been a lot of Nazi activity here, so watch for sniper fire. Questions?"

There's only silence. We've all been through this drill many times before.

"Good luck, gentlemen."

The tank commanders and platoon leaders return to their men and split in three different directions. Roads that were nothing but a sloppy mess a few months ago are now as dry as a popcorn fart. A cloud of dust curls from behind the wide tracks as the tanks clatter along. With early-spring branches plastered all over them, our tanks look more like rolling bushes.

"Radio dispatch. We need the signalman to cut all wires. No live communication in or out," Colonel Reid orders.

"Yes, sir," Private Rottman says, screwing the radio handle as if he were turning an eggbeater.

I start Betsy. *Hang in there, old girl. Get us back in one piece.* Colonel Williams cinches his helmet to keep it from bouncing off in the open-air buggy.

At the sound of three companies nearing their town, a small group of what appears to be civilians wave white kerchiefs. Maybe they're going to give us the key to Merkers.

Colonel Reid, with Colonel Williams next to him, meets them with guns drawn and the barrel of a Sherman pointed in their direction. I stay a respectable distance behind.

"Ackerman." Colonel Williams waves me forward. "Find out the status. Who are these people?"

I learn they include the mayor, a councilman, and a couple of businessmen. Their biggest concern is saving their little burg from total destruction. "The mayor says there aren't any troops here. The Nazis left within the last twenty-four hours, and the townspeople are willing to cooperate." I question them further until I'm convinced they aren't hiding anything. "I told them we need safe passage into town or we'll blow the whole place to smithereens." No matter what, we'll still go in cautiously. There are a lot of men's lives on the line.

"Okay. Tell them to gather their cameras, binoculars, guns and ammo. All of it gets piled in the middle of town, an open market or something like that," Colonel Reid says. "We'll follow the tanks in."

Within two hours, a small patch in the town square is heaped four feet high with loads of Zeiss binoculars and Belgian Brownings. I'd give my left nut to snag one of those Browning shotguns as a souvenir. Colonel Williams told me anything I needed I could box up and send home, and he'd sign for it. Well, I just can't do it. It's all legal and everything, but it would be cheating the American people. They didn't send me over here to line my own pockets. Nope, I just can't do it, but damn, it sure is tempting. Maybe just one Browning.

BOOK VII:
CATHERINE AND ERVIN –
TWO LIVES INTERSECT

APRIL 7, 1945

Chapter 23

A young woman walks along the sun-drenched road. She seems dreamlike and out of place. An MP stops her. She gestures with her hands; he shakes his head. Her stick-like arms hug the front of her dress, emphasizing her protruding belly. I am fascinated and shocked by her appearance. If this war were on a different continent, that could be my wife and my baby.

The woman tries desperately to communicate with the MP. He waves me over. Her hair is dark brown, more from not being washed for a long time rather than its actual color, but she has a certain beauty—a beauty that doesn't show as much on her face as it does in the lift of her chin and the set of her shoulders.

"I don't know what the hell she wants," the MP says. "She started out in French and then switched to German. You know the language, Ackerman. You talk to her."

"Start at the beginning," I say slowly in German, hoping to calm her.

"I'm going to have a baby."

I can see that.

"I want to have my baby here."

"We'll get you some place safe."

The MP waits a few steps away. She looks over her shoulder several times.

"Are you okay, miss?"

She glances at the MP again.

"Come on. I'll take you to my commanding officer. We'll get you to a medic."

A faint smile crosses her face.

"I'll take things from here, sergeant."

The MP shrugs. He seems relieved to be rid of a pregnant woman he can't understand.

She and I walk in silence. There are lots of things I think about asking her, but I hold off because she looks as fragile as a newborn filly trying to stand for the first time.

Eventually, I try some friendly small talk. "What's your name?"

"Catherine."

"I'm Ervin. Are you by yourself?"

She nods.

"Where'd you come from?"

"I walked from a place near Merkers."

"No, I mean, how did you end up here? You're not German. I'm guessing you're French."

"*Ja, Französisch*. I was slave labor for the Nazis."

"Slave labor?"

"Yes, I escaped from a mine not far away."

I pull a Hershey's bar from my jacket pocket and hand it to her. "Looks like you could stand something to eat."

She holds it in her hand, turning it and staring at its rectangular shape.

"It's chocolate. Part of my provisions."

She looks at me, her eyes watering in the cool April air. After carefully removing the brown wrapper, she takes a bite.

The dark brown candy sticks to her parched lips. "There's treasure buried there," she says. With amazing recall, she recounts the staggering amount of loot and how it was buried, and then explains how she escaped when the Nazis abandoned the mine.

We walk slowly as I take in everything she's told me.

I point to Colonel Williams sitting on the hood of the battered Jeep. "There's my commanding officer." This will knock his socks off.

We approach the colonel as he puffs on a Camel. "Colonel, you won't believe it, but this young lady says there's gold buried in a mine not far from here."

"Really?" He turns toward her, his eyes scanning her up and down. "Where'd you get that information?"

She looks upset and confused. "She's French and doesn't speak any English. She was slave labor for the Nazis and worked in the mine."

"Does she know if anyone's still there?"

"She said she was the last one out."

"I'll be damned." He drops his cigarette and crushes it with his boot, twisting it in the dirt. "Operation Safehaven. Intelligence has been snooping around for months. They assumed the Nazis were hiding their plunder underground, but they always came up empty-handed."

"Well, we found the needle in the haystack. She'll give me the exact location if she can have her baby behind our line."

"You find out where it's buried. If she can stand the trip, I'll have someone take her to the field hospital. Otherwise, I'll get Fogle to do the duty right here. I doubt he's ever delivered a baby, but I'm sure it's the same no matter what language you speak, right?"

"I bet he can figure out which end without her telling him."

The colonel's shoulders shake with laughter as he calls to a private to hustle over.

I ask her whether she can make it to a hospital and about the mine's whereabouts.

After thinking about her options, she decides to stay put for now and not venture too far from our post.

"That's probably a good idea," I say in agreement. Based on the way she's holding her middle, I'm not so sure she won't have her baby right here in front of me.

Having settled on a plan, she seems relieved. She describes the twists and turns in the road and what the gate at the mine's entrance looks like. "The elevator doesn't work any longer. There's a hole that was boarded up not far from the shaft. You'll know it's the place because most of the slats have been knocked out. A wooden ladder inside that hole will take you to the cache."

"*Merci*," I say.

The colonel puts his hand on the private's shoulder. "Escort this young woman to Corporal Fogle and see she gets the help she needs. Tell him she doesn't speak a lick of English either."

"Yes, sir. Right away, sir," the private says, tipping his head to her. As she slowly walks away with the young soldier, she turns and glances back. Although the corners of her mouth lift only slightly, her smile reaches to her eyes.

"Okay, Colonel. There are a couple of extra flashlights in the backseat. You can bet your bottom dollar we're gonna need 'em," I say.

We hop in Betsy and I drive like a bat out of hell. The road is as rough as a cob and we bounce most of the way there. We pull up to a brick building. Her directions were right on the money, and the description of what the place would look like was spot on. We leap out of the Jeep and walk through a tall iron gate. "She told me there'd be a side shaft next to the elevator—not far from this gate."

Colonel Williams points to a hole in the ground. "Probably over there. We'll double-check to make sure it's petered out."

Snooping around, I find a hefty cable sliced in two pieces and pull the elevator's steel lever. Nothing happens. "Looks like we'll have to use the ladder."

"I was afraid of that."

I point to some broken boards. "I bet that's the other shaft." We hurry over and I kick out a couple of pieces to make a larger opening.

He switches on his light and looks down. "She didn't happen to say how far we had to go, did she?"

"No. Just that it was a long way."

I clip the flashlight back on my belt and enter the black hole. I can't see my hand in front of my face. I only know the colonel is above me by the sound of his boots scuffing against the wooden rungs. Loose dirt crumbles and floats downward each time my boot brushes the side, but there's no sound of anything reaching the bottom.

"I tried to count how many steps we'd come, but I lost track," the colonel says. "How in the hell did that girl make it to the top of this? Are you sure she wasn't with anyone?"

"She said she was alone, but she looked scared and kept glancing at the MP. Maybe she thought she'd get somebody else in trouble. I can't believe she was by herself either."

"Guess it doesn't really matter now. A person can do almost anything if they have to."

"Amen to that," I say.

We continue down the blackened opening. My hands ache and I feel blisters starting to form. I sure hope this ladder holds. Gradually, I feel a change in the air. I unclip the light and shine it below. "There's a space dug out right here." I find good footing and aim the beam for the colonel.

"This must have been cut out when they were digging the mine. Probably a good place to store equipment and supplies."

"It's a good spot to take a break." I direct my light down the shaft. "It's still as black as the ace of spades." We rest and listen for any sounds. I'm not interested in coming across any surprises, so I check the clip of my .45 sidearm to make sure she's fully loaded and rack the action to put one in the chamber.

"Okay. We're not going to make it to the bottom by sitting around here. Let's get moving, Erv."

I turn off my flashlight and clip it to my belt and start down again. The ladder creaks with each move I make.

"You notice that, Colonel?"

"What?"

"Salt. I can taste it in the air."

"That makes perfect sense. A salt mine would be a perfect place to store valuables. Would keep moisture out of the air."

The temperature drops slightly with each step. We must be getting close to the bottom.

I pull my light out again. "This is the end of the road."

Boxes are braced against the battered door, and I push the crates aside to clear a path. I point my flashlight across the ceiling and around the walls. "Hopefully the batteries will hold out in this thing." To the left is a tunnel; we head through and I notice a wall of bricks that looks out of place in a salt mine. I walk up to it. "What do you make of this?"

The colonel takes a closer look. "The mortar's got a green tinge to it—which means it's not cured yet." He rubs his hand along the wall. "I'd guess it was bricked not more than a couple of days ago."

I shine the light around and a glint of gray steel catches my eye. "Check this out. It looks like a door to a vault. Only a lot bigger than any bank safe I've ever seen."

"That's exactly what it is, but we won't be able to crack that baby open ourselves. We'll have to find another way in—maybe break through the brick from this side."

"There's a kerosene lantern, but I don't see anything we could use to get through that wall. I'll go back and look for a sledgehammer or something," I offer.

"Okay, but make it snappy. I'm not too fond of being down here without much light."

After a short spell of shinning up, my muscles burn and don't feel like they'll support me much longer, so I decide to distract myself by counting steps. I lose track at around five hundred. Sweat stings my eyes. I figure the bigger, hollowed-out space is maybe halfway. That's my gauge. This time I don't stop there to rest. There's a treasure and I can smell it.

I crawl out of the shaft and skedaddle back to Betsy and start her up. There's got to be a maintenance shed around here. I notice a building with wide doors that sort of looks like a garage. I get out and roll the big wooden door to one side. Nobody locked anything. Must not have been expecting company. I poke around and find a three-foot crowbar. It will do the trick. I jump back in Betsy and wind my way to the shaft's entrance. With the crowbar in one hand and the other on the rickety-ass ladder, I make my way to the bottom. My damp shirt sticks to me like ugly on an ape.

"Colonel?" I call, pointing the beam along the walls.

"Over here," he says, sitting against the brick. "I tried to find something to start chipping at the wall. Nothing but a few metal plates scattered around. Whoever was here must have left in a big hurry."

"Yeah, everything above was as wide open as church on Sunday. Anyhow, this should work." I slam the sharp edge of the bar into a mortar crack.

After a dozen or so whacks, the colonel takes a turn. Our progress is slow, but between the two of us, we eventually bore a hole about the size of a cannon ball. He inspects the opening. "Shit. There's another wall. There could be three or four walls for all we know. We could be at this until morning and still not get through. We need to get some dynamite."

"I'll get Maxwell. He's slow, but he's an ace demolition man."

"Good. But this time I'm going with you. I'll get an electrician to restore power to this place."

"Yeah, without an elevator, it's a nut buster. I'm sweating like a one-handed fan dancer."

When we reach the top, we both rest for a minute or so, and then hustle to the Jeep. I put her in drive, high-tailing it back lickety-split, dropping the colonel off at his tent.

The next place I stop is the guard house. "Anybody seen Maxwell around here?"

The MP points in the direction of the mess tent. "Last I saw he was chowing down."

Maxwell is a barrel-chested guy with stubby fingers. Never have understood how he manages to tie those tiny wires with fingers as thick as cane poles.

"Hey, Maxwell," I call out over the din of clattering plates and silverware. He saunters over after scraping leftovers from his rust-brown tray into a black barrel.

"Whatcha want?" Maxwell says with a Southern drawl as thick as taffy.

"Colonel Williams needs you for a special job. Grab your demolition gear. We've got some bricks to move. Meet me at the MP gate in fifteen minutes." Maxwell moves almost as slow as he talks, so I imagine the colonel and I will beat him there.

I jump in the Jeep and hot-foot it over to the colonel's tent, but not before I stock up on new batteries—got to have stronger light. As I pull up, the flap to the colonel's tent flies open.

"Wait a second," the colonel says, quickly disappearing behind the canvas.

A minute later he returns and hops in the passenger side. "I sent a request to get the power back on. Let headquarters know it was a top priority."

"Sounds good. Maxwell's supposed to meet us at the gate."

Maxwell stands at the guardhouse, wearing a heavy field jacket and a dark green bag slung over his shoulder. I guess any place outside of Louisiana feels like an icebox. As soon as the Jeep comes to a stop, he heaves the bag in the back seat and climbs in. I cringe as I imagine the whole shebang, Jeep and all, going up in a cloud of smoke higher than a cat's back. All of a sudden now that he's got a bag of dynamite, he's in a hurry.

"What's the 'signment, colonel?" Maxwell quizzes.

"It's a big deal. You ready to do some climbing?"

"Climbin'? Nobody said nothin' about climbin'."

"Take it easy. Ackerman's been up and down this thing twice."

We ride the rest of the way in silence with Maxwell's arms crossed over his chest. He's either cold or disgusted, or both.

"The hole's over there. We have to use the ladder until headquarters can bring somebody to get the elevator running," the colonel says.

"How far?" Maxwell scrunches his brows as if worried about the answer he might get.

"You're gonna be drinking tea in China," I say. "You need everything in that bag?"

"Yup."

As wide as Maxwell's shoulders are, I wonder whether he'll make it through the opening. The colonel starts out first, and I put the light on Maxwell until he gets his footing. I bring up the rear.

Occasionally, Maxwell, who moves like blackstrap molasses, calls out that he needs a break, probably so I don't step on his noggin. All three of us wait in the dark until Maxwell stops wheezing.

I sure hope we don't land at the bottom in a big heap. I'd hate to have a stick of dynamite stuck where the sun don't shine.

"Ain't never been down nothin' like this before," Maxwell says, as he reaches the mine's floor.

The colonel flashes some light in the hole we chipped out. "There's at least two brick walls. You need to punch a space big enough for a man to crawl through. No need to blow it all to kingdom come."

Maxwell unpacks his bag and starts to work. "Only need 'bout half a stick. You'll be okay just around the corner when she goes." In about five minutes, he's ready to detonate.

We go around the corner, crouch, and cover our heads. I've seen Maxwell blow up plenty of stuff, but never anything that might come down on me. I sure hope he knows what the hell he's doing.

Maxwell yells, "Fire in the hole." After hitting the plunger, there's a sharp crack from the explosion, and sound rumbles through the tunnels.

When the dust settles, a gap clean through the two walls, about the size of the door on my '37 Chevy, appears through the fog.

"I can't see shit. These rinky-dink flashlights don't do nothin'," Maxwell grumbles.

I move the flashlight's beam around the room. "There's a kerosene lantern right there. You got a match, dynamite man?"

"Here," he says, taking one from his pocket.

I fetch the lantern and hold the flashlight in my mouth while I lift the glass, strike the wooden match on the back of my pant leg, and ignite the braided wick. The lamp casts a hazy, buttery glow around us, dust particles still glistening in the air. The blast made a sizeable hole in the first wall and blew a cavity big enough to get through in the second.

"Let's see what's in there," the colonel says, threading himself through the opening.

I ease myself inside. "Holy smokes! Look at this, Colonel."

"What the hell is it?" Maxwell asks, pulling through and dragging the lantern.

The colonel scans the stacks and stacks of Reichsmarks lining the walls. "You blew us into the First National Bank of Hitler. That's what the hell this is. If the communication about Operation Safehaven is accurate, and if what that French girl told Erv holds any water, we'll find the Nazi's entire gold reserve down here. If there's another way in from here, I sure don't see it. Not that they would have drawn a map for us or anything like that. My guess would be it's behind that steel vault door."

"It's exactly like she said." I turn slowly and try to imagine the value of the room's contents. "It's kind of like that rhyme my sis used to tell us younger kids. There was this part about a king in the counting house counting out his money. I feel like a king in a counting house." Betty isn't going to believe this. Hell, nobody will believe it!

"You got that right. This is what the Nazis were fighting for," the colonel says.

The stillness in the cavern makes the hair on my neck and arms tingle. "Yeah, and we've been fighting for that French girl and lots of others just like her."

Colonel Williams nods in agreement. He breaks the calm with rapid instructions that vibrate off the walls. "There's still lots to be done, but we'll head up for now. I'll get a hold of General Eddy Manton. He'll inform Patton about this. You can bet the Old Man will make sure we go through this place with a fine-toothed comb."

Maxwell stands with his arms crossed over his chest. "I'm stayin' right here until they get that elevator goin'. I ain't climbin' that shithouse ladder again."

"Quit your bellyaching and get moving," the colonel orders. "You're not staying down here, and that's all there is to it."

BOOK VIII:
TREASURE ENTOMBED

APRIL 1945

Chapter 24

When General Patton's call comes in for Colonel Williams, the silence in the officers' tent is like that of a honky-tonk just after a nun walks in. "Colonel Williams reporting, sir," he says into the handset, which had been resting in a green metal case—the kind that looked like a tackle box I'd seen in a Monkey Ward's catalog. "Yes, that's right, sir. Three of us went down and saw it for ourselves."

"Well, listen up, Williams. I've been burned too goddamned many times on rumors. If any bastard breathes a word about gold before we've got it confirmed, he'll be begging for God's mercy because I sure as hell ain't gonna give him any." General Patton's forceful voice travels through the receiver while the colonel holds it six inches from his ear.

"Yes, sir. General Patton, sir."

"Good. I told Eddy to get somebody to blast that goddamn vault door open. I don't care how you have to do it. I want to see that fuckin' Nazi loot with my own two eyes."

"Yes, sir. We'll get it open and be ready to take you down there."

"I'm leaving right now. I'll be at the site tomorrow morning at 0900. That's all, colonel."

Colonel Williams gingerly places the receiver in its cradle and looks around the tent. Everyone lets out a deep sigh of relief before officers start issuing orders left and right. I can't keep track of who's giving directions and who is supposed to take them.

"Good thing we've got the elevator working. I don't know if we could prod Maxwell down there to blast more holes," the colonel says in a sarcastic tone.

"Oh, he'll go. Having Old Blood and Guts here is like having the Pope over for Sunday dinner. Maxwell will do whatever needs to be done or those sticks of dynamite won't be able to blow him far enough," the one-star says, in a feeble attempt to clear the tension.

"All right. Let's get moving. We've got a lot of work to do before Patton gets here. We need to make sure the mine and shaft equipment function properly and that German officials from Merkers are available," the colonel says. "Erv, you'll need to be on hand to interpret if Patton wants to question any of them."

I swallow hard. "Yes, sir."

No one got much sleep that night. At least, I know I didn't. Couldn't stop thinking about interpreting for a three-star. My gut got twisted like braids on a schoolgirl.

The next morning we stood around like a batch of boys lined up outside the principal's office as 0900 came and went. Still no Patton. At about 0930, communication comes in that the general is greeting General Eisenhower and General Bradley at Hersfeld Headquarters. You don't get any more VIP than that. From there, the three will fly to Merkers along with Colonel "Bernie" Bernard, who handles foreign money matters for the Department of the Treasury. Colonel Williams and all the other stars and bars within a hundred-mile radius will be ready and waiting to escort them to the mine.

Several hours later, a Jeep bearing a plaque with a circle of five gold stars and a couple of other Jeeps without any decoration arrive at the mine site. Guards from three companies of the First Battalion, with the assistance of one platoon of heavy machine guns and two sections of light tanks, are posted at the main entrance and several other openings that had been discovered. Special guards are also stationed at essential operations, like the electric plant, transformers, and the mechanism that operates the elevator. The mine's sealed tighter than rusted lug nuts on a deuce-and-a-half cargo truck.

With salutes and hand pumping all around, the bigwigs meet and proceed to the main entrance of the mine. The generals, Colonel Bernard, Colonel Williams, two German bank officials, the elevator operator, and I make the trek down. A later elevator will bring a photographer and a couple of men from the newspapers.

"Ask him if this thing's safe," General Patton says, first looking at me and then at the elevator operator.

"*Ist das sicher?*" I quiz the slender old man.

"*Ja, ja.*"

General Patton gives him a skeptical look and eyes the single cable dangling above us suspended from the dark hole. "If this cable snaps, promotions in the United States Army would be considerably stimulated."

General Eisenhower pulls up his shoulders. "Okay, George, that's enough. No more cracks until we're above ground again."

The elevator lands with a dull clunk. Everyone piles out except me and the operator. I wait for a minute and then sidle over to the colonel, still trailing behind the others. I feel like a turd in a punch bowl at a school dance. I've gotten really comfortable with the colonel, but well, he's a colonel. Guess the higher-ups put their trousers on one leg at a time just like I do—only theirs are starched and pressed.

The group enters what is now being called Room No. 8. General Eisenhower seems the most moved by what he sees. He stands with his hands on his waist and shakes his head as he surveys the bounty. "What kind of inventory do you have so far?"

Colonel Williams scans the faces of the men standing before him. "From what we've gathered from paperwork in the vault, we've found

Hitler's Fort Knox." He pulls out a clipboard and starts to reel off the contents. "What we're certain of right now is that there are 8,198 bars of gold bullion; 55 boxes of crated gold bullion; hundreds of bags of gold items, jewelry and the like; over 1,300 bags of gold Reichsmarks, British gold pounds, and French gold francs; 711 bags of American twenty-dollar gold pieces; 9 bags of valuable coins; 2,380 bags and 2.76 billion in Reichsmarks; 20 silver bars; 40 bags of silver bars; 63 boxes and 55 bags of silver plate; 1 bag containing six platinum bars; and 110 bags from various countries, along with additional sacks of gold and silver coins and foreign currency that we haven't had time to total yet." He comes up for air and continues, "We haven't even inventoried the art work and museum pieces." He looks at General Eisenhower. "If you don't mind me saying so, sir, I'd get an expert in here to figure that one out."

General Eisenhower gestures in agreement.

General Bradley lets out a short whistle.

"Holy shit! Can you believe this, Ike?" General Patton says in his high-pitched voice. "We're standing here with the whole fucking German treasury and then some. Those thieving bastards."

There must be words the German bankers understand because they both put their hands behind their backs and stare at their shoes, slowly inching themselves away from the big wheels. I can't blame them. Patton is the kind of man you wouldn't want to piss off. I'm glad I'm playing for his team.

"George, why, when you heard about all this, did you want to put on a censorship stop and keep it classified?" General Bradley asks. "What would we do with all this money?"

"Well, Brad, I'm of two minds. On the one hand, the gold could be cut into medallions and every sonofabitch in the Third Army given one. Or the Third Army could hide the loot until peacetime when military spending is tight and then dig it up to buy new weapons."

Eisenhower looks at Bradley and grins. "He's always got an answer."

As the men scout around and make comments to each other, Colonel Bernard, our official tour guide, asks everyone to follow him as he explains about the art pieces and treasure and how plates were used for printing Reichsbank currency. While they look at the stacks of money, a German banker announces in broken English that these were probably the last reserves and would be expected to pay the German Army.

General Bradley interjects, "I doubt the Nazis will be meeting payroll much longer." The German banker only shrugs.

Near the end of the hour-long inspection, General Eisenhower notices German writing on the wall. "What's that supposed to be?"

"It says," I start out slowly, "the state is everything and the individual is nothing."

General Eisenhower shakes his head. "What an appalling doctrine."

"It's a shitty mess. That's what it is," Patton says.

The group walks a little farther, and General Bradley makes a sweeping motion. "If these were the old free-booting days when a soldier kept his loot, you'd be the richest man in the world." General Patton chuckles.

Yeah, that might be true, but I think I'm the one who's rich—a guy raised on the Nebraska plains who just happened to speak German and just happened to come across this gold and treasure. And the girl who told me about it, she might very well have helped us round the corner on what will end up being the last leg of the war. Leaders aren't always the ones who write the endings.

The bunch of us, which also includes the newspapermen and a Signal Corps photographer, gather around the elevator and take turns returning to the surface. Once at the top, Generals Eisenhower, Bradley, and Patton are escorted to their Jeep by Colonel Bernstein.

I take a whiff of fresh air and realize I've had one helluva ride these past couple of days. I don't think it's all going to sink in for a while.

The colonel and I walk to our old, beat-up Betsy. Finding the gold feels about like taking a hammer and breaking Hitler's piggy bank. Yeah, that should do in the thieving coward. I'm glad I had a hand in kicking the lousy bastard squarely in the balls.

As we hop in, the colonel jolts me out of my daydream. "The 90th can't spare any of us, so we've been ordered to move out from this circus and join the division's other units." There's a hint of disappointment in his voice. "We'll head out in the morning. Czechoslovakia's calling our name."

I pull in next to his tent, and he jumps out. "See you in the morning, Erv."

"You betcha." The colonel grins at my familiar tone. He seems like an old friend. Sure glad the mucky-mucks didn't hear me.

When I get to my quarters, I join the other guys as we prepare to pull up stakes. I cram my fatigues into my duffle along with everything else I've dragged across this countryside—my weapon and ammo, of course, and my ragged, sawed-off toothbrush that's seen better days. I've made it through five countries and still have my unopened, Army-issued "individual chemical prophylactic packet," or what I call wishful thinking in a bag. It came with ointment you squirt up a place where Mother Nature says things should be going the other direction, a soap-cloth, and instructions. In the Army, there are directions for everything—come hell or high water. That's the size of it—everything to my name. Anyway, I'm going to turn in early. It's been a long day. I'm bushed and my dogs are barking, but I can't stop thinking about that French girl and her baby who are in the care of the American Army now. I feel proud when I think about her trust in me—the trust in my country. I know the medic will take good care of her, and her baby will be just fine.

Eventually, I fall asleep to the sound of my fellow bunk lizards wheezing, snoring like buzz saws and occasionally letting a fart or two rip. But shortly after midnight, when all of us are tightly bedded down for the night, the peace and calm is interrupted by an announcement that circulates through base like a raging windstorm. President Franklin D. Roosevelt is dead.

Chapter 25

We move south, hugging the western border of Czechoslovakia. We face little conflict, but when we do, we squash it with Tough Ombre ease. At almost every turn, we take on more German prisoners, like when we rounded a corner and surprised three young German soldiers standing on the side of the road. They could have easily been mistaken for my kid brother Tommy, who regularly milled behind the school house with his chums, trying to bum a cigarette he wasn't supposed to be smoking. One of the young soldiers had torn a piece of his undershirt and was drawing figure eights in the air with it.

"Drop your guns. I want to see your hands," I say in German.

They follow my command.

"Walk forward."

Again, they do as they're told.

"Where's the rest of your company?"

They mostly look down and say very little. It's as if there isn't energy to do much else. "They're separated from their unit—say they don't have ammo and haven't eaten in days," I report to the colonel.

"Send them to Sausage Hill at the back of the line with the rest of the prisoners," the colonel orders to two privates standing nearby.

"Yes, sir," Private Hays says as he and Private Sullivan search them and escort them away.

We continue on, patrolling the dense woods. Our plans are once again altered, on the morning of May fourth, when a German with the 11th Panzer Division enters 90th lines waving a white flag. This time it's a more formal encounter, and he hands a paper to General Price. He reads it to himself before reading it aloud to us: "The development of the military and political situation makes it desirable to me to avoid further losses on both sides. I have therefore ordered the major, the bearer of this note, to negotiate with you the cessation of hostilities. Signed, Wend von Wietersheim, Lt. General and Division Commander."

General Price pauses, neatly refolds the paper and sticks it in his pocket. "Hot damn. They're giving up faster than a two-dollar whore." He looks at the smirking men standing nearby and then takes a more serious tone. "Blindfold this Kraut, major, and take him to Division HQ. They can verify the terms of this surrender. In the meantime, get ready to roll. The good citizens of Prague have risen against the Nazis. They've seized the radio station and are begging for our help. We're going to give it to them."

On the way to Prague, we clear a route through the heavily wooded Regen Pass in the Sudeten Mountains to allow the 4th Armored to rush through and make a mad dash for the capital. The infantry will follow them into Prague and hopefully shit-can the German Army once and for all.

Tall timbers line the roads and winter's snow still covers the tall peaks. Being a guy from the flatlands of Nebraska, this terrain looks like God up and spewed His guts out in big old piles of rock and dirt. Even with this out-of-the-world scenery, I can't wait to leave and smell hay being spread out for the horses in the barn. That'll be one sweet day.

We inch forward through the slush of a spring thaw and come upon trees laid across the road. After we lift the timber out of our way and march several hundred yards, the column abruptly halts without warning.

"Now what's the holdup?" an impatient corporal says.

"It's probably information on a need to know basis, and you don't need to know," another soldier says.

Snickers drift through the line of men. "Yeah, that's the story of my life," the corporal replies.

"Stow it, buddy. Here comes the general," I say.

General Price swaggers to the highest point to ensure his voice will carry over us, takes a long draw on his cigar, and puffs out a cloud of smoke. "All right, men, give a listen. Division Headquarters just received new information and I'm damn sure you'll want to hear it." He clears his throat and begins. "The German High Command signed the unconditional surrender of all German land, sea, and air forces in Europe to the Allied Expeditionary Forces and simultaneously to the Soviet High Command at 0141B Central European Time. All forces will cease active operations at 0001B 9 May, 1945."

It's May 7, 1945. We stop right there in our tracks and never take another step toward the Czech capital. We now stand on the liberated soil of Czechoslovakia. On the liberated soil of Europe. The war is over. That's that. Plain and simple. It's what we've been waiting and praying for, but right now the words don't even make sense. I've imagined this every day I've been here, but now that it's real, I'm as numb as a pounded thumb. Some fellas start crying like little girls from the joy of the whole thing. One guy shakes my hand, but my arm feels as if it isn't attached to my body. It's a dream, isn't it? No, it can't be. There's the colonel. He's smiling and hugging everyone in sight.

The colonel makes his way to me and slaps my shoulders until my teeth rattle. "Erv, it's over! The war's over! We made it in one piece."

The news doesn't really sink in until instructions for shipping out filter through the ranks. Our first task is to count our points for discharge from the Army. I have ninety-four, more than enough to be cut loose, but I still have to wait my turn and go with my outfit. To be furloughed stateside, or de-mobbed, an enlisted man needs eighty-five. You get one point for each month you've been in the service, one point for every month overseas, five points for combat decorations, and twelve for each child you have under eighteen. It doesn't matter if you have a passel of curtain-crawlers; a guy can only take credit for three. For once, men who always denied they had a kid are trying to take credit for offspring from every fling they can remember. Everyone else is bucking for a last-minute medal, if they can finagle one.

Several men pull out dollar bills or anything they can find to write on and start asking buddies to sign them as keepsakes to take home. Seems like a good idea even though I don't think I'll ever forget some of these mugs.

By the time the ruckus dies down and guys have settled on how many points they have and that they aren't going to squeeze out any more, the commanding officer calls for formation. Men who were starting to get kind of squirrelly get serious and take it down a notch.

"At ease, men," the captain begins. "If I call your name, step forward." He looks at his clipboard. "Pfc. Patsy Abagnali, Pfc. Ervin Ackerman, Pfc. Joseph Akhiezer."

I move forward. The captain continues reading names, but I don't really hear them. "Okay, you men are going home. Do what you need to do to pack up." He points in the direction of the large convoy belching exhaust nearby. "Those trucks will load at 1400."

Boom. It's official. Freedom is seventy-five feet away. One guy passes out. I make a dash to my tent to get my duffle and then search for Colonel Williams.

Having to say goodbye to the colonel is more jarring than facing the end of the war. We've been through a lot together, covering a thousand miles across this continent. Even though I have six brothers, it's a brotherhood like none I've ever known in my life. I see him standing outside his tent, a Camel dangling from the corner of his mouth.

"Hey, Colonel. I'm going home!" I shout, waving my arms in the air.

He smiles that shit-eating grin of his. "That's what I hear."

"So, what are your plans, Colonel?"

"Well, seeing that I'm an officer with time on my hitch, I'll either be dispatched to the Pacific to fight the Japanese, or I'll stay here as part of the occupation forces. Don't know which way it's going to go."

"Sure hope you get to finish out here."

"Yeah. That's what I'm thinking. It's a bigger can of worms over there if what I hear is true."

I think on what he said and wonder about my brother Ed.

"Well, Erv, when you get stateside and if you're ever in the D.C. area, be sure to look me up. My dad's in the Bethesda book. Same name as mine. He'll know where to find me."

I sling my bag over my shoulder. "You bet. And don't forget you're always welcome in Nebraska, if you ever get to my stomping grounds. I'll even chase one of those chickens down for you." I give him a smile and a snappy salute.

He grins and puts two fingers to his cap.

I can't think of when I felt so good about something and yet kind of crappy at the same time. I'm going to miss the old bird. Oh well, it'll be harvesting time soon, and I'm finally going home. Nothing crappy about that, especially seeing as how I'm still in one piece. It will be a long haul, with the first leg of the trip being a train ride to the port of Le Havre, France.

When I reach the port, there's a smell of fish in the air and the sound of seagulls squawking above. By the time we shove off on this old banana boat, we're packed tighter than ten pounds of feed in a five-pound sack, but I don't really care. I'm on my way. I wonder how many of the guys I came over with made it out alive and are headed back. There are so many men who died. Not only men—so many people all over Europe are gone. People died who didn't do anything more than get up in the morning to live their lives. But there have been victories too—like the French girl's revenge on the Nazis. I have to smile when I think about her baby, who's probably several months old by now. It's amazing how life can begin in the shittiest of circumstances. All I know is that a lot has happened in the past year or so. It's going to be hard to go back and forget everything I've seen and everything I've been taught to do. I was trained to kill—now I just have to live with it. But for the next week or so, I'm going to look out at this big ocean and think about Betty, and nothing else but Betty. And I'm not going to fight any more wars unless it's a war against fighting wars.

EPILOGUE

The call came out of the blue to the author of *Finding Safehaven*.

It came from Julie Bartok, who had taken over the reins of the Dog-Eared Page, a Denver institution in the indie bookstore business, after the original owner decided to retire with more than forty years at the helm. The invitation was for a book signing on *Finding Savehaven*, her recently published book. The offer sent an electric shock through her body. She was thrilled and rattled at the same time.

Julie said her husband would call later in the week to discuss details and answer any questions. When her husband called, he explained that an author's remarks at a book signing were usually short—a session of mostly questions and answers, a comfortable discussion. So in spite of the battle the author waged against the butterflies in her stomach that fluttered their way to her throat, she agreed.

When the *Meet the Author* event came, she walked around the windowless room while people arrived. She tried to make a connection with someone, any-one, in an attempt to calm her nerves. Her heart started to beat with the steady rhythm of a drum roll. She listened while the owner made announcements for upcoming events. She was so interested in scanning the faces in the audience that she missed most of Julie's introduction and didn't come to until she heard the word "author." The word still sounded foreign to her. She wasn't even sure her name had been mentioned. She walked to the podium and gripped its cold metal sides. A curtain of shelves with neatly placed books formed her backdrop.

She thanked Julie for inviting her and looked out over the audience gathered on a sub-zero February evening. She said it was a privilege to be in the company of so many who shared a common interest in World War II history. She pointed out what most of them had likely surmised from the bookstore's program—it had taken her a long time to write the book. Her husband, whom she said was the life of the party, often joked that she had spent more time writing the book than it did for the armies to actually fight the entire war. She was calmed by their hearty laughter.

Although the audience might not assume it based on her husband's quip, he was her most ardent fan and fiercest supporter. Without him and the critique group she belonged to, the book would never have been written, let alone published. Several of her fellow writing group members were there. She thanked them and said she was eternally grateful, acknowledging their amazing talents and unending support. A second dose of applause was the tonic she needed to feel at ease, centered.

She knew she could have used all of her time talking about the trials of being a writer, but the audience had come to hear about the book. *Finding Safehaven* was based on a true story—her father's story. She had written it to tell of his integrity, his courage, and the discovery of gold and art treasure buried in a salt mine outside Merkers, Germany. This was the story he had told her from the time she was a little girl until his passing. Despite the deterioration of his mind brought on by Alzheimer's disease, his memory of the experience never faded.

As a soldier in the Army during World War II, her father, whom almost everyone called Erv, had landed at Normandy on the shores of Utah Beach, marched through Luxembourg, and fought at the Battle of the Bulge in Belgium. Shortly after crossing into Germany, history intersected his life with that of a young French woman, Catherine Revaux. When Catherine stumbled into the American Army's post, she tried desperately to communicate with an MP, but he had no idea what she wanted and asked Erv to interpret her second language, German. Erv's mother's insistence on speaking their native language and a chance conversation with a fellow soldier had landed him a plum assignment as an interpreter in the Army. It would most likely be the good fortune that saved his life.

With the German Catherine knew, Erv translated her plea and discovered what she so desperately wanted. She told him she was pregnant and wanted to have her baby behind Allied lines, fearing capture. She had worked as slave labor in the Kaiseroda salt mine. She recounted the Nazis' staggering plunder and how it was entombed. Their meeting was brief. This was the only time he would ever see her. Erv and his commanding officer went on to find the gold and treasure she told him would be there.

The author told the audience that after she read a segment from her book, she would open the presentation for questions. This was the part she always hated. Reading. Reading out loud in front of people. It was a custom pressed upon members of the writing group she belonged to. It was good practice, but it hadn't gotten any easier. When reading aloud, she always felt a strange vulnerability. As a writer, it was much easier to comfortably sit and write instead of talk. She'd rather chew glass.

She read several pages. When she stopped, the silence was deafening. She wanted to run out of the small room as if her hair were on fire. No one got up to leave, but watching them fidget in their seats and give her blank stares told her they weren't ready to ask questions, either. Finally, a brave soul (probably an employee of the Dog-Eared Page) asked whether it was easier to write a book or sell one. She smiled. A feeling of relief temporarily washed over her.

After answering the first question, she pointed to the woman with her hand up in the third row and invited her to speak. The woman wondered what advice she would give a beginning writer.

Her response was to join a critique group. It was the best investment of time a writer could make—her group's encouragement had been invaluable, and writers of all levels could learn so much from their different perspectives. In terms of editing their work, she said they'd find the last error when they stopped looking. A titter rippled through those who could easily relate to the trials of endless polishing.

She gave the audience another recommendation—make sure they had confidence and trust in early readers and took the advice that felt right. She added that some things they would change, some things they would stick with. But most importantly, she encouraged them to find their own voices. Write the stories they wanted to write.

The next questions were more about the publishing world instead of World War II or the book, but she answered them as best she could. It was funny, she told them—when a writer gets published, everybody believes the author possesses a magical key to the current idiosyncrasies of the entire publishing industry. But it just wasn't so.

Eventually, the questions veered toward what she'd written, with a few wannabe-writer questions sprinkled in. Most inquiries centered on when she began writing, how she came up with names of characters, how much of the book was true, what was the hardest part of being a writer—and did she have any other advice.

An elderly man in the audience looked like he had a burning question, but never raised his hand or spoke. Whenever she looked his way, he simply stared. Did she know him? His look was intense—almost to the point of being unnerving.

When the questions ended, she offered to sign the books people had brought or to sign ones that could be purchased. The man who looked as if he had a question on the tip of his tongue but never asked it, hovered near the line of people buying books—even though he carried a copy held tightly against his handmade sweater. There was something different about the way he dressed. Maybe he was a professor. He looked like an academic without the proverbial leather patches on his sleeves. He appeared to be in his late sixties, early seventies—mostly because of his graying hair. His physique was lean, like a runner or cyclist. His clothes were tight, not the loose-fitting t-shirt variety worn in a college town. If it weren't for his salt-and-pepper colored hair pulled into a tight ponytail, he would have looked much younger.

The crowd thinned out and the last two people were her husband and the gray-haired man she'd started to think of as a stalker.

She asked if he wanted her to sign his book.

He extended his hand for her to shake and introduced himself as Étienne.

She told him she was pleased to meet him and again asked if he wanted her to sign the copy he clutched under his arm.

He stammered out a "no," but then said what he really meant was "yes," but that he wanted to talk to her.

She looked at her husband. What did this man want?

Étienne moved to one of the chairs in the front row and gestured for her to join him. She pulled a chair around so she could sit facing him. Her husband stood nearby.

"I am the child from your book."

His words stopped her. She had to remind herself to breathe.

He repeated his name—Étienne—and explained he had been in Fort Collins visiting friends at the University. He had planned to contact her by phone, but when he saw a poster in a coffee shop that she'd be in Denver doing a reading and speaking about her book, he had to attend.

She could barely comprehend his words. This was Catherine's son. Her book was about his mother!

His mother had told him the story of the American soldier she had met after she escaped from the Nazis at the salt mine. She never forgot his kindness in a world that had been so cruel. "The experiences of the war were etched on her soul," he said.

The author was stunned. She was physically stunned. She had always hoped to find out what had happened to Catherine and to her child—find out more about what they'd gone through. And now she was sitting talking to Catherine's son. It was difficult for her to believe any of this was real.

A friend of Étienne's had read her book and knew it must have been written about his mother from the stories he'd shared. His friend had given him a copy.

"I feel as though I knew her," she said.

Étienne shifted in his chair. "Of course there is fiction, no?"

"Yes, historical fiction." Was she dreaming this? She ran through things in her mind to orient herself. Sitting in a room at the Dog-Eared Page talking to a man who was the unborn child in her book! "Please tell me about her."

Étienne began, "She met my father during the war. They planned to get married, but they were separated when the Nazis sent her to work at a camp in Germany."

"Please. Go on."

His voice grew softer. "After the war, she talked to people, posted notices—anything to try to find him. Every street corner, any possible place to see him; a knock on the door provided the prospect he might be standing there. She never gave up hope. She tried to find her best friend, too, but decided she must have perished at the camp like so many others. There were rumors about mass graves, but no evidence of her was ever found. When my grandmother passed away, we moved to the U.S. It was a new life for us, a place to start over with fewer reminders of my father, of everything. I was the thread that bound them together. She always said I was so much like him." A warm smile crossed his face. "She often wondered what happened to your father."

"Yes, yes, of course. After the discovery at the mine, the Army brought in Patton, Bradley, and even General Eisenhower. They arrived with an entourage of military people to inventory the gold and art, which was eventually shipped out. My father and his division moved on to Czechoslovakia. When the war ended, he received orders to return to the States—to my mother and sister.

Several years later, he took a job as a civilian on a military post, where he was injured in a horrible accident caused by the negligence of a young man hired that very day. I was a child at the time. It was so ironic that he made it through the entire war without a scratch and then spent months in a Veteran's Hospital back in the States. Anyway, there were a lot of things from the war he wouldn't discuss, but he always talked about the discovery of the gold. He was a hero to me—he disagreed and said he wasn't. He merely thought of himself as a soldier. To him, the heroes were the ones who never came home. He's gone now. So many things I wish I would have asked him."

There was recognition in Étienne's eyes, as if he had also wished the same thing. "My mother is gone now, too."

"Yes, they're both gone, but they were witnesses to the extraordinary things that can happen to ordinary people."

He took a deep breath. "So true." He placed his hand on her shoulder. "The story will live on."

"I'd like to sign your copy."

He handed it to her, and she pulled back the cover to the title page.

To Étienne,
With gratitude.